Presented by:

J. Ellington Ashton Press

www.jellingtonashton.com

&

Hold the Line

BY D.A. ROBERTS

CODE NAME:

WILD HUNT

BOOK TWO

CURSE OF THE

WENDIGO

BY

D.A. ROBERTS
THE END IS ONLY
THE BEGINNING

HAG
HORROR
AUTHORS
GUILD
MEMBER

3

BY D.A. ROBERTS

Edited by: J. Ellington Ashton Press Staff

Cover Art by: Michael "Fish" Fisher

http://jellingtonashton.com/

ISBN: 9798696278100

"I GREW UP FASCINATED BY THE CONFLICT BETWEEN GOOD AND EVIL, AND THE GREAT MIDDLE BETWEEN THE TWO. I'VE SPENT MOST OF MY LIFE IN THAT GREAT MIDDLE ... RUNNING TOWARDS THE EVIL, RESOLVED TO BE "THE GOOD" IT WORRIES ABOUT WHEN/IF IT SLEEPS. ROBERTS' WRITING IS LIKE STEPPING ON A TREADMILL WITH A MAD (BUT GOOD) SCIENTIST SITTING IN A DJ BOOTH SMOKING A CIGAR AND SAYING 'LET'S SPEND A LITTLE TIME BOUNCING INSIDE THE VIRTUOUS VIOLENCE SETTING' AND SEE WHAT THE KID DOES.' I GREW UP WHERE HE WRITES ABOUT ... AND NOW I WONDER ABOUT ALL THOSE LITTLE PRIMAL NUDGES I FELT WHILE WALKING THROUGH THOSE WOODS .... "

R. CLINT BRUCE
FORMER SPECIAL OPERATIONS OFFICER — NAVAL SPECIAL WARFARE
USNA GRADUATE
DECORATED ATHLETE AND ENTREPRENEUR

By D.A. ROBERTS

SPECIAL THANKS TO

JOSH DALTON

STEVE MONROTUS

AND

CLINT BRUCE

FOR ALL YOUR HELP AND ADVICE

Table of Contents

BY D.A. ROBERTS

PROLOGUE

"The hand of the aggressor is stayed by strength
— and strength alone."
Dwight D. Eisenhower

1100 Hours CST
12 February
Rocky Lake
Michigan's Upper Peninsula

Kerry "Pocket Doc" Davis was cold, despite the thermal layers he was wrapped in. The wind was nasty and blowing in from the north from Canada. He knew they were only a few miles from the Canadian border, as the crow flies, but it was through some of the densest woods in the lower forty-eight states.

There were six of them trudging through the snow that was almost up to their knees. Doc was wearing a yellow parka with matching thermal pants and thick boots. The black balaclava around his face only blocked out part of the cold. He could feel ice forming in his beard.

With him were five men he met several years ago in Duluth, Minnesota. He'd been teaching a Live Fire Med Class with Officer Down drills, Single-Hand Shooting drills, and Tourniquet drills. They were all SWAT officers and they'd become close friends almost immediately. When they invited him up for some ice fishing, he'd jumped at the chance. Now, he was rethinking the decision since he had no idea how cold it was in northern Minnesota in the winter.

The men were Sergeant Michael Freeman, Corporal Stan Brokatansky, Corporal Jim Sheffield, Sergeant Julian Pelletier, and Corporal Bert Anderson. They were all ex-military before joining the Duluth Police Department with three of them in the army and two marines and all had seen combat in Afghanistan and Iraq. Even though Doc had been in the Air Force, he was a combat medic and they all appreciated a good medic. Besides, as a combat medic, he'd been seconded to Army Special Forces for part of his career. It was at that time when he'd met a certain Army Ranger named Will Greyeagle.

"Come ice fishing they said," Doc muttered, his voice full of sarcasm. "It'll be fun, they said. You guys forgot to mention the part where it's colder than Antarctica here. Jesus, I think my nuts have crawled up inside me. I'll have to spend a month in south Texas to get them to come back down."

"Come on, Doc," said Sheffield. "I thought it got cold in Colorado."

"It does," replied Doc. "But this isn't just cold. This is ball shriveling cold. How do you idiots live up here? Besides, I was born in Mississippi. I'm not built for the cold."

"You know," said Pelletier, "we do have summer up here, too."

"Yeah, this year it was on a Tuesday," said Anderson.

Everyone but Doc laughed at the joke. They all had grown up in northern Minnesota and the winters didn't bother them that much. It was just time to ice fish, hunt, and play hockey. Things they'd all been doing since they were children.

"Just imagine how good those fish are gonna taste when we get back to the cabin," said Sheffield, chuckling.

"I'm more interested in the Scotch I have in my bag," said Doc. "That'll warm me up more than any fish."

"Look," said Pelletier, pointing ahead of them. "There's the fishing cabin. We'll get inside, get the fire going, and cut the ice so we can get started fishing. You'll be warm in a few minutes."

"I may never be warm again," muttered Doc, shaking his head.

The tiny ice fishing cabin was about fifteen feet by fifteen feet and sat out on the thick ice of Rocky Lake. It wasn't anything fancy, just a big box with a slanted roof that had been built on skids so it could be slid off the ice when spring came. There were a couple of small windows and a single door. The only other feature was the metal chimney pipe protruding from the roof.

Opening the door, they looked inside before they entered. It wasn't uncommon to find a wild animal inside, so they checked first just to be safe. Once they saw it was clear, Sheffield entered and lit the lanterns. Once it was lit up, they all headed inside and started dropping their backpacks. Freeman started bringing in firewood, stacking it beside the woodstove.

Brokatansky opened up the stove and started getting some kindling in place, then lit it. Once it was burning, he added a few sticks of wood and soon it was crackling as the fire started in earnest. Shutting the door, they let the heat start building up before they all began shedding their layers of thermal gear.

By the time that Pelletier had cut through the ice with the saw, the room was beginning to warm up. Doc dropped a hose into the lake water and used the hand-pump to run a few gallons of water through the inline filter. Once that was done, he poured water into the metal coffee pot, added coffee grounds, and put it on the stove to percolate.

"Coffee's on," said Doc, glancing around at everyone.

Soon, they were all laughing and fishing, telling jokes and swapping stories of their time in uniform. They ate lunch while they fished, feasting on premade cold cut sandwiches. Their luck was good and they were slowly but steadily pulling fish from the lake in good numbers. They were having so much fun that no one was paying attention to the time.

"Shit," said Pelletier.

"What?" asked Doc.

"It's almost dark," said Pelletier, glancing out the window.

"It shouldn't be a problem," said Sheffield. "We're only a little over a mile from the cabin and it's a clear trail."

"That's not the problem," said Brokatansky. "These woods are dangerous after the sun goes down."

"What do you mean?" asked Doc, dreading the answer.

He immediately thought of a year ago when he and his friend Will had faced the Dogmen in Missouri. He hoped that wasn't what they meant by dangerous. He began thinking of defensible positions and whether or not they could hold out here in the fishing cabin.

"The trail between here and the cabin is pretty broken," said Brokatansky. "People wander off the trail and get lost in these woods every year. Most of the time, they're never found. It's really easy to get lost up here and it's damned near twenty miles to the nearest town."

"What about animals?" asked Doc. "Anything up here particularly dangerous?"

"There's all kinds of animals," said Sheffield. "Elk, deer, bears, although they should all be hibernating. We even have the occasional wolverine and mountain lion. Why? What were you expecting? Bigfoot?"

They all laughed except Doc.

"Call me paranoid," said Doc, "but I like to be prepared."

"No worries," said Brokatansky. "Let's put everything away and get back to the cabin. I want to cook some of these fish."

They might have all laughed when Doc worried about the animals, but all of them opened their packs and started putting together their AR rifles. Doc took out his custom Noveske and put it together quickly, then checked to make sure his SIG was still on his hip.

They put the fish into a cooler for transport and everyone busied themselves putting their cold-weather gear back on. Once that was in place, they put out the lanterns and headed out the door. Brokatansky brought up his AR and scanned in both directions along the lake.

Sheffield grabbed the rope to the sled that they used to bring the firewood and put the cooler on it. Slinging the rope over his shoulder, he headed out behind Brokatansky and Pelletier. Doc came next with Freeman and Anderson bringing up the rear. Despite their jokes about being out after dark, Doc noticed that they were all quiet and had their weapons at the ready. Taking his cue from them, Doc brought his rifle into a low-ready position and started sweeping the area.

The moon was already high in the sky and the sun was a mere sliver on the western horizon. The night was cloudless and cold, but the wind had died down. Doc was astounded at the clarity of the stars twinkling in the sky above them. Despite the cold, he had to admit there was a rugged beauty to this place.

Brokatansky quickened his pace and headed for the edge of the frozen lake. Once they reached where the trail entered the dark woods, they slowed down and warily watched the deep shadows. The only sound they could hear other than their footfalls was the whispering of the wind through the trees.

"We should have gone back to the cabin before it got dark," whispered Freeman. "These woods always give me the damned creeps after dark."

Doc noticed that the forest was eerily quiet. It was winter and there were no sounds of insects to be heard, but that wasn't it. There was something sinister about the darkness that surrounded them. Doc felt a familiar sensation running through the primitive part of his brain. He'd felt it before when he'd encountered the mysterious Dogmen. It was the feeling of being hunted.

Glancing around, Doc noticed that he wasn't the only one who was noticing it. Everyone was gripping their weapons tighter and bringing them up closer to their shoulders. They all felt something hungry watching them from the deep darkness. Whatever it was, they all understood that it was malevolent and they were all on the menu.

From somewhere in the distance, they heard the sound of wood breaking. It echoed through the woods making it almost impossible to tell exactly where it had originated. The trees were so thick that only in rare spots did the moon break through the branches to reach the forest floor. In some places, you couldn't see your hand in front of your face.

Most of the trees were coniferous Jack Pines and didn't lose their needles in the winter, although the trees that did seemed to stand like ominous skeletons in the moonlight. Just as Doc turned his head, panning the trees, he thought he saw one of the trees move. Glancing back quickly, there was nothing where he had been certain a tree stood only moments ago.

He played over the image in his mind. It wasn't one of the Dogmen. For one, it was gaunt and twisted with small branches at the very top. It certainly didn't look or move like a Dogman. He would have sworn it was a tree, but it was gone and trees don't move on their own.

Up ahead, the woods grew denser as they passed through a thick grove of Jack Pines. Doc didn't remember passing this way when they went to the lake earlier, but this was his first time here. Brokatansky had been coming here for years, so Doc trusted his sense of direction.

Once they entered the grove, Doc noticed that even their footfalls seemed to be muted. The very air was oppressive and stifling, making him feel like strange hands were reaching for him from every shadow. He was trying to shake the feeling when he heard the scream from behind him.

"Goddamn it!" bellowed Anderson. "Something just grabbed Freeman!"

These were not men prone to running from threats. Every man here had spent most of their adult lives running towards danger when most men would have run away. Instead of panicking and running for their lives, every one of them pulled the charging handles on their ARs and headed for Anderson.

"Where did he go?" roared Pelletier.

"It picked him up and dragged him into the trees," said Anderson, pointing upwards.

Clicking on their tactical lights, they all began sweeping the trees for any sign of Freeman. Above them, they could hear something moving in the branches and the wheezing cries of Freeman. Then, there was a wet crunching sound and Freeman stopped making noise.

Doc panned his light along a section of trees and illuminated a nightmare. Looking down at him from about twenty feet up was a creature out of a horror film. The head was skeletal and looked like a deer's skull complete with antlers. Despite the deer skull, it had massive needle-sharp teeth in its mouth. The body was gaunt and withered, almost as if it was nearly starved to death. The beast's grey mottled skin looked taut and pulled thin over an almost skeletal frame and it smelled like it had crawled out of a grave.

There was fresh blood on its mouth, face, and hands. Freeman was gripped in its left hand while it was tearing chunks of flesh from his chest cavity with its right. Shoving a handful of organs into its mouth, it began chewing while staring directly at Doc.

"What the fuck is that?!" screamed Doc, bringing his rifle up and firing.

14

The rounds struck the beast in the chest and it dropped Freeman, letting him fall through the branches to land in a heap at the base of a Jack Pine tree. Pelletier and Brokatansky opened fire on the creature and it leaped from the tree into the darkness. In seconds, they lost sight of it as it moved off through the trees at high speed. It shrieked as it ran, a high-pitched multitoned scream reminiscent of tearing metal. Then, it was gone.

"Goddamn, that thing's fast!" yelled Sheffield.

"Fuck!" snapped Brokatansky. "Freeman's dead! Get him on the sled and let's get out of here!"

Everyone took a knee and faced outwards, providing cover while Doc tossed the cooler with the fish off to the side. Doc quickly put Freeman onto the sled and strapped him in. Seconds later, they were heading off through the trees as fast as they could safely go in the broken terrain.

"We've got to get to the cabin," said Anderson. "We've got snowmobiles there and more guns. Plus, there's a SAT phone so we can call for help."

"What the fuck was that thing?" demanded Doc.

"I thought they were just a legend," said Pelletier. "My grandfather used to tell me stories, but I thought he was full of shit."

"What stories?" asked Doc. "What did he say it was?"

"He called it a Wendigo," said Pelletier. "It's some kind of Indian monster that eats people. I thought it was bullshit."

"Can we kill it?" asked Doc, still looking around in the darkness.

"I don't know," said Pelletier. "Did you hit it?"

"Yeah," said Doc. "I put at least six rounds into that thing."

"And it didn't even fucking slow it down," said Brokatansky. "We don't have the firepower to bring it down. We've got to get out of here."

"If we can get to the cabin," said Pelletier, "it should be gone by morning. They don't come out during the day."

"Are you sure?" asked Doc.

15

"Yeah," said Pelletier. "I think so. Fuck, I can't remember, but I think they only come out at night."

"That fucking thing is fast," said Anderson. "Did you see how quickly that thing vanished into the trees? We'll never outrun it, not even on a snowmobile."

Brokatansky moved to duck under a low-lying branch when it suddenly moved and grabbed him by the head. With a blur of motion, it pulled him up into the trees and the screaming began. They heard the distinctive sound of tearing flesh and something wet hitting the ground.

"Fuck!" snarled Anderson

Doc panned his light up and saw the beast already ripping into Brokatansky's throat. Blood erupted into the night, steaming as it made contact with the cold air. Taking quick aim, Doc started putting round after round into the beast. He was instantly joined by the others.

Shrieking that strange multitoned scream again, the beast dropped Brokatansky and leaped from the tree. It dove right on top of Anderson, taking him to the ground and ripping his head off in a single move. The ripping of flesh and popping of bone was loud in the darkness and Anderson's scream stopped as abruptly as it began. Doc was at a distance of fewer than ten feet and proceeded to empty the magazine. Dropping the empty mag, he quickly reloaded.

Pelletier stepped forward and fired into the beast's head at almost point-blank range. The creature shrieked and swung its long, cadaverous arm at him, striking him just below the knee. Doc could hear the bone snap and knew immediately that it was more than one bone. The blow knocked him flying through the air, landing almost on top of Doc and impaling him on a broken tree branch.

"Get him out of here!" screamed Sheffield. "I'll hold it off!"

Sheffield started firing at the beast as it slowly stood up. Glancing down, Doc saw instantly that Pelletier had a compound fracture of the left leg. Bone was protruding from the thermal clothing and the blood was already starting to freeze.

Dropping his backpack, Doc quickly pulled out the medkit that he always carried. It was one of the same Dark Angel Medical kits that he used when he fought the Dogmen with Will. Those memories came

16

flooding back in an instant as he pulled out the parts of the kit he was going to need to stabilize Pelletier before he could move him.

"You've got to buy me some time," said Doc. "I have to stabilize him before I can move him."

"No promises," yelled Sheffield. "I'll do my best. Work fast!"

Turning to fire at the beast, Sheffield began trying to draw it off. The beast just looked at him with eyes that seemed to glow an unnatural red. Doc couldn't tell if it was reflected moonlight or if they just glowed on their own. The beast began to slowly move towards Sheffield, who kept firing at it. Doc knew it could easily overtake Sheffield at will. It was toying with them.

Doc quickly placed a tourniquet above the knee to stop the blood loss, then applied a SAM[1] splint and ACE wraps to the broken portion of the leg to stabilize it. Before he could stop him, Pelletier pulled the piece of wood out of his stomach and tossed it into the snow.

"Damn it," thought Doc. "I wish he'd left that in."

Glancing at the wound, Doc could see blood and a portion of the intestine sticking out. Grabbing the plastic wrapping from the splint, Doc pressed it against the open wound and bound it with an IZZY or Israeli Pressure Bandage. It wasn't pretty, but it was going to have to hold until he could get him to a safer place to work on him.

Glancing up, Doc could see Sheffield still circling away from the creature, putting as many rounds into it as he could. The beast just kept advancing on him with the bullets seemingly having no effect. Doc had the impression of a cat playing with a mouse. It seemed to be mocking Sheffield by letting him shoot as much as he wanted, knowing it wouldn't be hurt.

Grabbing the sled, Doc pushed Freeman's body off and pulled Pelletier onto it. It bumped over rocks and logs hidden in the snow, but they were moving. Pelletier groaned in pain as they bounced along, but it couldn't be avoided.

"I'm sorry, man," said Doc.

---

[1] SAM splints are moldable splits that can be applied quickly to a broken limb.

"Just get me the hell out of here," said Pelletier through clenched teeth.

Doc started pulling the sled down the trail as fast as he could safely go, hoping he was heading in the right direction.

"Sheffield!" shouted Doc. "Let's move!"

"Go!" roared Sheffield. "I'll catch up!"

The last glimpse Doc got of Sheffield, he was trying to draw the creature away from them, heading deeper into the darkness of the trees. Doc began trotting as quickly as he dared, trying to make sure he stayed on the trail. There was enough moonlight filtering through the trees and reflecting from the snow that he could see clearly.

In the distance, he could hear Sheffield firing. When the firing stopped, the screaming began. Doc knew that the creature would be coming for them next. Leaning into the rope, he pushed as hard as he could, hoping that the cabin would come into view with each passing step.

From the darkness behind him, he heard the beast scream, followed by the sounds of breaking branches as it rapidly headed in his direction. He couldn't be more than a couple of hundred yards ahead of it, so he knew it wasn't going to take long before it caught them and ripped them both to shreds. Behind him, he heard Pelletier begin firing his rifle.

"It's coming!" shouted Pelletier. "Run!"

Doc could feel his heart thundering in his chest from the exertion in the extreme cold. He knew he wasn't going to be able to keep up this pace much longer. Suddenly, he rounded a bend in the trail and the cabin was less than thirty yards away. Putting everything he had into the effort, he sprinted for the door.

Dragging the sled right up the porch steps, he was glad that they had left the door unlocked. Swinging the door open, he pulled Pelletier inside and started shutting the door. Glancing up, he saw the beast emerge from the trees and look directly at him. With a horrifying scream, it raced towards him with frightening speed.

Slamming the door shut, Doc dropped the crossbar in place and prayed that it would hold. The beast hit the door with enough force to shake the entire front of the cabin, but the door held. There were crossbar brackets at the top, middle, and bottom of the door. Doc wasted no time in dropping them all in place.

The windows to the cabin were still covered with the wooden shutters, preventing the creature from bursting through the glass. The fire had burned low, but there were still coals at the bottom. Stirring them up, Doc threw several logs onto them, then went to check the back door. It was still bolted shut and had three crossbars still in place.

Moving back into the living room, he checked on Pelletier. He was out cold but was already showing signs of a fever. Doc knew that peritonitis would set in within twenty-four hours due to the abdominal wound. He only hoped that the bowel hadn't been perforated. That was going to require surgery and they were miles from the nearest hospital.

"Hang on till morning, brother," Doc said quietly to Pelletier. "When the sun comes up, I'll pull you out of here with the snowmobile."

Almost on cue, Doc heard the sound of splintering wood and tearing metal. Looking through the cracks in the shutter on the front window, Doc could see that the creature had broken into the shed where they kept the snowmobiles.

"What the fuck are you doing?" said Doc.

One by one, the beast was pulling the snowmobiles out into the snow and destroying them.

"Son-of-a-bitch," hissed Doc.

Remembering the SAT phone, he ran into the kitchen and grabbed it from the table. Punching in a familiar phone number, he hit dial and waited, hoping that he could get a signal through. After the third ring, he heard a familiar voice.

"Hello?" said Will Greyeagle.

"Will!" Doc almost shouted. "I need your help!"

"Doc?" said Will. "Where are you? What's going on?"

"I went ice fishing in Minnesota with some friends," explained Doc. "We were attacked by this creature. I think Pelletier called it a Wendigo. It killed four of my friends and we're trapped in a cabin."

19

"Ok, slow down," said Will, concern in his voice. "Can it get inside?"

"I don't think so," said Doc. "At least, I hope not."

"What's it doing, right now?" asked Will.

"From the sound of it," said Doc, "it's having angry sex with my snowmobile. The goddamned thing is destroying our only means of escape."

"Are you the only one left?" asked Will.

"No, it's me and a guy named Pelletier," said Doc, "but he's hurt pretty bad. He's likely going to need a surgeon, and soon."

"Can you stabilize him?" asked Will.

"Already on it," said Doc. "I'll do my best for him, but we can't hold out for very long. We can't try to hike out. Pelletier would never make it. The snowmobiles are trashed. It's only a matter of time before this thing finds a way inside."

"Hang tight, Doc," said Will. "I'm on my way."

"No offense, buddy," said Doc, "but if you could hurry, that would be great. We're on the western end of Rocky Lake, about a mile north of the shore. If you find the ice fishing cabin, we're almost directly due north of that."

"I've got your GPS coordinates from the call," said Will. "We'll be inbound ASAP. Its 1930 hours now. If you haven't heard from me by 0600, call me back. Hopefully, I'll have news before then and I'll let you know. I'll call you back when we're close. Stay buttoned-down and don't go outside, no matter what you hear. Don't open that door until I get there."

"Thank you, brother," said Doc.

"I seem to remember you jumping a plane to come to help me, once," said Will. "I'll be there as fast as I can. Just hang on."

"Will," said Doc, "If Pelletier doesn't get to a hospital in less than forty-eight hours, he probably won't make it. The faster he gets there, the better his chances of survival."

"You're the best medic I know," said Will. "Keep him alive and we'll be there."

"Brother," said Doc, suddenly serious, "if you don't make it, please tell Angie I…"

"Check that shit right now," said Will. "We're coming. Just stay locked down and we'll get to you."

"Thank you, brother," said Doc.

"Don't thank me, just yet," said Will. "Just hold on and I'll get the first bird out of here. I'm on my way."

"Will," said Doc. "Most Rikki-tik[2] would be appreciated."

"Solid copy," said Will.

Doc hung up the phone and glanced out through the crack in the window. Pieces of the snowmobiles were scattered all over the area. Not a single machine was intact. There was no way he could escape on foot, especially not dragging Pelletier on the sled. They would never outrun the Wendigo.

There was no sign of the beast. Doc looked around the area but couldn't see it anywhere. He was beginning to think that it had left, but then he saw the red glowing eyes. They were back in the trees, in the deep shadows. They were watching the cabin, waiting for the chance to come in after them.

"Most Rikki-tik," whispered Doc, putting his hand on the grip of his pistol.

Unpacking his bag with the full trauma kits, he started cleaning and treating the wounds. Starting an IV with antibiotics, he covered Pelletier with a space blanket and checked his temperature. He was already elevated and he was turning a sickly grey with sweat on his brow.

"Hang on, man," whispered Doc. "Help's on the way."

---

[2] Most Rikki-tik – military slang meaning "Immediately if not sooner."

Chapter One
On the Tarmac

"It doesn't take a hero to order men into battle.
It takes a hero to be one of those men who goes into battle."
General H. Norman Schwarzkopf

2200 Hours CST
12 February
Fort Leonard Wood, Missouri

First Sergeant Will Greyeagle stood on the tarmac at the post airport on Fort Leonard Wood. There was a flurry of activity going on around him as they waited for the transport aircraft that would ferry them to the airstrip belonging to the 148th Fighter Wing of the Minnesota Air National Guard.

Their transport, a US Air Force C-5M Super Galaxy would transport three of their helicopters and an advanced group from Team Odin. The group consisted of 1SG[3] William Greyeagle (Call Sign: Fenrir), SSG[4] Cody *Tapuche* (Call Sign: Kodiak), SSG Frank Margolin (Call Sign: Huntsman 2-6), SSG Samantha Pennebaker (Call Sign: Shieldmaiden), TSGT[5] Miranda Masterson (Code Name: Valkyrie) and SGT[6] Liam McGregor (Call Sign: Huntsman 2-9). Flight crews for the choppers would be going as well.

Will started the ball rolling as soon as he got off the phone with Doc. He'd gone straight to Major Saunders and Captain Clark. With one phone call, Major Saunders got clearance to put an assessment team in the air to evaluate the situation. They were going to insert via helicopter and help extract the civilians who were in danger. If they confirmed the presence of the cryptid, the rest of the team would be on-site within twelve hours.

The advance team was already preparing to board their transport as the rest of the team began mobilizing. They would land on the same

---

[3] 1SG – First Sergeant
[4] SSG – Staff Sergeant
[5] TSGT – Tech Sergeant
[6] SGT - Sergeant

airstrip in Minnesota four hours behind the advanced team. The Mimic Units were already en route and would be ready to deploy as soon as confirmation was received. Team Odin was mobilizing. A cover story had already been prepared, stating that they would be conducting search and rescue exercises in the remote wilderness of Minnesota.

"Everything ready?" asked Captain Clark as he approached Will.

"Yes, sir," said Greyeagle, glancing at his clipboard. "The C-5M is on final approach and should be landing in a few minutes. We're ready to begin loading as soon as it finishes taxiing."

"Ordinarily, I'd take the assessment team in," said Clark, "but since you know Mr. Davis personally, I'll oversee the deployment of the Mimic Units."

"Copy that, sir," said Greyeagle, nodding. "Doc was an SF medic when I met him. Saved my life a couple of times back in Afghanistan."

"Think we should recruit him for the team?" asked Clark.

"No, sir," said Will. "His wife would kill me for even asking. He does run a medical training and supply company called Dark Angel Medical, though. We need to stock his kits and have him run Combat Lifesaver courses for the teams."

"Seriously?" said Clark. "That's the guy? Holy crap, I've been carrying their kits for years. In fact, the last time I got shot up as a cop, it was one of those kits that saved my life."

"He'd be thrilled to hear that, sir," said Greyeagle.

"I'm looking forward to meeting him," said Clark.

"Sir," said Greyeagle, "I believe him when he said he saw a Wendigo. He was with us last year when we fought the *Oolonga-Doglalla* near Lebanon."

"The what?" asked Clark.

"*Oolonga-Doglalla*," said Will. "It's the Cherokee word for Dogmen."

"So, this isn't his first cryptid encounter?" asked Clark.

"No, sir," said Greyeagle.

"I'll make sure the Major's aware of that," said Clark. "We'll step up the timetable on the deployment of the rest of the team. I'll start placing the Mimic Units as soon as we hit the tarmac in Minnesota."

"Thank you, sir," said Will.

In the distance, they saw the blinking lights of an approaching aircraft. Their ride was coming in for a landing. As it grew closer, they could hear the deep roar of the gigantic turbine engines. In less than a minute, the leviathan of the air touched down and began taxiing towards the end of the runaway. Once it had decelerated and turned, it headed directly at the hanger where the flight crews were standing by to begin loading the two UH-60 Blackhawks and the MH-6 Little Bird helicopters.

No sooner had the behemoth C-5M Super Galaxy come to a full stop, the nose cone of the aircraft began lifting to open the massive cargo bay. The Air Force flight crew in green Nomex coveralls and thick jackets came running down the ramp and came directly over to Clark and Greyeagle.

"Someone call for a ride?" asked the crew chief, grinning.

"Thanks for coming on short notice," said Clark. "This is First Sergeant Greyeagle. He'll be leading the team you're taking. How soon can you get back in the air?"

"Tell your people to start loading, sir," said the crew chief. "We're going to get the ground crew to start the refueling. We're wheels up whenever you're ready."

There was a flurry of activity as they began loading the helicopters and securing them inside the aircraft. Two fuel trucks came out to the enormous aircraft and began topping off the tanks. Clark nodded at Greyeagle and started to turn away.

"Let me know if you need anything," said Clark. "I'm going to see if I can expedite the rest of the team."

"Yes, sir," said Greyeagle.

When the helicopters were all secure, Greyeagle began checking items off the clipboard as they loaded supplies, weapons, ammunition, and additional gear. Once it was all secured, he headed up the ramp and onto the aircraft. The fuel trucks were just pulling away and all three of the choppers were loaded and secured.

"We're all loaded and ready to go, sir," said the crew chief, trotting over to Greyeagle. "The skipper says he's good to go on your order."

"Let's roll," said Greyeagle.

"Copy that," said the crew chief, turning away and talking into his headset as he headed deeper into the aircraft.

The flight crew double-checked the load was secure, then hit the door controls to close the nosecone. Greyeagle watched as it lowered into place and saw the indicator lights go green to indicate a positive lock.

As Greyeagle headed for the passenger seating area, he noticed that the rest of his team was already there with their gear. Kodiak had already brought his gear up there for him. The flight crews for the helicopters that were being transported were already in seats and kicked back, ready for the flight. Through the skin of the aircraft, he could hear the turbines begin spooling up. Taking out his cellphone, he sent a quick text message to Doc.

"Going wheels up now," he said. "Landing in Duluth in a couple of hours. Are you holding ok?"

"We're good," Doc replied. "Pelletier is stable, at the moment. I haven't heard the creature in a while, but I know it's still out there. I've barricaded the doors. We'll hold."

"See you in a few hours," said Greyeagle. "Text if anything changes."

"Solid copy," Doc said.

Greyeagle slid into his seat as the gigantic aircraft began to taxi back towards the runway. The crew chief came up to the passenger area and handed Greyeagle a headset.

"Here you go, sir," said the crew chief.

"Thanks, chief," said Greyeagle. "What's this for?"

"So you can keep in touch with the pilot," said the crew chief. "If we don't hit headwinds, we should be touching down in Duluth in about

25

an hour and a half. They're still on Central time so we should have you unloading before midnight."

"Thanks, chief," said Greyeagle, slipping the headset on.

"If you all need anything," said the crew chief, "just let us know."

As he walked away, Margolin turned to Greyeagle and smiled.

"I gotta say, Top," said Margolin. "The accommodations in a C-5 are a hell of a lot better than in the back of a C-130."

"No argument there," said Greyeagle. "Next time we fly overseas, I'm asking for one of these."

Margolin leaned back in his seat and closed his eyes. Greyeagle was always impressed with the ability of the American soldier to fall asleep anywhere the moment they have more than five minutes to kickback. Glancing around, Greyeagle noticed that the rest of the team was already asleep and they hadn't even taken off yet.

Ninety minutes later, they were on the final approach to Duluth and the 148th Fighter Wing. Greyeagle started kicking boots and waking everyone up. Grumbling, they all started coming around and grabbing their gear.

"We'll be on the ground in two minutes," said Greyeagle. "Let's get this bird unloaded so it can go back to base to begin loading more of the team."

"Gotcha, Top," said Margolin.

The others all nodded and started getting ready. The big aircraft banked and lined up on the runway and they all heard the landing gear lowering into place. The whine of the turbines changed pitch as they began their descent to the ground below. Approaching with a cup of coffee, the crew chief handed the cup to Greyeagle and smiled.

"On the ground in two minutes," said the crew chief. "Just an FYI, it was twenty-eight degrees in Missouri when we left. It's negative eight degrees in Duluth."

"Thanks, Chief," said Greyeagle. "Guess we'd better get out our parkas."

"You think this is bad," said the crew chief, "try landing at Minot, North Dakota. Frankly, I'd rather land in McMurdo."

Greyeagle chuckled. The chief took a seat quickly and Greyeagle covered the styro cup of coffee with his hand so the landing wouldn't make him spill it. He was shocked at how smooth the landing was with the C-5M. Despite all the time he'd been in uniform during his career, this was his first time in a C-5M. He would recommend doing it again. Margolin was right. It was by far and away better than flying in a C-130.

"Just out of curiosity," said the crew chief, "do you mind if I ask how you got those scars on your face?"

Greyeagle reached up and touched the scars that covered most of the right side of his face, remembering the night he'd almost lost his eye fighting a Dogman in Louisiana, just a month before. Although the scars were completely healed, they were still fresh to him.

"Bear attack," said Greyeagle. "We were on a training exercise in Alaska when we got too close to a grizzly. I was lucky to survive."

"Damn," said the crew chief. "That had to hurt."

"You have no idea," said Greyeagle, nodding.

"I'm going to head down and get my people moving," said the crew chief. "We'll get you unloaded as fast as we can. I know you guys are on a timetable."

With that, the crew chief headed off towards the cargo deck. Greyeagle grabbed his bag and headed towards the front part of the aircraft. The others followed along behind him and no sooner had they reached the flight deck, the big nose cone began opening. The frigid air hit them like a blast in the face.

"Damn!" said Margolin. "This feels like Oklahoma all over again."

"Let's hope not," said Valkyrie. "Oklahoma was a shit show."

Greyeagle knew that they were referring to the incident late last year in which Team Odin encountered a tribe of Bigfoot-like creatures while attempting to recover a missing Air Force drone. The team had taken extensive losses during the mission, but that was before he and Cody *Tapuche* had joined the team. He was hoping that this time would turn out much different.

27

The cold didn't bother Greyeagle or *Tapuche* as much as it bothered the others. The *Hotamétaneo'o* could withstand temperature extremes that would kill most normal people. Although both Greyeagle and *Tapuche* could both still change forms, they had agreed not to unless it was a life or death situation. Not everyone on the team even knew that they could.

Heading down the ramp, they noticed that while there was quite a bit of snow on the ground, the stars were clear and bright above them. Extended weather forecasts were calling for cold yet clear weather for the next several days in the area where they would be operating.

There was a pair of Humvees waiting for them and Greyeagle tossed his gear into the back of the first one. The others followed suit and a young Air Force Airman exited the driver's side door of the lead Humvee and approached them.

"First Sergeant Greyeagle," said the Airman.

"That would be me," said Greyeagle.

"I'm here to take you all to the hanger we're using as a staging area for your team," said the Airman.

"What about the gear that's still on the aircraft?" asked Greyeagle.

"Our people will take care of unloading it all and bringing it to the hanger," said the Airman. "Your General Dalton called our base commander about an hour ago and we're instructed to give you all whatever help you need."

"I'll have to thank the General when I see him," said Greyeagle, heading for the passenger side of the vehicle.

Behind him, the rest of his team were climbing into the two Humvees. *Tapuche* climbed in right behind Greyeagle and settled into the seat. More Humvees were arriving to pick up the flight crews as they were pulling away. It was just a short drive to the large hanger where they were already beginning to stage equipment for Team Odin. Six of the Mimic Units had already been delivered.

"We're deploying the Mimics again?" asked Margolin. "I sure hope they improved them from the last time."

28

"I read the file," said Greyeagle. "They upgraded the armor, equipment compliment, added a full trauma unit and a maintenance unit. I think they took their lessons to heart."

"I hope so," said Margolin. "No offense, Top, but you weren't there for the last one. Forgive me if I don't have a lot of confidence in those things until I see it for myself. You should have seen the Battle of the Shieldwall. Fucking epic."

"No offense taken," said Greyeagle. "Honestly, from what I read of the mission briefing, I'm not sure how far I trust them, either."

"We had six for the last deployment," said Valkyrie. "How many are we getting this time?"

"Major Saunders was promised twelve units," said Greyeagle, "but he had to promise not to blow these up."

That drew a round of chuckles as they exited the Humvee and headed into the hanger. They were shown to a conference room where large urns of coffee, cold cut sandwiches, bags of chips, and donuts had been put out for them.

"Sorry about the crappy food," said the young Airman. "We didn't have time to get the cooks in before you arrived. We'll have a full hot breakfast set out for you before sunrise, though."

"This is crappy?" asked Margolin, heading for the table. "This is five-star hotel shit in my book."

"We're used to MREs and stale coffee," said McGregor.

"This is the Air Force, sir," said the young Airman, smiling. "We don't serve stuff like that."

"Boy did I join the wrong branch," muttered McGregor, heading for the table of food.

"That's what I've been trying to tell you idiots," said Valkyrie, following McGregor.

The rest of the team headed over with them.

"She's in the Air Force?" asked the Airman, nodding at Valkyrie.

"Technically, yes," said Greyeagle. "Our team recruits from all Tier One, Two, and Three Special Forces Units, regardless of service. She's considered seconded to us, but her original branch of service was Air Force. Tech Sergeant Masterson was a sniper in the ParaRescue teams."

"I'm in the selection process for the PJ's," said the young Airman. "I hope I make the cut."

"I can't say much about them," said Greyeagle. "You'd have to ask her about it."

"If you don't mind me asking," said the Airman, "what unit were you in before this one?"

"I was with the Rangers," said Greyeagle.

"Hey Top!" yelled Margolin. "There's like four kinds of meat and three different kinds of cheese on these sandwiches! This shit's better than Subway! Holy shit! Is that spicy brown mustard?"

"Uh, sergeant," said the Airman. "There are pickles, tomatoes, and other veggies in that blue box to put on your sandwich."

Margolin looked back with a wide grin and pointed exaggeratedly at the table.

"We should eat like this at our base, Top!" he said.

"I'll put in a request to the Major," said Greyeagle.

"Top," said Valkyrie, "you'd better get over here before Margolin eats it all."

"Don't worry," said the Airman, "there's like six more boxes of food in the other room. Eat all you want."

Greyeagle just shook his head and took a seat by the gear. Reaching into his bag, he brought out his clipboard and started double-checking that all of their equipment had arrived. After several minutes, SSG *Tapuche* sat next to him with a big sandwich on his plate and a couple of bags of Doritos.

"You should get something to eat, Top," said *Tapuche*.

"I will," said Greyeagle. "I want to check our inventory to make sure nothing got misplaced. We need all our gear to pull this off."

30

"This might be our only chance to eat real food for a few days," said *Tapuche*.

"Good point," said Greyeagle. "I'll get a sandwich in a minute, assuming Margolin doesn't eat it all."

"First Sergeant Greyeagle," said a voice behind them.

Greyeagle stood up and turned to face the newcomer.

"That's me," said Greyeagle.

"I'm Captain Rick Musgrave," said the man. "I'm your Little Bird pilot. I thought I'd let you know that the choppers are all unloaded and we'll have them pre-flighted and ready within the hour."

"Copy that, sir," said Greyeagle.

"Just one question, Top," said Musgrave.

"What's up, sir?" said Greyeagle.

"We're just wanting to know if you're going to want to go in before sunrise or wait until it gets light out before we lift?" asked Musgrave.

"What's the travel time from here to the coordinates?" asked Greyeagle.

"We can be on station in about an hour," said Musgrave.

"I want to be on station the second we have enough light to see by, sir," said Greyeagle. "The quicker we get the wounded out, the faster he can get the treatment he needs."

"Copy that, Top," said Musgrave. "I'll get with the other pilots and work out a timetable. I'll get with you when we've got a working schedule. By the way, our radio designations for this are Eagle 1-1 for the Little Bird and the Blackhawks are Eagle 1-2 and Eagle 1-3."

"Thank you, sir," said Greyeagle. "Make sure you tell your people that they put food out for us. It's on that table over there."

"I'm sure we'll all hit that before we go wheels up," said Musgrave. "Is there a place we can do a preflight briefing?"

"Yes, sir," said Greyeagle. "There's a room just behind that door. We'll be ready when you are."

31

Musgrave headed back to the far side of the hanger where the crews were still prepping the three helicopters. Greyeagle noted that all of the rotors had already been put back in place, having been folded back to fit inside the bit C-5M. Flight crews were going over all the systems and double-checking electronics to make sure nothing had been damaged during shipment.

Once the inventory was completed and Greyeagle was certain all of their gear had arrived safely, he headed over and made himself a sandwich. As he sat down, he saw Valkyrie sitting on the floor with her legs folded beneath her, carefully going over her sniper's rifle. It was custom built for her and Greyeagle could tell that she lovingly maintained it. It was an amazing piece of technology from Phoenix Weaponry. It was a .45-70 with a Vortex Viper PST GEN2 5-25x50 scope.

Although Team Odin was fully capable of stealth missions, this was a rescue mission against a known aggressive cryptid. They were carrying their heavier weapons. All of them except for Valkyrie and Kodiak were carrying Wilson Combat .458 SOCOM rifles with mil-spec[7] lowers that allowed for full-auto or three-round bursts. They all had Trijicon ACOG[8] 4x32 ROC riflescope mounted.

SSG *Tapuche*, Code Name Kodiak, was carrying an XM214 minigun in 5.56mm. The backpack carried the ammo for it, holding two 500 round magazines of linked ammunition that fed the minigun through a flexible chute. Ordinarily, the XM214 was crewed by two people, but Kodiak could carry it and still run. His strength was already nearly legendary on the team.

Once everyone had eaten, Greyeagle began opening the containers that held their gear. Soon, everyone had set up their plate carriers, customized their ammo storage, and added trauma kits. They all were wearing arctic camouflage due to the snowy conditions of the environment where they would be operating.

Once the armor was adjusted and in place, they started breaking out the weapons. Greyeagle had left his personal weapons in his locker back

---

[7] Mil-spec – military specification
[8] ACOG – Advanced Combat Optical Gunsight

at the base. They would all be carrying the team issued weapons so they could easily exchange magazines and support each other.

Putting the Guncrafter Industries Glock .50 GI on his right hip, he took out the knife that had been custom made for him by the Mohawk twins. That went on his right hip. Grabbing two of the Winkler Knives Sayoc tomahawks from the box, Greyeagle clipped both of them to the molle tabs on the back of his armor where he could reach back with either hand and grab one.

Opening the single-point sling, Greyeagle slipped the Wilson Combat .458 SOCOM on and adjusted the fit until it hung perfectly. All around him, the rest of the advanced team were doing the same. Breaking out the ammunition, Greyeagle began loading all of his magazine pouches and securing everything in place. Slapping in a live magazine, he closed the dust cover on the rifle and let it hang against his chest.

Reaching behind himself, he grabbed the long ponytail and rolled it up, then tucked it behind his armor. No sense letting it hang loose to catch on a tree limb on the way down the rope. He glanced over and noted that Kodiak was doing the same thing.

The young Air Force Airman approached, looking at everyone's equipment with wide eyes.

"This isn't a training mission, is it?" asked the Airman.

"What makes you say that?" asked Greyeagle.

"No blank adaptors, First Sergeant," said the Airman. "You're all loaded with live ammo."

"Good eye," said Will. "What's your name?"

"Airman First Class Timothy VanZant," said the young man.

"Alright, I'm William Greyeagle," he replied. "This is a classified mission and we're not allowed to discuss it. If you make the PJ selection process, you might find yourself eligible for this team. If you need a recommendation for the PJ's, you tell them to contact First Sergeant Greyeagle with the Wild Hunt. I'll be keeping an eye on your career, VanZant. You're a sharp kid and we could use people like you."

"Thank you, First Sergeant," said VanZant, grinning broadly. "I will."

"Alright, now you can't be here for our briefing," said Greyeagle. "You're not cleared. Thank you for all your help."

"My pleasure, First Sergeant," said VanZant.

With that, the young man headed quickly out of the area.

"That was really nice of you," said Valkyrie.

"He's a smart kid," said Greyeagle. "If he makes the PJ selection, I'd give him a shot for team tryouts."

"Are you going to give him a recommendation for the selection process?" asked Valkyrie.

"Yes," said Greyeagle. "I have a good feeling about him. Besides, I've recommended men for Ranger School for less."

"Still," said Valkyrie. "That was good of you to do."

"Not really," said Greyeagle. "He's going to have to do all the work. I'm just giving him a nudge."

Valkyrie didn't say anything else, but her respect for the new First Sergeant had just gone up considerably. She now understood what the Captain saw in Greyeagle. Although mysterious, he was a good soldier with great instincts. She was still a little scared of him, though. She'd been there, that night in Louisiana. It had been her bullet that took out the Rougarou.

Once they were done, Greyeagle glanced at his watch. It was almost time for the briefing. He noted that the flight crews were all heading into the conference room, most of them still eating as they walked. Margolin was on his third sandwich.

"Alright, people," said Will. "Let's move. I want to be in the air ten minutes after we finish the briefing. Hooah?"

"Hooah!" snapped the others.

Greyeagle turned and headed for the conference room, slipping his FAST helmet on and clipping the chin strap. Thirty minutes later, the meeting ended and everyone headed out for their respective aircraft to begin the mission. The ball was now in play.

The three choppers were already spooling up their rotors when Greyeagle and the others headed out onto the tarmac. A team of Air Force medics was aboard each of the Blackhawks while the members of Team Odin all headed for the Little Bird.

The Little Bird would go in first with the advanced team dropping in at the cabin utilizing the HRST[9] method. Their job would be to secure the site and prep the wounded man for extraction. Once they were ready, the first Blackhawk would lower the litter to the ground. The patient would then be secured to the litter and lifted to the Blackhawk.

Then the choppers would leave the area immediately. The second Blackhawk would provide air support if needed, or take over the role of patient extraction should the first chopper become unable to complete the task. If everything went according to plan, the choppers would be on station less than two minutes. The assessment team's job would be to prevent any attempt to damage or destroy any of the choppers.

Greyeagle stopped at the side of the Little Bird and did a quick check of the team as they climbed aboard. Once he was satisfied that everyone was accounted for, he gave the pilot a thumbs up and climbed in. Seconds later, the Little Bird lifted into the night sky.

Circling wide of the area, the Little Bird gave them a good view of the entire area and of the two Blackhawks lifting to join them. Once they were all in the air, they moved into formation and the Little Bird pilot took the lead. Checking his course, he headed out towards their destination. If their timing was correct, they would arrive fifteen minutes after sunrise. Taking out his SAT phone, Greyeagle sent a text to Doc.

"We're wheels up from Duluth," said the text. "On-site just after sunrise. How are you holding out?"

The reply was brief.

"Holding," it said. "Hurry."

---

[9] HRST method – Helicopter Rope Suspension Technique – a method for rappelling or FAST roping into an area when helicopter landings are either impractical or impossible.

By D.A. Roberts

CHAPTER TWO
RANGERS LEAD THE WAY

"I don't know what effect these men will have upon the enemy,
but, by God, they terrify me."
The Duke of Wellington

0730 Hours CST
13 February
Rocky Lake, MN

They were coming in at a higher altitude to avoid giving away their presence. They reasoned that people might recognize the sound of the choppers but the creature probably wouldn't pay any attention to it until it got close. So, there was no sense in giving themselves away until they were ready.

"Five minutes to your LZ[10]," said Captain Musgrave, glancing back at Greyeagle.

Clicking on the radio, Musgrave contacted the other choppers.

"Eagle 1-1 to all units," said Musgrave. "Beginning our run in five minutes. How copy?"

"Eagle 1-2 copies," said a voice.

"Eagle 1-3 copies," said another.

Greyeagle just nodded and turned to his team holding up five fingers. Everyone nodded and started doing a quick weapons check. Once that was completed, they slid open the side doors to prep the ropes. Instantly, the temperature in the helicopter dropped by thirty degrees.

"Fuck!" snapped Margolin. "That'll wake you up."

That drew a few nods and chuckles. It would have been difficult to hear with the air rushing through the doors but Margolin wasn't quiet. Besides that, they all were wearing headsets that they would have to remove before dropping down the ropes.

---

[10] LZ – Landing Zone

"Alright, boys and girls," said Greyeagle. "Here's the stack order. Portside rope is Valkyrie with me on the Starboard rope. As soon as we hit, I want Kodiak on port and Margolin starboard. Last is Pennebaker port and McGregor starboard. Any questions?"

No one spoke up.

"Alright folks," said Greyeagle. "We're going hot. Lock and Load!"

All around the cabin, charging handles were pulled and weapons were now hot with only the safety preventing them from being able to be discharged. Glancing down, they could see the frozen surface of Rocky Lake coming up beneath them. Only one ice fishing cabin was on the entire lake, so they knew they had to have the right one. Due north of the fishing cabin, they could see a plume of smoke rising into the air from a chimney. The roof of the cabin was barely visible through the trees.

"Looks like this is going to be tight," said Greyeagle. "Watch out for the trees when you drop."

"Gotcha, Top," said Margolin.

"We have no idea what kills a Wendigo," said Greyeagle. "There's too much out there that conflicts with other versions of the legend. So, we're gonna try it all. Stay alert and stay close."

"Hooah!" said Margolin.

The Little Bird banked north and started dropping altitude.

"Eagle 1-1 is beginning his run," said Musgrave. "Eagle 1-3, take up covering position, over."

"Eagle 1-3 copies," said the other pilot.

Greyeagle could see the Blackhawk moving into an approach that would allow them to provide cover fire with their miniguns if they were to come under attack.

"Here we go," said Greyeagle, grabbing the rope.

Flaring out to a stop, the Little Bird hovered directly in front of the small cabin. Pushing the thick rappelling ropes out, they weren't fully uncoiled before Greyeagle grabbed the rope and dropped from the side of the chopper. Valkyrie went at the same time.

As soon as they hit the ground, Greyeagle kicked away from the rope and brought up his rifle. Valkyrie moved up onto the porch of the cabin and brought up her rifle to scan the surrounding trees. Greyeagle brought his rifle up into high-ready, flicked the safety off, and began scanning the shadows beneath the canopy.

Margolin and Kodiak hit the ground next, instantly moving away and bringing up their weapons. Seconds later, Pennebaker (Code Name Shieldmaiden) and McGregor hit the ground. Shieldmaiden instantly headed for the door of the cabin. The thick ropes dropped to the ground and the Little Bird lifted straight up and cleared the area.

Inside, they could hear heavy furniture moving as the door was being cleared. They could see deep claw marks on the door and on the wooden shutters that covered the windows. Before the door was open, the Eagle 1-2 was hovering and beginning to lower the litter.

Doc emerged from the door of the cabin and glanced around at the group. He had his AR slung across his chest and his plate carrier in place. There was blood on his sleeves and his plate carrier.

"I'm damned glad to see you," said Doc, glancing around the group.

Shieldmaiden and Doc went back inside and carried Pelletier out, moving slowly so as not to cause him any unnecessary pain. Fortunately for them, he was unconscious. Loading him into the litter, they secured him in place and gave the medic that was hanging out the door of the chopper the go-ahead to move. As the litter began lifting, they heard a monstrous roar from deeper in the woods. It was moving in their direction.

"Here it comes!" shouted Greyeagle.

The creature crashed through the trees about sixty yards away and headed directly at them. Instantly, Greyeagle and the others opened fire. The creature was impossibly fast and was managing to dodge most of the fire when there was a loud boom. Valkyrie had waited for the right moment and put a round right in the beast's chest.

They were using special silver-tipped rounds since one of the legends had said silver was the beast's weakness. The impact of the round spun the beast around and they could see a look of shock on its face as it stumbled, but the pain was short-lived. Rolling behind a tree, the beast roared and ran off into the deep shadows beneath the canopy.

"Direct hit," said Margolin. "I guess we can take silver off the list."

"It hurt it," said Greyeagle, "just not enough to stop it. The silver has a limited effect."

Above them, Eagle 1-2 successfully brought Pelletier inside the chopper and it immediately lifted, gaining altitude as it cleared the area. Seconds later, they could hear the sounds of the rotors fading as they headed back to base.

"Alright folks," said Greyeagle. "We're on our own until the rest of the team hits the ground."

"Great," said Margolin. "Just the six of us against that fucking thing."

"Seven," said Doc.

"What?" asked Margolin.

"Seven," repeated Doc. "I'm in this fight, too. Those were my friends it killed."

"That's what I figured you'd say," said Greyeagle. "That's why I brought you one of our rifles and extra gear. Let's get inside and figure out our next move."

Activating his comm, Greyeagle spoke as he glanced around the surrounding woods.

"Fenrir to Thunder-God," he said.

"Thunder-God," said Clark. "Go ahead."

"We have confirmation," said Greyeagle. "Visual confirmation of hostile. Negative result from silver ammunition. Over."

"Solid copy, Fenrir," said Thunder-God. "We're deploying the Mimic Units now. Target location is approximately seven klicks west of your current position. Will transmit coordinates upon completion. Over."

"Copy that," said Greyeagle. "We're going to assess the situation here and engage only if necessary. See you when you get here. Fenrir out."

"Solid copy, Fenrir," said Clark. "Thunder-God out."

Heading inside the cabin, Greyeagle felt the eyes of the creature watching them. It was cautious now since it had felt that wound. Normal rounds did very little or nothing to the beast, but silver had gotten its attention. It would be more careful in how it attacked them, next time. Greyeagle knew full-well that there was going to be a next time. The beast was watching them, waiting for a chance to strike.

Moving inside, they shut and secured the door behind them. With a nod at Margolin and McGregor, Greyeagle turned to verify the door was secure. Margolin and McGregor moved off through the cabin to check other exits and to evaluate the security of the building as well as look for defensible positions.

Doc slid into a chair and leaned back. He looked exhausted and seemed to have aged since the last time Greyeagle had seen him. The experience had been rough on him.

"Doc, are you ok?" asked Greyeagle.

"I'm good," said Doc. "Tired but good. I'm just happy you got Pelletier out of here before the infection got too bad. If they get him to a good doctor, he should recover. His law enforcement career might be over. That leg was pretty bad."

"We got here as fast as we could," said Greyeagle.

"So, what's with the military unit?" asked Doc. "Last I know, you were doing the Native American thing. What happened?"

"It's a long story, brother," said Greyeagle with a shrug. "I was recruited into this team. They hunt all kinds of creatures like this."

"I heard a few rumors about teams like that existing," said Doc, "but I thought it was all rumor."

"They're real," said Greyeagle. "I'm not sure how much I can tell you, though. It's all above Top Secret."

"Well," said Doc, gesturing around him, "I think I already know about the team and you can attest that I know these things exist."

"Fair enough," said Greyeagle. "The Code Name for the group is The Wild Hunt. We're part of Team Odin. The rest will be here in a few hours."

"Outstanding," said Doc. "I guess I'm unofficially part of the team, for now."

"Looks that way," said Greyeagle. "Let me grab you some gear."

Greyeagle opened a bag and handed Doc a full kit with pistol, rifle, ammo, armor, and uniform. While Doc was getting into the gear, Greyeagle met with the rest of the team.

"The building's secure, Top," said Margolin. "It's pretty solid. We can hold for a while."

"There's plenty of supplies here," said McGregor. "We won't go hungry."

"I've got a good vantage point up in the loft," said Valkyrie. "I can open a small window and get a good field of fire on the front of the cabin. If it comes from that direction, I'll know it."

"I can set up at any point," said Kodiak. "I can lay down suppressive fire on any arc."

"Alright," said Greyeagle. "I think we're secure, for now."

"Since the silver rounds didn't work," said Valkyrie, "what do you want to try next?"

"Let's switch to incendiary," said Greyeagle. "We'll see how he likes it burning hot."

"Fuck yeah," said Margolin. "Smoke his ass."

"Everyone cover your area," said Greyeagle. "We only have to hold until the Mimic Units are online. Then we're going to head for them."

"That's going to be a dangerous trip," said Valkyrie.

"I'm counting on the creature not being out much during the day," said Greyeagle. "If he is, he'll be easier to see."

"Maybe," said Valkyrie. "One version of the legend says that they move incredibly fast and can blend in with their surroundings."

"Well, we know they're fast," said Greyeagle. "We all saw that. Here's hoping the blending thing isn't real."

"I know he's your buddy, Top," said Margolin, nodding at Doc, "but can he keep up?"

"Doc was a Special Forces medic when I met him," said Greyeagle. "Saved my life a couple of times. Plus, last year, he hunted Dogmen with me and some friends of mine."

"I'd say that would cover it," said Margolin. "That helps out considerably."

"He's a shooter," said Greyeagle. "He'll more than keep up."

"Outstanding," said Margolin. "Can we keep him?"

"Let's get to our positions," said Greyeagle. "I don't think it can get inside, but let's not give it the chance."

"We've got you, Top," said Valkyrie.

With that, they all headed to different points throughout the cabin. Greyeagle headed back to the living room to check on Doc and found him peering through the cracks in the shutters. He was wearing the full Team Odin kit and had replaced his 5.56mm Noveske AR with the team's .458 SOCOM rifle.

"Looking good, Doc," said Greyeagle, softly. "See anything out there?"

"Not a damned thing," said Doc. "That's the weird part, too. Yesterday deer were moving around and I even saw a few rabbits. Today there's nothing. I don't even hear birds."

"It's still out there, somewhere," said Greyeagle. "I don't think it's bothered by the dark. I was hoping it hid during the day, but that might not be the case. The team has a research crew that checks legends and history books, looking for the stories on how these things are killed. The problem is, there's just too many versions of the Wendigo story out there. We'll keep trying until something works."

"It didn't seem to like the silver rounds," said Doc.

"Like, no," said Greyeagle. "Although they didn't seem to hurt it that bad, it did feel them. That's something, at least. By the way, does this place have a basement?"

"I have no idea," said Doc. "We just got here yesterday afternoon and I didn't exactly get the grand tour. I know that the lofts upstairs are the sleeping areas. Other than that, your guess is as good as mine."

"I'll have a look around," said Greyeagle. "Places like this usually have a root cellar or something similar because they can't refrigerate food without electricity."

"Makes sense," said Doc.

"Are you alright, Doc?" asked Greyeagle.

"Physically, yeah," said Doc. "That thing never hurt me. I'm numb right now, but I won't be later. That thing killed four of my friends."

"I understand," said Greyeagle. "We'll get it, I promise. Stick to the group and don't try any solo stuff. It's teamwork that'll bring this thing down."

Doc turned and looked at him, nodding slowly.

"I got you, man," said Doc. "We play this by the book. I still hope I'm the one that gets the final shot."

"Hey, look at it this way," said Greyeagle. "Uncle Sugar[11] is buying the ammo. Shoot it as many times as you want."

"How long do we have to wait here?" asked Doc.

"Until Team Two hits the deck and the Mimics are in place," answered Greyeagle.

"Mimics?" asked Doc. "What the hell are those?"

"Long story, brochacho," said Greyeagle, smiling. "You'll see them in a little while. Margolin refers to them as the Insta-FOBs, because you can build a FOB[12] in a matter of hours."

---

[11] Uncle Sugar – play on the words Uncle Sam and Sugar Daddy referring to something paid for by the government. Usually heard by military retirees referring to their retirement check every month. The Uncle Sugar check.
[12] FOB – milspeak for Forward Operations Base

44

"I bet that comes in handy," said Doc.

"I hope so," said Greyeagle. "This is the first time I've used them. I guess they didn't hold up well in their last deployment. Supposedly, they've upgraded since then. We'll see."

"Lowest bidder," said Doc with a chuckle.

"Just like the rest of our gear," said Greyeagle with a shrug. "Here's hoping it stands up to the hype. I don't think the Wendigo is going to make this easy on us."

"Easy?" said Doc. "When has anything gone easy when the two of us get involved. Hell, the night I met you was one of the biggest shit-shows I've ever had the displeasure of being part of. What a clusterfuck."

"We survived," said Greyeagle. "A lot of good men didn't, though. Even when it sucks, we keep fighting. That's who we are."

"Embrace the Suck," said Doc.

"Embrace the Suck," echoed Greyeagle.

"Aw fuck!" snapped Margolin.

Turning around, Greyeagle and Doc saw Margolin putting his gear down and dropping to do pushups.

"What's he doing that for?" asked Greyeagle.

"Standing orders, Top," said Valkyrie. "Ever since he showed up at a briefing wearing a shirt with that slogan on it, Sar-Major says he has to drop and do a hundred pushups every time someone says it."

"Now, I've gotta do a hundred pushups," grumbled Margolin.

"Nope," said Valkyrie. "Two hundred. They both said it."

"Fuck!" hissed Margolin, starting his pushups.

"Don't cheat," cautioned Valkyrie. "Sar-Major always knows when you try that."

Margolin said nothing. He just kept knocking out pushups rapidly while Valkyrie secretly kept count.

CHAPTER THREE
MIMIC

"Who dares, wins. Who sweats, wins. Who plans, wins."
British Special Air Service (SAS)

0958 Hours CST
13 February
Rocky Lake, MN

"Two minutes to LZ, Captain," said the pilot to Clark.

"Copy," said Clark, holding up two fingers to the rest of the occupants of the transport helicopter.

"Two minutes, Team Two!" roared Gideon.

"Two minutes, Team Four!" echoed Captain Hernandez.

Teams Two and Four of Team Odin were ready to deploy. They were to secure the Landing Zone or "LZ" for the placement of the Mimic Units. Their target LZ was a large clearing several hundred yards west of Rocky Lake.

"Hammer 2-1 to all Hammer Units," said the pilot over the radio, "we are two minutes from target. Standby for Mimic deployment. All Units, how copy? Over."

"Hammer 2-2 copies," said a voice.

Clark listened as seven more of the big Chinook helicopters checked in, Hammer 2-3 through Hammer 2-9 all confirmed their compliance. Clark knew that this was going to be critical on the timing. By the time they had finished dropping the first eight of the Mimic Units, the next four would already be on their way. The first eight would form the ground level of the FOB. The next four were to lock in place on top of the other eight. The difficult part would be keeping the area secure until the Mimics were all in place.

Banking around over the lake, Clark got his first look at the snow-covered landscape. While not as rugged as the Ouachita Mountains of Oklahoma, they were no less remote. They were more than twenty miles from the nearest town of any actual size and only a few miles from the

Candian border. They were all alone out here and any assistance would only be coming from the air. There wasn't even a logging road for more than ten miles in any direction.

Beginning his descent, Hammer 2-1 brought the big Chinook in over the clearing and touched down in the middle of the area. He was careful to stay well away from the trees, just in case the creature was to take a shot at the aircraft. As soon as the wheels hit the ground, the ramp at the back of the chopper started lowering.

"Lock and Load!" roared Gideon. "Teams Two and Four going hot!"

The sound of numerous charging handles being pulled at the same time filled the air. The ramp lowered to the ground and the rotor wash was kicking snow up into the air and driving it into their faces and eyes. Clark had planned for that exact thing, ordering the entire team to deploy with the polarized goggles to prevent eye injury from projectiles or snow blindness due to the sunlight reflecting from the thick snow.

As the teams rushed out of the chopper, they all started deploying to cover the area. Dropping down in preplanned zones, they quickly established interlocking fields of fire. Clark and Hernandez came down the ramp at the same time with Gideon and First Lieutenant Murdock directing the movements of Team Two, while First Sergeant Delmar and First Lieutenant Keogh directed Team Four.

"We've got the north side of the clearing," said Hernandez.

"I put Murdock in charge of the south side," said Clark. "I'll be overseeing the placement of the Mimic Units."

"Got it," said Hernandez. "We'll cover you."

Hammer 2-1 climbed into the sky and banked back to the south. Clark knew that it was already heading back to pick up another Mimic Unit module. Hammer 2-2 was already lining up to lay the cornerstone of the Mimic placement. If everything went according to plan, they would have the modules in place and be going online in two hours. The clock was now ticking.

"Thunder-god to Fenrir," said Clark, activating his comm. "Teams Two and Four are on the ground. Mimic placement is beginning. Standby for additional instructions. Over."

"Solid Copy, Thunder-god," said Greyeagle. "Standing by."

"Fenrir, what's your status? Over," said Clark.

"We're stable," said Greyeagle. "No additional contact at this time, over."

"Copy, Fenrir," said Clark. "Thunder-god out."

Snow began to kick up into the air as Hammer 2-2 begin descending, bringing in the first piece of the Mimic Units. Lowering it into place, they cut the swing-load cables loose and climbed back into the sky. Clark immediately directed his ground crew to begin removing the cables and clearing the rigging to prepare for the next section to be added. Above him, Hammer 2-3 was already moving into position.

Clark continued to coordinate as unit after unit was lowered into place and secured with the locking mechanisms. Checking the status of the other units, he found that the last four were inbound and should be on station in twenty minutes. The ground level was all in place and the onboard systems were already synching up. The full system wouldn't be brought online until Teams One and Three arrived in the final chopper.

"Contact!" roared someone over the radio. "We've got movement in the trees."

"Sound off!" replied Clark. "Last call station give your designation!"

"Huntsman 4-5," came the reply. "Positive contact. Subject has not attempted to close."

"Huntsman 4-5, this is Broadsword," said Hernandez, "hold your fire unless it becomes hostile. Do not engage at this time."

"Copy that, Broadsword," said Huntsman 4-5. "Standing by."

Clark glanced at the clipboard and saw that per the assigned positions, Huntsman 4-5 was on the North West corner of the clearing. Tossing the clipboard to one of the placement team, Clark pulled out his binoculars and headed around the edge of the Mimics to see if he could get a view of the creature.

"Thunder-god to Viking," said Clark over the radio.

"This is Viking," said SSG Marcel Hendrix. "Send it. Over."

48

Viking was the team's newest sniper, recently assigned to the team from the US Army Green Berets. Although he was combat-proven, Clark had chosen to keep him with the team when Valkyrie had gone with Greyeagle on the rescue. As good as he was, Valkyrie had proven to be a better shot on the range. He sent his best sniper with Fenrir because they were going to be in the middle of the fight without immediate support.

"Viking," said Clark, "identify target on the northwest sector. Do not engage unless it becomes hostile."

"Copy that, Thunder-God," said Viking. "Acquiring target. Over."

"Viking," said Clark. "Be advised, silver ammunition has minimal effect. Switch to incendiary tipped rounds. Over."

"Copy that, Thunder-god," said Viking. "I'm on it. Over."

Clark began sweeping the area again with the binoculars. In the deep shadows beneath the trees, he could see movement but nothing clear enough to verify the target. Whatever it was, it was being cautious. It was getting a look at them before it made any moves.

"Thunder-god to Fenrir," said Clark.

"Go ahead," said Greyeagle.

"The subject has approached our position," said Clark. "You should be in the clear, at the moment. Over."

"Negative, Thunder-god," replied Greyeagle. "We're still seeing movement in the trees. Subject is still on site. Over."

"Fenrir interrogative," said Clark. "Can you verify? You're certain it's still there? Over."

"Affirm," replied Fenrir. "Subject still on site. Confirmed. Over."

"Copy that, Fenrir," said Clark. "Stand by for further instructions. Do not attempt to move yet. Over."

"Copy that," said Greyeagle. "Fenrir out."

Clark took a deep breath and glanced around. Reaching into his pocket, he took out a can of chewing tobacco and put in a large pinch to soothe his nerves.

"Thunder-god to all units," said Clark. "Be advised, there is more than one creature. Say again, there's more than one. Over."

"Broadsword acknowledges," said Hernandez.

"Fenrir acknowledges," said Greyeagle.

In the distance, Clark could hear the rotors of incoming helicopters. Glancing in that direction, he could see the first Hammer Unit returning with a Mimic module beneath it.

"Hammer 2-1 to Thunder-god," said the radio.

"Thunder-god, go ahead," said Clark.

"We are inbound to your position, ETA two minutes," said Hammer 2-1. "How copy?"

"Solid Copy, Hammer 2-1," said Clark. "We're ready for your arrival. Over."

"Huntsman 4-5 to Broadsword," said Huntsman 4-5.

"Go ahead," said Hernandez.

"Subject is moving off into the trees," said Huntsman 4-5. "I have lost visual. Direction of travel is northeast. Over."

"Copy that," said Hernandez. "All Huntsman units be advised subject is on the move. Over."

"Thunder-god to Mjolnir," said Clark.

"Go for Mjolnir," replied Gideon.

"As soon as we're clear with Mimic placement," said Clark, "come to my position. Over."

"Copy that," said Gideon. "Over."

In fifteen minutes, the remaining four Mimic modules were put into place and locked. The final Chinook landed on the snow and Teams One and Three disembarked. Immediately, Team One headed inside the Mimic Units to begin bringing the systems fully online. Gideon approached Clark just as the final chopper began lifting into the air.

"You wanted to see me, sir," said Gideon.

"Yeah," said Clark. "If there are more than one of those things, then we can't take it for granted that there's only two. We have to assume several of them."

"Safe assumption, sir," said Gideon.

"As soon as they've got the Mimics online and Team Three is in place," said Clark, "we're taking Team Two and we're going to get the others. I won't risk them coming with just the six of them."

"Good idea," said Gideon. "I'll spread the word and make the preparations."

"Make sure everyone makes the switch to incendiaries," said Clark. "Also everyone needs to bring both Gladius and tomahawk on this one. We have to be prepared for the possibilities that guns just don't work."

"How soon do you want to be ready?" asked Gideon.

"As soon as All-father gives us the all-clear," said Clark. "I'll go brief him now. I want to be moving in ten minutes. We need to have everyone back inside the wire before nightfall."

"Attention all units," said Major Saunders over the radio, "Valhalla is online. All units, Valhalla is now online."

"There's my cue," said Clark, grinning.

Gideon nodded and headed for the team while Clark ducked inside the Mimic Units. Entering the Command Module, Clark found Major Saunders and Command Sergeant Major Hammond checking systems. CSM[13] Hammond was running checks on the perimeter camera systems while Saunders did a Comms check with base. Wilder was at the computer console running systems checks to verify everything was working correctly.

"Clark," said CSM Hammond. "Good to see you, son. How's it look out there?"

CSM Hammond smiled and held out his hand. Clark handed him the can of chewing tobacco and the older warrior took a large pinch before handing it back. It had become a running joke with the two of them since CSM Hammond's wife wouldn't let him buy it anymore.

---

[13] CSM – Command Sergeant Major

"Snowy and cold," said Clark. "Kinda like last time."

"Fuck, let's hope not," said CSM Hammond.

"Well, we've already confirmed there's more than one creature," said Clark. "No engagements, since Fenrir's initial contact."

"How many do you think there are?" asked CSM Hammond.

"No idea," said Clark. "Two for certain. We have to assume there's more than that."

"What's on your mind, son?" asked CSM Hammond.

"I'm planning on taking all of Team Two to rendezvous with Fenrir's team," said Clark. "Since we know there's more than one, I thought it better to have more firepower to bring them home. A small team could get overwhelmed easily by several creatures."

"And you're waiting to ask Levi for permission," said CSM Hammond.

"Pretty much," said Clark.

"I take it your team is already prepped and ready to go?" said CSM Hammond.

Clark just smiled at him.

"Go get your people, son," said CSM Hammond. "Levi won't be off the radio for a while. I'll brief him when he's done. The quicker you get moving, the quicker you get back. Your team doesn't need to be out there once the sun goes down."

"Copy that," said Clark, grinning.

"We'll have the coffee ready when you get back," said CSM Hammond, with a wink.

Clark headed out the door and ducked through the supply module, taking the most direct path outside. He could tell that the Mimics had been seriously upgraded since they last used them in Oklahoma. It was clear that the armor was thicker and there were more modules. They had twice the number of modules than their last deployment.

When Clark exited the Mimic Units, he saw that Team Three was already putting in firing positions for their heavy weapons. Lieutenant

Elliott was placing his team for maximum coverage of the surrounding trees. By placing the Mimics in the middle of the large clearing, they had almost fifty meters of kill zone established in every direction.

Team Four was already deploying concertina wire around the perimeter in double layers. Unless the creature could leap ten feet in the air and cover twenty yards in a single leap, it wasn't coming through the perimeter without being noticed.

All of the dog teams would be deployed inside the wire to help detect the approach of the creatures. This time, they weren't going to let the creatures get close enough to attack the Mimic Units directly. They were already changing their strategy for Mimic Deployment and it would continue to evolve as they learned more about them.

When the team formed up, Clark called the senior staff together. He met with Gideon and Lieutenant Murdock a few feet away from the rest of the team.

"Alright folks," said Clark. "We have a green light. We're going after the others. We're moving fast and taking no chances."

"Where do you need us?" asked Gideon.

"Murdock," said Clark, "you take the point with Huntsman 2-1 and 2-2. We're spacing at ten-foot intervals and everyone covers each other. Watch the trees. These things tend to try to drag prey up into the treetops. Gideon, you bring up the rear with Huntsman 2-7 and 2-8. I'll be in the middle with Runestone on comms. Do not be drawn away from the group. We stick together and we come back as a team."

"Copy that," said Murdock.

"Gotcha, boss," said Gideon.

"We're weapons hot until we're back inside the wire," said Clark. "We're clear to engage if you have a clear shot."

Murdock and Gideon both nodded, then headed off to brief their men. Clark activated his comm and stepped away from the group.

"Thunder-god to Fenrir," said Clark.

"Go ahead," said Greyeagle.

"Stand by for extraction," said Clark. "We're coming to get you. Do not exit your cover until we're on site. How copy?"

"Solid copy," said Greyeagle. "We'll be watching. Over."

"Be ready to move on our arrival," replied Clark. "I want to be inside the wire long before dark. Thunder-god out."

Heading back to the group, Clark pulled the team together and brought out his map.

"Alright folks," said Clark. "We're going after Fenrir and the others. Since we now know there's more than one creature, we're not taking any chances. We're proceeding due east from here to the lake. Once we reach their ice fishing cabin, we follow the trail due north right to the cabin. Stay with the group. Do not pursue these creatures. They are deceptive and intelligent. You're clear to engage but do not do so unless your target is confirmed. Don't be shooting at shadows."

That drew a few chuckles.

"Alright," said Clark. "If there are no questions, let's get moving. The sun goes down early here in the winter. We're about four miles from the cabin but we're not going to be moving fast. Especially once we hit the trees. Be safe, watch each other's backs, and DO NOT leave the group."

"Hooah!" shouted the team.

"Hooah!" replied Clark. "Murdock set the pace and let's move."

Murdock took his group and headed for the wire. Team Two's dog teams were on guard duty at the makeshift gate and let them through without an issue. Keeping their spacing set, Murdock set a good pace. Fast enough to cover ground but slow enough that they were easily able to constantly sweep the surrounding trees.

Thirty yards past the gate, they entered the thick trees. They only had about a hundred yards to go before they reached the lake and were clear. While they were in the clear, they had little concern for being ambushed. However, inside the thick trees, they were inside the creature's domain and they all knew it. Despite the sun in the sky, the woods were still shrouded in deep darkness. They were now on their own.

Chapter Four
Ambush

"War to the knife and the knife to the hilt."
Unknown

1215 Hours CST
13 February

The moment they hit the trees, the point men split watching the trees and both sides of the trail. Moving in a crouch, the team stayed low to avoid branches. They were all prepared for the Wendigo hiding in the treetops and dragging victims to their doom.

Traversing the section of woods took less than fifteen minutes, but felt like much longer. Clark felt himself relaxing slightly when they passed from the darkness of the trees and back into the open as they approached the frozen lake.

"Mjolnir to Thunder-god," said Gideon.

"Go ahead," said Clark.

"We've got movement to the north," said Gideon. "It's keeping its distance, but it knows we're here. Over."

"Copy that," said Clark. "All units, stay alert. Thunder-god out."

Clark glanced to the north but didn't see any signs of movement.

"Valhalla to Thunder-god," said Saunders.

"Go ahead," said Clark.

"Eye in the sky now going up," said Saunders. "We'll relay information as it comes in, over."

"Copy that," said Clark. "If you can locate the subjects, please advise. Over."

"Solid copy," said Saunders. "Valhalla out."

Ahead, they could see the single ice fishing cabin on the lake. The trail they would take to the cabin was due north of that. Clark motioned for the new team sniper, Staff Sergeant Marcel Hendrix (Call Sign:

56

Viking), to move up beside him. Keeping his voice low, Clark began relaying instructions.

"When we reach the ice fishing cabin," said Clark. "I want you and two others to stay back and set up to engage if we need you."

"Yes, sir," said Viking. "Once you're inside the trees, I won't be able to track you."

"I realize that," said Clark. "What I want is to have you in place in case we have to come back on the double. Huntsman 2-4 and 2-5 can stay with you."

"Copy that, sir," said Viking.

Clark relayed the instructions to Huntsman 2-4 and 2-5, motioning for them to remain with Viking.

"Valhalla Actual to Thunder-god," said Saunders.

"Go ahead," said Clark.

"We're tracking at least three motion tracks heading in your direction," said Saunders. "We don't have a confirmed visual, but the movement patterns indicate large subjects. Over."

"Copy that," said Clark.

"Two will be on the west side of the trail," said Saunders, "and one on the east side."

"Understood," said Clark. "Thunder-god out."

Covering the distance to the ice fishing cabin, Clark called for the team to stop. Viking and his two guards cleared off the snow from the roof of the small cabin. Once cleared, Viking climbed up and set up his firing position with a clear view of the tree line. Clark waited until they were set up and ready before giving the order to move out.

Heading for the trees, they moved slowly and deliberately, waiting for any sign of the Wendigo. They could feel themselves being watched, but the creatures never made any move to show themselves. With each step they took, the air seemed to grow thicker and the tension continued to mount.

When they reached the edge of the trees, Lieutenant Murdock crouched down and peered into the treetops. Signaling for the team to come to a stop, Murdock took the time to study the trees before approaching. After a moment, he began moving forward in a crouch. The rest of the team slowly followed, staying low and scanning left, right, and up with each step. There was no sound coming from the trees other than the whispering of the wind through the pines.

"Valhalla to Thunder-god," said Saunders.

"Go ahead," said Clark.

"Motion has stopped," said Saunders. "We've lost track of the subjects. Over."

"Copy that," said Clark. "Proceeding with caution. Over."

"We'll maintain the eye in the sky and update if we see anything, over," said Saunders.

"Copy," said Clark. "Out."

Moving into the darkness, the team continued to sweep left, right, and up with every step. Once in the trees, the silence was oppressive with the only thing disturbing the utter stillness being the soft crunching of boots on snow. It took a few seconds for their eyes to adjust to the shadows and tension was high.

Clark kept his head on a swivel as he moved beneath the dark canopy. Every twig that moved in the breeze seemed magnified as he peered desperately into that stygian darkness, looking for the threats to his team. There was a rustle of dry sticks which was followed by an almost inaudible sound that made the hairs on the back of his neck stand up. It sounded like bones tapping gently against each other.

Turning his head rapidly, he zeroed in on the spot with uncanny accuracy. There, in the deep shadows, was a shape that was nearly invisible in the gloom. It was pressed close to the side of a large tree peering at them with just the barest slits of its eyes. It was in those bare slits that Clark caught the hint of red.

"Contact left!" he shouted.

Snapping his rifle to his shoulder, he zeroed in the ACOG on the spot and felt the safety snap off as he prepared to fire. Just as he was

58

taking up the slack on the trigger, the creature moved impossibly fast. Leaping from the tree, Clark saw the figure fully silhouetted against the sparse light filtering in through the treetops. It was at that moment he saw the shimmering effect and instantly recognized what it meant. They could cloak themselves.

Leading his target, Clark let fly with a three-round burst of the powerful .458 SOCOM rounds. These were incendiary rounds and he hoped that they would cause more damage than the silver rounds had. The first two rounds missed due to the incredible speed of the beast, but the third round found its mark.

Grunting in pain, the beast's trajectory was altered and instead of landing among the branches of a large Oak, it slammed into the trunk with considerable force. Several more rifles sounded as others began taking shots at the beast.

Howling in pain and fury, the beast vanished into the trees and was soon lost from sight. They could still hear the odd tearing metal sound of the creature's screams as it sped off into the distance.

"They can cloak!" roared Clark. "The goddamned things can cloak!"

Quickly the team formed a circle with their backs towards one another and began scanning the trees around them. They all had their weapons up and were scanning for targets. With the knowledge that the creatures could virtually turn themselves invisible, every shadow and shape had to be studied closely. The threat level was now incredibly higher than they had expected. None of the legends had suggested that the creatures could cloak.

"Valhalla to Thunder-god," said Saunders over the radio.

"Go!" said Clark, not taking his eyes off their surroundings.

"The drone detected gunfire and movement," said Saunders. "What's your status? Over."

"We engaged one creature and it fled," said Clark. "One hit confirmed but more possible. Over."

"To what effect?" asked Saunders. "Over."

"Incendiaries hurt it," said Clark, "but not enough to put it down. Over."

"We're still tracking the movement," said Saunders. "Whatever you did, it's clearing the area as fast as it can. Over."

"Monitor where it goes," said Clark. "It might lead us to its lair. Over."

"Copy that," said Saunders. "Out."

They continued to watch the trees for several minutes without anything else presenting itself. Clark glanced around and above them before making his decision. They were burning daylight and this was now the last place he wanted to be when the sun went down. With the creature's cloaking ability, finding it at night would be almost impossible without using thermal imaging and no guarantee would work against them.

"Stay sharp, folks," he said. "Let's get moving."

The team started moving again, cautiously watching every shadow and tree. Murdock took point with his two escorts flanking him. They were approaching a thick stand of pine trees when Clark saw Murdock's hand go up giving the signal to stop. The team froze instantly and Clark could hear the creaking of gloves tightening on the handles of weapons.

The team knelt into the snow and brought their weapons up, covering every angle of approach. Murdock turned and made eye contact with Clark, then held up two fingers pointing at his own eyes. He'd seen something. Motioning for Clark to come up to him, Murdock turned back towards the stand of trees and brought his weapon up into a ready position. Clark made his way up to Murdock and knelt beside him.

"What have you got?" whispered Clark.

Pointing ahead, Murdock leaned close to keep his voice as low as possible.

"I see blood ahead," said Murdock. "There's quite a bit of it on the ground near the base of a tree."

"That's probably where they were attacked," whispered Clark. "Do you see any movement?"

"No," replied Murdock, "but that's the perfect ambush spot. It's darker than the surrounding trees and it's where it was waiting for the men that were attacked. We won't be able to see it in there."

"If we go off-trail," said Clark, "it's going to slow us down. We might not make it back before dark."

"If we go through there," said Murdock, "we might not make it back, at all."

"The map doesn't show how big this section is," said Clark. "We've got no way to know how far we'll have to go to avoid it."

"Therein lies the rub," said Murdock. "We walk into a possible ambush or we chance not getting back before dark. Hell of a choice to have to make. Glad you're the one that's gotta make it, sir."

"Gee, thanks," said Clark.

"Seriously, though," said Murdock. "We're damned if we do, damned if we don't. Unless you've got another solution I'm not considering."

Clark thought for a moment, considering all available information. He knew that a decision had to be made quickly because they were wasting daylight with every passing second.

"We go through," said Clark, frowning.

Turning to the team, he motioned for them to get where they could hear him.

"Alright folks," he began, "we're going through an area where an ambush is highly possible."

Everyone nodded as they glanced behind him towards the thick pines.

"Load your grenade launchers," said Clark. "It might not kill one, but I bet it gets his attention. From this point on, we're at free fire. If you see it, engage it."

There were eight of them that had the under-barrel mounted M320 grenade launchers, including Gideon and Clark. They all quickly loaded their launcher tubes and readied them for use.

61

"Let's move," said Clark.

Murdock nodded and headed back to the point position. Crouching low, he crept into the trees and swept every direction. The team closed the distance, keeping within arm's reach of the next person. This made it easier to respond to help anyone who'd been attacked.

Clark constantly swept the trees as he moved beneath them. Just ahead of him was the team communications specialist, Senior Chief Petty Officer Santana Alvarez (Code Name: Runestone). He was recruited into the Hunt from the US Navy SEAL Team Six and had been with the team for almost two years.

Runestone was watching the trees and providing cover when they all heard the radio hiss with a garbled communication. As Runestone shifted his attention to try and clear up the signal, there was a sudden rush of movement from directly above him. Hidden among the branches, a Wendigo slashed downwards, cutting into Runestone's vest and face.

Before the creature could attempt to drag him up into the trees, Clark shot it in the neck at almost point-blank range with his rifle. The massive .458 SOCOM round slammed into the beast with tremendous force.

Dropping Runestone, the beast fell to the ground shrieking in pain and rage. The multitoned tearing metal sound was painful to everyone around the beast from both the tone and volume of the scream. Ignoring the pain, Clark shot it twice more in the chest. The shrieks stopped almost instantly.

Looking down at the smoking wounds in the beast's torso, Clark could see that the incendiary rounds were causing massive damage but he couldn't tell if the creature was alive or dead. Not taking any chances, he shot it once more in the head. The force knocked the skull face off the head. It wasn't part of the creature. It was the skull of an elk that it had crafted into a mask.

The features beneath the mask were horrifying. It was clear that it had once been human. The skin was leathery and drawn tight over the bones of the skull. The lips looked like they had been ripped or chewed off. The bluish-purple tongue lolled out of the mouth and seemed to have strange pustules on it. There was a tattoo over the thing's left eye.

The skin was withered but you could still make out the details of the tattoo. It was a black bird's wing that covered one eye.

"Looks like the incendiary rounds will put one down," said Clark.

Runestone was on the ground, his hand cradling the deep laceration to the left side of his face. The newest medic on the team, Staff Sergeant Norman Meredith (Code Name: Caduceus) immediately ran over to Runestone to start first aid. Caduceus had been recruited in January at the team tryouts in Washington and came to the team from the US Army Green Berets."

The rest of the team formed a defensive perimeter around the wounded man and brought their weapons up. Clark continued to watch the beast on the ground, still unsure if it was dead. There was massive trauma to the head and chest cavity, but the creature was not natural. It was a supernatural creature and there was no way to know if it was going to stay down or for how long.

"Gideon," said Clark, loud enough to be heard.

Gideon moved over next to Clark and kept his weapon trained on the creature.

"What's up, boss?" asked Gideon.

"Do you have any thermite in your pack?" asked Clark.

"I think so," said Gideon, taking off his pack and checking. "What have you got in mind?"

"One of the books said that you had to cut out its icy heart and burn it," said Clark. "I think a thermite grenade placed on the chest should burn anything in the area."

"That it might," said Gideon, grinning. "Here you go, sir."

Gideon slipped his pack back on, then resumed covering the creature in case it tried to get up.

"Caduceus," said Clark. "How's Runestone?"

"He's going to need quite a few stitches, sir," said Caduceus. "He won't be winning any beauty pageants and he's gonna have a hell of a scar, but he'll live."

63

"Can he be moved?" asked Clark.

"I've got pressure on the wound now," said Caduceus. "We need to get that stitched up as soon as possible."

"Can he make it to the cabin?" asked Clark. "We're sitting ducks here."

"I can make it, sir," said Runestone.

"Give me two minutes and I can close it with superglue," said Caduceus. "It's gonna hurt like a bastard, though."

"Do it," said Runestone.

"Two minutes," said Clark.

Caduceus set to the task of cleaning out the wounds with peroxide, then beginning the process of closing them with a tube of medical adhesive. To his credit, Runestone barely made a sound during the entire process.

"Done!" said Caduceus. "It needs to be double-checked once we're in the clear, but he's mobile."

"Alright folks," said Clark. "Let's get moving."

Murdock took point again and they headed deeper into the thick pines. Once the team was moving, Clark pulled the pin on the thermite grenade and stuffed it into one of the open wounds in the middle of the creature's chest.

"Fry motherfucker," whispered Clark.

They moved away, heading off into the trees when the thermite ignited. The creature began flailing and screaming again. It hadn't been dead the entire time. Digging at its chest, it tried in vain to pull the burning thermite from its chest, catching its hands-on fire in the process. As the bright glow engulfed the creature's entire torso, it burst into flames. The shriek of pain died away as the creature became completely immolated in flames.

In the trees around them, they heard at least four more shrieks as other creatures sounded their fury at the death of one of their own. None of them would get closer and as the dying creature's screams ceased, they could hear the creatures moving off at a high rate of speed. They had just been put on notice. The humans could kill them, now. The game had just significantly changed.

Despite the creatures moving away, the team did not let its guard down. From the roars and screams of the creatures as they fled the area, they knew this was not over. In fact, it was far from over. They were going to be back. They were coming back for blood.

As they moved deeper into the trees, Murdock called for them to come to a stop. Clark could see Murdock step off the trail, then return holding an AR-style rifle. It had been nearly snapped in half at the magazine well but was held together by a single section of the aluminum lower receiver.

Murdock reached up and put the remains of the rifle in the pack of one of Huntsman 2-2. Once it was secure, they continued through the trees. They passed two spots where there had been a great deal of blood spilled in the snow. They did not find any bodies or even pieces. The creatures were very thorough at taking everything they could eat.

Motioning for Clark to approach her, the other team medic was crouched beside a pool of blood. Staff Sergeant Samantha Pennebaker (Code Name: Shieldmaiden) had come to the team before Clark had and was originally in the US Air Force ParaRescue teams.

"What do you have?" asked Clark, kneeling beside her.

"This spot here," she said, pointing.

"Its blood," said Clark. "What about it?"

"I can see the impressions in the snow where one of the men fell," said Shieldmaiden.

"Okay, so what's the problem?" asked Clark. "Sorry, but I don't follow."

"There's not enough blood here to have been fatal," said Shieldmaiden. "I think he was alive when he was dragged away."

"I believe that would have been a guy named Sheffield," said Clark. "Fenrir told me that he was the only one that was taken but not confirmed dead."

"Then I would guess that he's alive," said Shieldmaiden. "Or, at least, he was when he was taken."

"There was something in one of the legends that suggested they occasionally took people alive to eat later," said Clark. "Like stocking food for a long winter."

"Then, unless they've eaten him since then," said Shieldmaiden.

"There's a chance he might still be alive," finished Clark. "If there's a chance, then we have to try and find him."

"Yes, sir," said Shieldmaiden, smiling.

"Leave no man behind," said Clark, heading back to the group.

"And that's why we like you, sir," whispered Shieldmaiden.

Taking her place back in the formation, they continued through the trees. As they rounded a bend in the trail, the cabin emerged from the darkness and they could see light again. Moments later, they all entered the clearing and headed for the front porch.

"Thunder-god to Fenrir," said Clark.

"Go ahead," said Greyeagle.

"We're on your front lawn," said Clark. "We've got a wounded man. Let's get him inside so he can get patched up before we head back, over."

"Solid Copy, Thunder-god," said Greyeagle. "We're coming out. Over."

"Copy that," said Clark. "Out. Break. Thunder-god to Valhalla."

"Go ahead," said a voice Clark didn't recognize.

He knew it had to be one of the new Combat Controllers that had been brought on board from the Air Force.

"We've reached objective one," said Clark. "Nothing additional. Over."

"Copy, Thunder-god. Valhalla out."

The door to the cabin opened and Greyeagle walked out onto the porch.

"We put on some coffee," said Greyeagle. "Who's hurt?"

A man Clark didn't recognize came walking out in the team uniform.

"Captain Clark," said Greyeagle, "this is Kerry Davis. We all called him Pocket Doc. Doc for short when the crap hit the fan."

"This is the guy from Dark Angel, right," said Clark.

"That's me," said Doc.

"Well," said Clark. "I've got a story to tell you. I'm alive because of your kits. It's damned good to meet you, sir."

"Glad to be of service," said Doc. "Now, how can I help? I heard you have a man wounded."

Caduceus headed inside leading Runestone. Doc and Shieldmaiden went with him.

"I think they've got this," said Greyeagle.

"I'm still getting to know Caduceus," said Clark, "but he seems solid. I think there aren't many wounds that those three couldn't treat."

"Let's hope we don't have to find out, sir," said Greyeagle.

While the medics patched up Runestone's face, Clark brought everyone up to speed on what they'd learned thus far. They now knew that fire would kill a Wendigo. The trick was putting them down long enough to burn them. That was going to prove to be the most difficult part.

Chapter Five
Darkness Falls

"Live for something rather than die for nothing."
General George S. Patton

1445 Hours CST
13 February

Runestone walked out of the cabin with a large bandage on his face. He gave Clark a thumbs up and started putting his gear back on. Doc, Shieldmaiden, and Caduceus emerged behind him and stood on the porch. Clark headed over to them and stopped a few feet away.

"How is he?" asked Clark.

"Well, we cleaned him up," said Shieldmaiden. "He had three nasty gashes in his left cheek and on his neck."

"We found a piece of a claw embedded in his neck," said Caduceus. "That would have caused a hell of an infection if we hadn't found it."

"Over sixty stitches to close it up properly," said Doc. "He's going to have a couple of interesting scars, but he'll heal."

"Good," said Clark. "Grab your gear and get ready to move. We're rapidly burning daylight."

With that, everyone started grabbing their packs and double-checking their gear. Weapons were checked and magazines were replenished so that everyone was operating with full ammo. While Clark was checking the map, Doc approached him and stood to his left.

"Something I can do for you?" asked Clark, not looking up from the map.

"I heard you think Sheffield might be alive," said Doc.

"We think so," said Clark. "We have no way to know for sure, but it looks like he was taken alive."

"I want to be part of the team who goes after him," said Doc adamantly.

68

"Greyeagle speaks highly of you," said Clark, smiling. "He says you would have been someone we recruited but he's scared of your wife."

"Hell, I am too," said Doc, chuckling. "She'd never go for it. But I certainly appreciate the thought."

"I have faith in Greyeagle," said Clark. "If he says you're capable, I believe him. The thing is, you aren't even supposed to know this team exists. We're about four steps above Top Secret."

"I've held clearances before," said Doc.

"Then I don't need to remind you of the danger in revealing the existence of this team," said Clark. "Do I?"

"Not at all," said Doc. "Besides, who the hell would believe me. If I start talking about seeing Dogmen and Wendigo, they'd book me a room in the Hotel Twinkie and give me one of those fancy jackets that lace in the back."

"Good point," said Clark. "Greyeagle trusts you. I trust him. You're in, for the duration. If there's any shit to take over it, I'll take it. If it was my friend out there, I'd want to be part of the rescue mission, too."

"I owe him that," said Doc. "I won't leave knowing he might still be out there."

"Then I'm going to expect you to act like a member of the team," said Clark. "That means following orders, like everyone else."

"It's your team," said Doc. "You lead, I'll follow."

"Good," said Clark. "Welcome to Team Odin."

"Mind if I ask more information than that?" asked Doc.

"I think you probably know too much, as it is," said Clark with a grin. "Once we get back to Valhalla, I'll give you the highlights."

"What's Valhalla?" asked Doc.

"You'll see," said Clark, chuckling. "As I said, you probably already know too much."

Gideon came up beside them.

"Sorry to interrupt, boss," said Gideon, "but we need to get moving. We've only got a few hours of daylight left. We didn't pack NVGs[14]."

"Get the team ready," said Clark. "Same positions. Keep Kodiak on rearguard with you and Greyeagle goes on point with Murdock. The rest to the middle."

"On it, boss," said Gideon. "I'll make it happen. When do you want to leave?"

"Be ready in five," said Clark.

Gideon nodded and headed out at a quick pace.

"Your Sergeant Major seems like a solid guy," said Doc.

"Gideon?" said Clark. "Yeah, he's a hell of a soldier. Just got promoted to Sergeant Major last month. Frankly, he earned it a long time ago. They've been bouncing it around since Oklahoma. I'm glad he finally got it."

Clark turned to check his gear when the radio came to life.

"Valhalla Control to Thunder-god," said a female voice he didn't recognize.

"Go for Thunder-god," said Clark.

"Thunder-god, we have a shift in weather patterns," said the voice. "A storm that was north of our position has shifted directions and is heading our way. Over."

"Copy," said Clark. "How long until it hits? Over."

"If it maintains current speed," said the voice, "we anticipate two hours at the most."

"Solid copy, Valhalla," said Clark. "We're going to be heading back. Please advise if there is any change in the weather. Over."

"Copy," said the voice. "Valhalla out."

"Gideon!" yelled Clark. "We're moving now!"

The team began grabbing gear and checking weapons as they began stacking in position. They were in position in less than thirty seconds.

---

[14] NVG – Night Vision Goggles

Every person double-checked the people around them. No one wanted to leave any gear behind. Clark held up his thumb. One by one, the rest of the team followed. Once every thumb was up, Clark nodded at Murdock.

"Set the pace, Lieutenant," said Clark. "We need to cover some ground as quickly as we can. We've got a storm inbound."

Murdock nodded and headed into the trees. Greyeagle locked eyes with Clark for a brief moment, then nodded and followed Murdock. As the team started moving into the trees, Valkyrie took her position beside Clark and matched his pace.

"Good to have you back, Valkyrie," said Clark with a grin.

"Glad to be back, sir," she said, nodding. "If you're going after the possible survivor, I'm going with you."

"Never doubted that for a second," said Clark without glancing her way.

As they entered the trees, training took over and they both began sweeping every angle of approach. Valkyrie had slung her sniper's rifle over her back and was using one of the custom made HK-UMP50's that the team armorer had crafted for the team. It was a standard military version of the HK-UMP45 but rechambered to fire the Guncrafter Industries .50 GI bullet. The team snipers carried them as a backup weapon and the dog handlers carried them as a primary weapon.

Murdock was setting a rapid pace and it was only a matter of minutes before they were passing the charred remains of the dead Wendigo. The fire had burned all the flesh away and left behind the odd skull mask. It was an elk skull that had been modified to wear. There were even crude leather straps attached so it could be tied to the creature's head. Margolin picked up the mask and looked into the empty sockets.

"Damn," said Margolin. "That thermite did a hell of a job. There are scorch marks all over it. Was this the thing's skull or just a mask?"

"I think it was a mask," said Clark.

"Put that thing down, you moron," said Valkyrie.

"Hell no," said Margolin. "The Cap'n took this bastard out. I'm putting this on the wall at Steve's place."

71

Clark just shook his head.

"You could tell him to leave it alone," said Valkyrie, grinning.

"And listen to him bitch about it all the way back?" said Clark, returning the grin. "Besides, if he hangs it there, no one would believe what it was anyway."

"We'll know," said Valkyrie.

"That's the important part," said Clark.

The passage back through the trees didn't seem to take near as long as the trip through. When they started getting glimpses of the lake ahead, Clark activated his radio.

"Thunder-god to Viking," said Clark.

"Viking here," replied Viking. "Go ahead."

"We're approaching your position," said Clark. "Over."

"Copy that," said Viking. "I see you. Over."

"We're coming to you," said Clark. "Thunder-god out."

As they emerged back out into the clearing and onto the lake, they saw Viking still panning the trees behind them with his scope.

"You're all clear, Thunder-god," said Viking. "I see no signs of pursuit. Over."

"Copy," said Clark. "Out."

Once they were clear of the trees and in the open, Clark could see the dark clouds forming in the north. He feared that they would get more snow like the blizzard they'd faced in Oklahoma. Then he saw the lightning flashing through the clouds.

"Shit," he hissed. "Thunderstorm."

"Don't tell me the Thunder-god is worried about a little thunderstorm," said Valkyrie, suppressing a chuckle.

"You do realize," said Clark, grinning, "that Thunder-god is a Code Name, right? I don't have a magic hammer and I can't control the weather. I'm no God unless it's of scars and bad decisions."

"Well, I know what to get you for your birthday," she replied, with a smile.

"I'm more worried about the rain turning to ice once the temperature drops," said Clark. "Ice makes everything worse."

Thunder rolled across the frozen lake, echoing off into the distance. The promise of the storm hung heavily in the air. Clark could feel the electricity growing in the air. There was something oddly unnatural about this storm.

"There is an ill feeling in this storm," said Greyeagle as he approached.

"Can the Wendigo control the weather?" asked Clark.

"In some versions of the legend, yes," said Greyeagle. "In some versions, it cannot be killed by anything but silver. Some say, not at all. The fact that you killed one with fire is a testament to their vulnerability."

"Yeah, thermite did the trick," said Clark. "But knocking it down to use it was the real trick. Those things can take a beating."

"The silver bullets we made for your team won't work on it," said Greyeagle. "They have to be pure silver to have a real effect on the Wendigo. This is a far more powerful creature than you've ever faced before."

"That explains why the bullets had only limited effect," said Clark. "We took out one, but that was as much luck as anything else. We have no idea how many there are."

"I noticed that about the bullets, as well," said Greyeagle. "Perhaps we can get the armorer to make some when we get back."

"If he has the silver to do it," said Clark. "That's not normally something we keep with us. Fortunately, all of our blades are etched with pure silver."

"Then they should be effective," said Greyeagle. "Are the tomahawks also etched with silver?"

"Yes," said Clark. "We had all the edged weapons done that way. Even my combat knife is etched."

73

"Good," said Greyeagle. "However, if the Wendigo is controlling the weather, we should expect it to attack during the storm. We should get inside the perimeter as fast as we can."

"I agree," said Clark. "Let's get everyone moving."

The team began forming back up for the last leg of the journey back to Valhalla. Since they were no longer in the trees, Murdock set a rapid pace retracing their steps back to Valhalla.

"Help me!" called a voice from the woods.

"That's Sheffield!" yelled Doc.

"Help me, Kerry!" called the voice.

Doc looked confused.

"What's going on?" he asked, glancing around.

"What do you mean?" asked Clark.

"That's Sheffield's voice, but he never calls me by my first name," said Doc. "He always calls me Doc. He thinks it's funny to say 'What's up, Doc?' all the time."

"The Wendigo could not know that," said Greyeagle. "It can mimic voices, but it cannot read minds."

"Then how did it know my name?" asked Doc.

"That's the real question," said Clark. "One thing is for certain. We're not going after that voice. It's trying to lure you into a trap."

"Uh, boss," said Gideon. "You might want to take a look at this."

Clark turned towards Gideon to find the older warrior looking at the approaching clouds. Looking up, Clark saw it. There in the leading clouds was the unmistakable shape of the Wendigo's face. It was plain to see with the lightning illuminating the clouds behind it.

"Fuck me," said Margolin. "How's it doing that?"

"The Wendigo are creatures of dark magic," said Greyeagle. "Who knows what they are capable of?"

"We need to get moving," said Clark. "Murdock, get us going!"

As the team headed out, Greyeagle moved up beside Clark.

"If they are controlling the weather," said Greyeagle, "as we believe, then there is one actively controlling it. Like a shaman of my people, one will be summoning this storm."

"If he's outside, we can find him," said Clark.

Nodding, Greyeagle headed back to his position in the formation.

"Thunder-god to Valhalla," said Clark.

"This is Valhalla Control," said a female voice.

"I need Valhalla Actual, over," said Clark.

"Go ahead," said Saunders.

"Do we still have the eye in the sky?" asked Clark.

"Affirm," said Saunders. "What do you need?"

"Have it look for one of the creatures standing in the open," said Clark. "Possibly near a fire or on a hill."

"Copy," said Saunders. "I'm assuming you'll explain why later?"

"Affirm," said Clark. "Can you locate? Over."

"That's affirmative," said Saunders. "We have one four klicks northwest of your current position, standing in the open on a hilltop. Over."

"Is the drone armed?" asked Clark.

"Negative," said Saunders. "All of our drones are too small to be armed. Over."

"Is there any chance we can get one called in?" asked Clark. "Over."

To their astonishment, another voice cut into the channel.

"This is Asgard Actual," said the voice. "We have an asset not far from your position. It can be on-station in ten minutes."

"Copy Asgard Actual," said Saunders. "We'll have our eye in the sky paint the target. Over."

"Understood, Valhalla," said Asgard. "Asset can give you one pass and it has to return to its assigned sector. Over."

"Thank you, Asgard," said Saunders.

"Solid copy, Valhalla," said Asgard. "Looking forward to reading this mission report. Asgard Actual out."

"Who the hell is Asgard Actual?" asked Valkyrie, looking wide-eyed at Clark.

"Asgard Actual is none other than Lieutenant General Joshua Dalton, himself," said Clark.

"Why is he monitoring our radio communications?" asked Valkyrie.

"Because he can, I suppose," said Clark. "But that's not what bothers me."

"What's that?" asked Valkyrie.

"Why do we have an armed asset in the air above US soil less than ten minutes from northern Minnesota?"

"We may never know the answer to that, sir," said Valkyrie.

"You're probably right," said Clark.

Turning back to the team, Clark cupped his hands around his mouth.

"Team Two!" roared Clark. "Move!"

The team increased speed and quickly covered the distance to the trees. Glancing at his watch, Clark knew that whatever the asset was, it should be coming in very soon. Looking up into the sky, Clark saw a Predator drone break from the clouds and streak over their heads at an altitude of about a thousand feet.

"Fuck me," said Margolin. "Was that a goddamned Predator Drone?"

"Yes, it was," said Clark.

Seconds later, they heard the whoosh of a Hellfire missile launching, followed by an explosion. As the Predator drone banked back over their heads and headed back into the clouds, they saw the fireball rolling into the sky to the northwest.

"Valhalla Actual to Thunder-god," said Saunders. "Target is destroyed. Say again, Target is destroyed. Over."

"Copy, we're RTB[15], over," said Clark.

"Copy," said Saunders. "See you inside the wire. Valhalla out."

"Check out the clouds," said Valkyrie.

Clark turned back to see the face of the Wendigo blowing away like smoke in a strong wind. The intensity of the storm seemed to be fading, as well. Although, it was still coming towards them.

"Well, the storm is weakening, but it's still coming," said Clark. "Those dark clouds are going to cover the sun. It's going to get dark soon."

"How soon?" asked Valkyrie.

"Not long," said Clark. "Half hour at the most."

"Then we need to get inside the wire," said Valkyrie.

Murdock hit the trees at the end of the lake and didn't slow down. They crouched and covered every angle, but they were pushing hard to hit the wire. Clark scanned the trees for any signs of movement but saw nothing. Thirty seconds later, he entered the trees.

Margolin panned upwards and turned a full circle as he kept moving. Clark followed his search but saw nothing in the canopy. Nothing was moving and no shapes stood out.

"Everything ok?" Clark asked Margolin.

"Yeah," said Margolin. "I just had a funny feeling."

Turning back to the team, they continued through the trees. Seconds later, they emerged from the woods and headed for the gate. Glancing back, Clark caught a faint shimmer in the trees with a brief flash of red eyes. There had been at least one watching them the entire time.

"Son-of-a-bitch," whispered Clark.

---

[15] RTB – milspeak – Returning To Base

Chapter Six
To the Rescue
"Fortune favors the brave."
Terence

1640 Hours CST
13 February

Clark walked into the Operations Module without removing any of his gear. Team Two had headed for the dining module to get some food and to take a break. They'd been on the move for hours.

"Welcome back," said Saunders.

Wilder handed Clark a steaming thermal cup of coffee which he accepted gratefully. Taking a long pull from the coffee, Clark closed his eyes for a moment to let the dark liquid soothe his nerves. With a sigh, he lowered the cup.

"Thank you," said Clark, nodding at Wilder.

"No problem, sir," she replied, heading back to the computer console.

The weather center was occupied by one of the two new Air Force weather specialists from Special Reconnaissance. Tech Sergeant Emily Drake (Code Name: Rainmaker) was at the console, busily monitoring the approaching storm front.

"Something on your mind, son?" asked CSM Hammond.

"I need to bring you all up to speed," said Clark. "There's been several new developments. Before I do, were you able to track the one that ran back to a lair?"

"Yes, sir," said Master Sergeant Thaddeus Jackson (Code Name: Overwatch), one of the new Air Force Combat Controllers. "We tracked it to a cave about five klicks northwest of here."

"Do you have GPS coordinates?" asked Clark.

"That's affirmative, sir," replied Overwatch.

"Good," said Clark. "I might need that later."

78

Clark spent the next several minutes explaining everything they'd observed since they left. Everyone listened without interrupting until he finished and sat back into a chair. Taking a long pull from his coffee, he waited for them to comment. CSM Hammond wasted no time.

"I know all the mumbo-jumbo shit," said CSM Hammond. "I get all that. It's a goddamned supernatural creature. Did I hear you correctly when you said you think one of the men might be alive?"

"Affirmative," said Clark. "Or at least he was when they took him. They may keep some alive to store for later. They're creatures associated with long winters and famine."

"David," said Saunders, glaring at CSM Hammond. "Don't you say it."

"Goddamn it, Levi," said CSM Hammond, "of course I'm gonna say it. If he's alive, we've got to go after him."

"Which is exactly what you were waiting to hear," said Saunders, glaring at Clark.

"It is the right thing to do, sir," said Clark, shrugging.

"Shit," said Saunders, shaking his head. "Of course, it is. I just hate sending you right back out into the meat grinder."

"Levi," said CSM Hammond, "haven't you figured it out, by now. That's where this kid likes to be. He can't help himself."

"Dan," said Saunders, suddenly very serious. "You don't have anything to prove. We all know you're good at what you do. You don't have to keep running into the thick of things."

"I know that, sir," said Clark. "But if I don't, then someone else has to."

"Why do you think it should be you?" asked CSM Hammond.

Clark was silent for a long moment. All eyes were on him and it made him more than a little uncomfortable.

"Alright," he said, softly. "A while back, I won an award that you all know about. I never felt like I deserved it. A lot of good people died that day. A lot of good friends of mine. I didn't do a damned thing that any of them wouldn't have done in my place. I just happened to be the one who survived. I think of that every day. I tried to turn the award down but I was told I couldn't. So, every time I wear this uniform, I try to be worthy of that award. To be worthy of the lives lost that day. I'm not trying to be a hero and I don't have a death wish. I just try to live up to their memory. To me, they deserved the award. Not me. I was just the guy that lived."

There was silence for a long time. No one spoke up. They were shocked at the honesty and sincerity that they had just witnessed. There was no bravado, no blustering. Just a man who was trying to live up to the legend that had been built around him.

"Alright, son," said CSM Hammond. "Put your team together and bring us the plan."

"I hope it's not your plan to go back out tonight," said Saunders.

"Maybe, maybe not," replied Clark, "but the longer we wait, the greater the chance that Sheffield will be dead before we can get to him."

"He's got a point, Levi," said CSM Hammond.

"Assemble your team and present your plan," said Saunders. "We'll decide after that."

"Thank you, sir," said Clark, heading for the door.

They all sat there in silence until Clark was well out of the area.

"I think that kid's gonna wind up *receiving* another one of those," said CSM Hammond, taking a sip of his coffee.

"You might be right," said Saunders.

"One of what?" asked Rainmaker.

CSM Hammond just smiled at her and took another sip of his coffee.

"Not my story to tell," said CSM Hammond. "Let's just say that the only award I've ever heard of that you can't refuse is one that's presented by the President, himself."

"Oh, my," said Rainmaker.

"Oh, my, indeed," said Saunders.

Clark made his way to the housing unit assigned to Team Two. Ducking inside, he found that the team hadn't turned in their weapons and was still wearing all of their gear.

"I thought you all were going to get some rest," said Clark, grinning.

"Are we all going?" asked Margolin. "Or is this a smaller party?"

"I can't take the entire team," said Clark. "We can't stealth run with an entire platoon. I need no more than six or seven people. We've got to keep it small."

Everyone exchanged glances. Clark saw in an instant that anyone on the team would go if he asked.

"This is not an order," said Clark. "This is going to be about the most dangerous thing we've done. So, if I call your name, there are no hard feelings if you don't want to go. Okay? None."

"I think the only ones that will be pissed," said Margolin, "will be the ones who don't get to go."

That made Clark chuckle as he looked around and saw the team all nodding in agreement.

"I'm going," said Valkyrie.

That wasn't up for negotiation and Clark knew it. He'd have to order her to stay behind and he wasn't sure she'd do it, even then.

"Okay, you're in," said Clark, grinning.

Viking got up and started grabbing his gear.

"What are you doing?" asked Valkyrie.

"If you're going, then I'll be on the roof providing overwatch until you're clear," he said, nodding at SSG Steve Killian (Code Name: Heimdall).

Heimdall grabbed his gear and started getting ready as well.

"You won't need a spotter on this mission," said Heimdall, "so I'll spot for Viking and help cover you."

"Thanks," said Valkyrie, grinning.

81

"Fenrir and Kodiak," said Clark, nodding.

They both stood up and started grabbing their gear.

"I'm coming, too," said Doc.

"Yeah, I figured that," said Clark.

"Who else?" asked Murdock.

"Gideon," said Clark. "Murdock, I want you to keep the team ready, just in case we need you to come get us."

"We'll be ready," said Murdock, smiling.

Gideon didn't say a word. He just picked up his gear and nodded.

"And me," said Margolin, grabbing his gear. "You're crazy if you think you're going without me."

"I'm sure one more won't make that much difference," said Gideon. "Besides, he's an idiot but he's our idiot."

"Thanks, Sar-major," said Margolin. "I think."

"Listen, folks," said Clark, addressing the entire team. "We're taking a small team out to rescue a missing man. That does not mean that the rest of you are standing down. If we fail or get cut off, it falls to you to come after us. Even if we succeed, the likelihood that we've seen the last of the Wendigo is low. I fully expect them to attack Valhalla sometime tonight. Be ready. Hooah?"

"Hooah!" shouted the team.

"Gideon," said Clark, handing Gideon his rifle. "Have the armorer switch out everyone's ACOG with thermal optics."

"Got it, boss," said Gideon.

"Alright," said Clark, "everyone that's going, get your gear ready and top off your ammo. I've got to brief All-father on the plan."

When Clark arrived back in the Command Module, they were all waiting for him. Hernandez and Elliott had joined them, as well.

"That didn't take long," said CSM Hammond.

"Yeah," said Clark. "It wasn't hard to get volunteers. The entire team wanted to go."

"You do seem to have that effect on them," said CSM Hammond.

"So, what's your plan?" asked Saunders.

"I was thinking that if Team Four put all their people together and started heading for the gate," said Clark. "It might draw their attention to that side of the clearing. And, while their attention is on Team Four, I slip out the back and go under the wire on the far side of the clearing with my smaller team. Hopefully, they won't even see us go."

"Alright," said Saunders, "assuming that works, then what?"

"We proceed to the coordinates of that cave," said Clark. "With any luck, we can be in and out of the cave before the creatures even know we were there."

"And if they discover you?" asked Saunders.

"Then we fight," said Clark. "If we get overwhelmed, we'll call for the rest of Team Two. They're already standing by."

"You're going to have to move fast," said Saunders.

"That's why we're keeping the team small," said Clark. "Also, I'm counting on Team Four keeping their attention focused on them for a while."

"These things are smart," cautioned CSM Hammond. "It won't take them long to figure out that they're not leaving the wire."

"Unless we do," said Hernandez. "We can take the team to the ice fishing cabin. Make it look like we're trying to go back to the other cabin. Guaranteed I can keep them focused on us for at least a couple hours."

"That's dangerous," said Saunders. "Leaving the wire might get you more attention than you bargained for."

"That's where my team comes into play," said Elliott. "We'll be standing by on the heavy weapons. If they get too close, we'll light up the night. We can put every sniper we have up on the roof and cover them."

"Alright," said Saunders, frowning. "Get everyone into position. Let's get these things' attention. Clark, get your team ready to move."

"We're ready to go, now," said Clark.

"Give me ten minutes and we'll be ready," said Hernandez. "Let us shake the trees and get their attention on us before you head out the back."

"I'll be listening for you to give the word," said Clark, tapping his earpiece. "We're going to remain radio silent to minimize noise. If we contact you, we've been spotted."

"Alright, let's move people," said Saunders. "Two hours should be enough for them to get there and back if they don't get noticed. Let's buy them at least two hours."

Clark headed over to the Combat Controller station and handed Overwatch his GPS unit. Overwatch quickly programmed in the coordinates for the cave and then pulled up the images they'd taken of the area with the drone.

"There are several game trails in that area," said Overwatch. "It should be easier to travel along one of those then it would be bushwhacking through the forest."

"Good point," said Clark. "What about this creek here."

He pointed at a small creek that cuts through the area and ran very close to the cave.

"Terrain might be a bit rocky," said Overwatch, "but the creek should be frozen. Might be a good path to try."

"That's what I'll aim for," said Clark. "It's lower than the surrounding terrain and it'll make it harder to see us. Unless that proves impossible for us to follow, that's the route we'll take."

"Copy that, sir," said Overwatch. "I'll get with Rainmaker and check the weather. If the wind isn't bad, we might be able to put a drone up and watch you on thermal. It might give you an advantage if they're coming your direction."

"It's worth a shot," said Clark. "Let me know if we've got an eye in the sky. I'm heading back to the team to finish checking our gear."

"Yes, sir," said Overwatch. "Good luck, sir."

"Thanks," said Clark, heading out of the Control Room.

As he approached the armory, he found his group was already there waiting for him. Smiling he headed over to the armorer's desk. Gideon handed him back his rifle with the thermal optic mounted.

"I have a question," Clark said, glancing over at SSG Hall, the team armorer.

"What's up, sir?" asked Hall.

"Do you happen to have any shotguns in the inventory?" asked Clark.

"I do," said Hall, "but I haven't made any of the specialized rounds for it. No one's wanted one, up until now."

"What kind of rounds do you have for it?" asked Clark. "Anything incendiary?"

"Well, now that you mention it," said Hall, "I've got about a thousand rounds of Dragon's Breath ammo. Will that do?"

"What type of shotgun do you have?" asked Clark.

"I've got a few AA12 Auto-Shotguns," said Hall. "I've also got a few of the M26-MASS[16] under-barrel mounted shotguns that I can mount on your SOCOM in place of that grenade launcher. I can load as many of the mags as you want with those Dragon's Breath rounds for either gun."

"Let's make the swap," said Clark. "Put the MASS on my rifle. I'll keep the shotgun loaded with Dragon's breath, just in case the shit hits the fan."

"Load mine the same way," said Gideon, placing his rifle on the desk.

In just a few minutes, SSG Hall had the shotguns mounted in place and was stacking loaded magazines on the desk.

"These mags are only five rounds," cautioned Hall. "Just remember that."

"Five rounds of Dragon's Breath should ruin anyone's day," said Margolin. "That's a lot of fire."

---

[16] M26-MASS – Modular Accessory Shotgun System

Clark did a quick weapons check and re-familiarized himself with the M26-MASS. Although he'd used one before, it had been a while and he wanted to make sure he was able to use it quickly. Once he was satisfied, he began putting magazines in pouches and preparing his gear. Gideon was doing the same thing on the other side of the desk.

Glancing around, Clark noticed that in addition to him and Gideon carrying the M26-MASS, Greyeagle and Margolin both had the M302 grenade launchers mounted. Kodiak was still carrying his minigun. What they lacked in numbers, they made up for in sheer firepower. He sincerely hoped they wouldn't need it.

"We should count on Sheffield being wounded," said Doc. "There's a good chance we might have to carry him back."

"We'll worry about that once we find him," said Clark. "Worst case scenario, Kodiak can carry him while the rest of us provide cover."

"Broadsword to Thunder-god," said Hernandez over the radio.

"Go ahead," said Clark.

"Teams Three and Four are in position," said Hernandez. "Standby to move while we go make some noise. Over."

"Copy that," said Thunder-god. "We're ready whenever you give the word. Thunder-god now going radio silent. Over."

"Overwatch to all units," said Overwatch. "Be advised, weather patterns are stable at this time. Eye in the sky is lifting. Will provide updates, as available. Over."

"Copy, Overwatch," replied Hernandez.

Clark and his team headed for the back exit, on the opposite side of the Mimics from the gate where Team Four was heading.

"All units," said Saunders. "This is Valhalla Actual. You may proceed when ready."

"Copy, Valhalla Actual," said Hernandez. "Team Four is Oscar Mike[17]."

---

[17] Oscar Mike – milspeak – On the Move.

Clark could hear the sound of the main entrance opening and the movement of the team exiting. They were making no attempt at stealth. Moving into the secondary exit module, Clark shut the door behind them and turned off the lights in the unit.

"Good call," whispered Greyeagle. "They won't see light when we open the door."

"Lock and load," said Clark, nodding at the team.

Everyone complied and readied their weapons.

"Broadsword to Valhalla," said Henderson, "we're approaching the gate, now. Over."

"Copy, Broadsword," said Saunders. "We see you. Eye in the sky is indicating four subjects moving your direction, over."

"Copy, Valhalla," said Henderson. "We're deploying flares over the woods near the gate to improve visibility. Over."

Clark smiled knowing they were pulling out all the stops to get the Wendigoes' attention on them.

"Valhalla to Broadsword," said Saunders. "Eye in the sky now indicates six subjects moving your direction. All motion is within a hundred meters of your position, over."

"That's a copy," said Hernandez. "We hear them coming. Thunder-god, you are a go at this time, over."

Clark didn't answer, he just turned to the door and punched in the unlock code. There was no audible cue as the door lock cycled. Clark pushed the door open a few inches and peered outside. There was no sign of movement in the darkness beyond the clearing.

Nodding at the others, Clark slipped outside and brought his weapon up in the high-ready position, scanning from left to right. The others filed out behind him and sealed the door behind them. To the east, they could see the red-orange glow in the sky from the flares.

Motioning for them to form up on him, Clark took the point and headed for the western edge of the clearing. There was a green ribbon tied to a section of the wire where two rolls had been secured together. It was easy for them to undo the wire and separate the two sections.

Slipping through, they secured the sections back together as they left. Moments later, they entered the trees and vanished in the darkness. Once they were away from the clearing, Clark motioned for them to stop so they could listen for any sign that they'd been noticed.

The seconds ticked by like hours as they sat in the deep darkness, forcing themselves to breathe slow and shallow to avoid too much noise. Clark could almost hear the blood pumping through his veins. After a tensely agonizing minute, they determined that they hadn't been seen.

Holding up his hand, Clark gave the signal for them to move out. Glancing down at the soft glow of the GPS, Clark set their trail towards the frozen creek. Once he had his bearings, he put the GPS away to avoid giving themselves away from the light. Cautiously, they moved slowly and watched their foot placement to minimize the noise they made. No one spoke.

The team was fanned out with Clark on point with Valkyrie right behind him. Next was Doc, then Margolin, followed by Kodiak and Greyeagle. The trees they were moving through were mostly Jack Pines, so their footfalls were softened by the bed of pine needles on the ground beneath the snow.

Fifteen minutes later, they found the frozen stream. The ground sloped steadily down to the stream and would keep them from being silhouetted in the trees as they moved. So long as they kept quiet, it was going to be very difficult to spot their movements. If Team Four could keep the creature's attention, then they had a good chance of reaching the cave without being seen at all.

Only, Clark knew that their luck was never that good. Murphy seemed to follow them wherever they went, and his law superseded any plan they could make.

Chapter Seven
Tooth and Claw

*"The bravest are surely those who have the clearest vision
of what is before them, glory and danger alike,
and yet notwithstanding go out to meet it."*
Thucydides

2030 Hours CST
13 February

Leading the group down into the creek, Clark tested the ice. The creek was frozen solid since it wasn't deep enough to have water running beneath the ice. It would make the rocks slippery, but they weren't in danger of slipping into frozen water and getting soaked. That could quickly cause hypothermia to set in and they would freeze to death.

"Attention all units," said Saunders. "Eye in the sky has the targets on thermal. They do not radiate heat but appear colder than the air around them. They will appear as the coldest spots on the IR. Over."

"Copy that, Valhalla," said Hernandez. "Thanks for the update. Out."

Clark glanced back the others and they all nodded that they'd heard it, too. That could work to their advantage. Clark activated the thermal optic and swept the area. There was nothing that stood out colder than the surrounding area. Once he was satisfied there wasn't any Wendigo in the area, he signaled for the team to move out.

"Broadsword to Valhalla," said Hernandez, "we're heading for the trees en route to the cabin, over."

"Good luck, Broadsword," said Saunders.

"Copy that," said Hernandez. "Broadsword out."

As much as Clark was grateful for the distraction they were causing, he hoped that no one would be killed just to provide it.

"God be with you all," Clark silently prayed.

Stepping around a fallen log, Clark saw something laying in the snow at the edge of the ice. Moving closer, he knelt beside it. He could tell that it hadn't been there very long. For one, it wasn't covered in snow and the elements hadn't ruined it. There in the snow was a long-bladed knife with a bone handle. It was different from any knife he'd ever seen and from the markings you could see it had been hand-forged. Motioning for Greyeagle to come over, Clark pointed at the knife. Greyeagle bent down to inspect it, then slowly picked it up.

Leaning close, Greyeagle whispered in Clark's ear.

"This should not be here," he said softly. "This is a ceremonial knife. It belongs to a tribal shaman. From the markings, I would say *Ojibwe*."

"What's it doing here?" whispered Clark.

"I would guess that we're not the only ones hunting the Wendigo," whispered Greyeagle.

"Well," whispered Clark, "here's hoping this isn't a bad sign. If they left their knife behind, are they still alive?"

"I certainly hope so," whispered Greyeagle.

"Alright," whispered Clark. "Hang on to the knife and let's get moving."

"If you see anything more," whispered Greyeagle, "please let me know."

Clark nodded and continued following the streambed. They continued in silence, watching the surrounding area for any sign of the Wendigo but found nothing. The woods were eerily silent and they felt completely isolated. As they rounded a bend in the stream, Clark stopped when he saw a small frozen waterfall. It was only about six feet in height, but it was going to be difficult to climb.

As they approached the waterfall, Clark could see a depression behind the falls that cut back beneath the stream into a small cave. Using his thermal optic, he scanned the interior and was shocked to see a heat signature inside. Laying on the ground was a Native American woman, wrapped in what appeared to be a buffalo skin. She didn't move or stir as they approached.

90

Clark signaled for them to stop and motioned inside the small cave. Valkyrie moved up beside him, already scanning with her optic. Margolin scanned with his optic, then started removing his pack and slipping out of the sling on his weapon.

"What are you doing?" whispered Valkyrie.

"Going in there," he whispered back. "Someone's got to check on her."

Clark nodded and the rest of the team formed a circle with their backs facing each other, covering every angle of approach. Margolin slipped behind the frozen waterfall and crawled about six feet back into the small cave to where the woman was laying. After a moment, Margolin began dragging her back out through the opening. Once he got her out of the cave, he motioned for Doc to come over.

"I think she's hurt," whispered Margolin. "Also, I think we figured out where the knife came from."

Doc nodded and started checking her over. After a few minutes, he nodded at Clark. Leaning close, Clark put his ear towards Doc so he could whisper his report.

"She's unconscious but alive," whispered Doc. "She's suffering from hypothermia and what appears to be a blunt force head trauma. Something hit her pretty hard. Also, her core temperature needs to be brought up, soon."

"Can she be moved?" whispered Clark.

"If she stays here, she'll die," whispered Doc. "We don't have any choice. Either she goes with us or she dies here, alone in the dark."

"Damn it," whispered Clark. "We need to get her back to Valhalla or she's not going to make it. We can't continue the mission and carry her along with us."

"I'll take her back," whispered Margolin.

"I'll go with him," added Gideon. "The five of you should be able to continue the mission without us."

"Alright," said Clark. "Move quick and quiet. Slip back in the same way we came out. I just hope you don't run into one of those things."

"Me either," said Gideon, "but if we do, I'll dump a few Dragon's Breath rounds into it and we'll run like hell."

"Good plan," said Clark. "Go. Watch your backs and signal when you're back inside the wire. We won't answer, but I want to know when you've made it."

"Got it, boss," said Gideon. "Come on, Margolin. Let's move."

Margolin shouldered his pack, then picked up the woman. He cradled her like a small child, careful to keep her wrapped in the buffalo skin. Gideon took up a defensive position and walked ahead of him, making sure the way was clear. Clark watched them go for a moment before turning back to the rest of the team.

"All we can do now is hope they make it," he whispered. "Let's get moving."

Clark found a rock to use as a step, then climbed up on top of the bank. Reaching back, he helped Valkyrie up and then continued to help the others while she kept the area covered with her rifle. As soon as everyone was up, Clark turned around and swept the area with his thermal optic. He breathed a sigh of relief to find that they still hadn't been spotted by the Wendigo.

Taking a glance at his GPS, Clark knew that they were at about the half-way mark. They were covering ground quickly, but time was ticking. If they weren't in and out of the cave before Team Four was back inside the wire, then it was just a matter of time before one of the Wendigo returned to the cave.

As they approached a bend in the creek, they saw someone leaning against the bank. Clark scanned but there wasn't a heat signature. He could tell that it wasn't a Wendigo but whoever it was, they were likely dead. Moving closer, Clark saw that it was another Native American, a male this time. He was slashed deeply to the chest, deep enough to see where the ribs had been broken. He'd managed to escape the Wendigo but died from his injuries.

"This man was killed by a Wendigo," whispered Greyeagle. "He's *Ojibwe*, like the woman. From the looks of it, he died within the last twenty-four hours."

"We'll know more when the woman can talk," whispered Clark.

"If she wakes up," said Doc, softly. "Head trauma on top of hypothermia. She'll have to survive the trip back and even then, it'll be touch and go. She needs a good doctor."

"Doc Olivetti is amazing," whispered Clark. "She's in good hands if they get her back in time."

Glancing around to make sure there weren't others, Clark nodded before signaling for them to get moving. Greyeagle reached down and gently took the fallen warrior's knife from his belt. He was already frozen, so he couldn't close his eyes. Whispering a quick prayer to his ancestors, he silently promised the fallen warrior that he would use his knife to help stop the Wendigo.

As Greyeagle began to follow the team, he made a quick note on his GPS to log the location of the fallen warrior. If they were successful in destroying the Wendigo, he would return for the body and take him back to his people so he could be honored properly.

As they moved through a section of brush that had grown over a narrow part of the ravine, they heard gunfire in the distance. Team Four had engaged the Wendigo. Signaling for the team to stop, Clark called them all close.

"Right now," he whispered, "Team Four is buying us time to succeed, risking their lives to help us save a missing man. Let's make this mission worthy of their sacrifice and hope that they don't take any casualties."

With that, Clark continued to follow the creek. They were getting closer with each passing step and they could feel it in the air. There was something about this place that was growing heavier the closer they got. Something evil was close.

"Mjolnir to Thunder-god," said Gideon over the radio. "We're inside the perimeter. We made it. Out."

Clark smiled as he moved, happy to hear that they had made it back safely. Glancing at the GPS, he could see they were within five-hundred meters of their target coordinates. They were almost there. Motioning for the team to come to a stop, Clark checked their surroundings with the thermal. Very soon, they were going to have to leave the creek and proceed directly towards the entrance to the cave.

Clark had the distinct feeling he was being watched. Glancing around, he couldn't find the source but the feeling just would not go away. Bringing up the thermal, he began sweeping the area thoroughly, searching the trees and the banks of the creek.

From behind them, he heard the sound of something cracking. It was an organic sound, but not from the trees. This was more like joints cracking on a person. Then it hit him, it was the sound a dead body made when you had to break the limbs loose from *rigor mortis* when you placed them in a body bag.

Spinning around, he could see that the others had heard the noise but it hadn't sunk in what it was. Behind Greyeagle, the dead Native American man that they had found was moving towards them with odd, jerky motions. He was transforming into a Wendigo.

Stepping wide to avoid hitting the others, Clark let his rifle drop to his chest as he drew his Winkler Knives Sayoc tomahawk and threw it as he was moving. The tomahawk flipped end over end and buried itself in the forehead of the dead man. The blade buried to the handle in the man's skull and smoke began to come from the wound because of the silver on the blade.

Everyone turned to see what Clark had thrown at and saw the dead man wobbling on his feet with the tomahawk protruding from his forehead. Although the blade hadn't put him down, it had stopped him in his tracks. The transformation to Wendigo was not complete and he wasn't yet at full strength.

Will drew the man's knife and turned, throwing it with uncanny accuracy. The blade buried to the hilt, striking the man right through the heart. Falling over backward, the body continued to move the legs and arms with those strange jerky motions, but it did not try to get up. Kodiak drew his Gladius and headed back to the fallen man. He quickly lopped off his head and moved it well away from the body.

"He is turning into a Wendigo," whispered Greyeagle. "I did not know that could happen. I thought the curse was passed when you ate human flesh. If it can be transferred from a wound, then we need to warn Valhalla about Runestone. He was wounded by one of the creatures, correct?"

"Yes," said Clark. "Do you think he might change?"

"I do not know," admitted Will. "This is magic beyond my understanding. We need someone like my grandfather."

"Will removing the head stop him?" asked Valkyrie.

"Again, I do not know," said Greyeagle. "Maybe it will or maybe it will only slow him down. The only truly effective way I know to kill a Wendigo is with fire."

"Put the head where the body can't reach it," said Clark. "We'll light it up on the way back. I brought plenty of thermite this time."

Kodiak recovered the knife and the tomahawk and returned them. Clark wiped his off with snow and then dried it on his pants leg. Putting it back into the Kydex scabbard, he nodded at the others and brought his rifle back up into high-ready.

"Let's roll," he whispered, then headed further down the creek.

They continued to follow the creek for another thirty minutes, moving slowly and checking every shadow. Once they reached the point where the creek turned back to the south, they knew it was time to leave the ravine and go directly towards the cave.

Clark scanned the surrounding area, then slowly made his way up the embankment. Once he reached the top, he went to one knee to cover the area while the rest of the team climbed out. Scanning the immediate area, there was no sign of the Wendigo or anything else. The woods were cold, desolate, and completely devoid of any sign of life.

As soon as everyone made it out of the ravine, Clark stood and began picking his way through the trees. He was starting to get the scent of decay and death. That could only mean they were close to the cave. Ahead, he was getting the first indication of a flickering light source.

"Do they have a fire?" he thought.

As they crept closer, he was beginning to see more glimpses of the light. There was a fire at the mouth of a large cave that angled back into the hillside to the south. He couldn't see inside from his position, but there was a large campfire built just outside the entrance.

Crouched in front of the fire was a man wearing the tattered remains of clothing. His skin was drawn and pale, stretched tight over his bones, making his ribcage stick out. Most of his hair had fallen out, leaving wisps of long, greasy black hair. It was impossible to tell anything about him from his features. They were pulled so tight on his skull that his face was just a mask of death. His lips were gone, either chewed off or torn off, leaving a gruesome death's head smile with teeth that were now sharp and rotting.

It was tearing the flesh from a bone. Although he wasn't sure, Clark thought it looked suspiciously like the thigh bone of a human. It was focused on eating and staring into the fire, completely oblivious to their presence. It just continued tearing pieces of flesh from the bone with a wet tearing sound, then chewing loudly on the meat.

"I hope that's not Sheffield," whispered Doc.

Doc raised his rifle but Clark put his hand on the barrel and gently pushed it down. Shaking his head at Doc, he pointed at his tomahawk. Doc got the message. They needed to do this quietly or they would attract too much attention. Leaning over, Clark whispered in Doc's ear.

"Move to the right and make your way to the far side of the fire," whispered Clark. "If you can get its attention focused in that direction, I can slip up behind him and take him out."

Doc nodded and began making his way through the trees. Greyeagle nodded at Clark and followed Doc, just in case he ran into trouble. Clark drew his tomahawk and waited. Valkyrie crouched beside him and drew her Gladius. She was ready to move when he was. Clark nodded and smiled at her.

A few moments later, a branch broke on the far side of the fire. The creature instantly stopped chewing and turned that direction. It looked off into the darkness for a moment, then turned back to the fire and resumed chewing.

After a moment, another branch broke, and then something shook the trees. The creature stopped chewing and sat the femur down next to the fire. It slowly stood up in a jerky fashion, twitching its legs and arms as it stood. It gazed off into the darkness and a chittering sound began emanating from the beast. Clark could see it was making the noise by clicking its teeth together rapidly.

Taking advantage of the distraction, Clark moved to the left and slipped in behind the creature. It was starting to turn back towards him when he struck, clipping the base of the skull with the tomahawk. The blade bit deep into the creature's neck, severing the spinal cord and dropping the creature like a puppet. As it began to fall, Clark yanked his tomahawk free and shoved the beast face-first into the fire.

Instantly, the beast was engulfed in flames and began shrieking like an air raid siren. The tearing metal, multitoned sound of the shriek echoed off into the distance.

"Well, there goes stealth!" said Clark, motioning for the others to move into the light.

Clark turned to look into the cave and saw that it was littered with bones and remains of things both familiar and unidentifiable. The smell that emanated from the cave was nauseating with the sickly-sweet reek of rancid flesh and decay.

"I'll cover the entrance," said Kodiak, taking a defensive position behind the fire and readying his minigun.

Clark nodded and headed into the cave. Inside were the remains of two humans who had been ripped apart. One was just a torso with a leg and the other had a torso and both arms. It was impossible to tell who they were, but from the condition, they had to be two of the missing men from Doc's fishing trip.

"I think this is Brokatansky," said Doc. "That looks like his watch."

"What about the other one?" asked Valkyrie.

"I can't be sure," said Doc. "Nothing to ID him by."

"Well, two are confirmed dead," said Clark. "I'm sorry, Doc."

"I already knew it," said Doc. "You don't survive the wounds I saw them take. Hell, I watched it tear Anderson's head off."

Clicking on his tactical light mounted on his rifle, Clark began sweeping the interior of the cave. It led back into the hillside about fifty feet and turned to the right.

There were several piles of bones and the remnants of animal hides littering the sides of the cave, but no movement. At least there weren't any more Wendigo, so far. That much was good.

Clicking on their tactical lights, Doc and Valkyrie flanked Clark and swept both directions. The smell inside the cave was horrifying, but they pressed further into the cave. They moved cautiously, watching every nook and cranny for any sign of movement.

Turning the corner, Clark froze and Doc wrinkled his nose. Valkyrie turned to the side and vomited on the cave wall. In the back section was dozens of body parts hanging from strips of leather or sinew, dangling from the roof of the cave. Some were covered with maggots and others looked like they had been smoked in the fire. Hanging towards the very back were two bodies that looked to be intact. On the ground behind them was a heap of furs and skins, piled into what looked like a crude bed.

"I think that's Sheffield," said Doc, gesturing to the body on the right.

"Let's find out and get the fuck out of here," said Clark. "Valkyrie, are you okay?"

"I will be," she said, wiping her mouth. "When this place is burning and I'm miles away. I also need a hot shower. And a vacation. I think this place will haunt me for a while."

"Me too," said Clark, making a sour face.

Doc moved through the hanging pieces, careful to not touch any of them. Most of them were pieces he could identify as human. Others were deer or elk, but some he had no idea what they were. A few looked like they were human but much too large to be a person.

"What the fuck is that?" whispered Doc.

Reaching the back of the cave, he found the two men who had not been fed upon yet. One was Sheffield and the other was Native American. Sheffield was bruised and bloody, but he was still alive. His pulse was weak but steady. The Native American man was not so fortunate. He didn't have a pulse and it looked like his neck had been broken.

Drawing his tomahawk, Doc motioned for them to come and help him. Clark nodded at Valkyrie before heading to help Doc.

"I've got this," he said. "Why don't you go check on Kodiak and Fenrir?"

"Are you sure?" she asked, relief in her voice.

"We've got this," he assured her. "Wait for us outside."

Valkyrie didn't say anything but there was gratitude in her eyes as she headed out of the cave. Clark watched her go for a moment before heading in to help Doc.

"I'll cut him down," said Doc. "Can you catch him?"

"I've got him," said Clark.

As their attention was focused on Sheffield, neither of them noticed the pile of skins begin to rise behind them. As it stood up, the furs fell away from it. A massive Wendigo rose, its head nearly touching the roof of the cave. It had to be close to twelve feet tall. The creature's eyes were glowing red as it turned to face the humans who dared to enter its cave.

Doc cut the strip of leather and Sheffield dropped. Clark caught him and lowered him over his shoulder. As they turned to head out of the cave, they saw the creature turning to face them.

"Go!" shouted Doc. "I'll cover you!"

Clark headed out of the cave with Doc walking backward right behind him. He brought his rifle up as the massive Wendigo let out a shriek that nearly made their ears bleed. The pain in their ears almost made them drop to their knees. It was by force of will that they both kept moving.

"It's coming!" roared Doc. "Move!"

As they ran towards the front of the cave, they could hear the heavy thuds of the creature's feet as it came after them. Just as they were reaching the front of the cave, they saw the others waiting with their weapons at the ready.

Diving to the right, Clark exited the cave with Doc right on his heels. As soon as they cleared the line of fire, they could hear the electric whine of the minigun spooling up to speed.

With a roar of fury, Kodiak opened fire and the minigun breathed fire like a dragon as it sent high-speed projectiles into the cave at a cyclic rate of nearly three thousand rounds per minute.

To its credit, the massive Wendigo took several more steps before Kodiak took off its legs and one arm with a sustained blast from the minigun. Once it hit the ground, Kodiak stopped firing and the barrels continued to turn for a few seconds before coming to a stop. Smoke poured from the barrels and drifted through the still night air. The entire area now reeked of cordite.

"Is it dead?" asked Doc.

"Fuck, I hope so after all that," said Clark, getting slowly to his feet. "Doc, check Sheffield while we finish that thing off."

Doc went to work on Sheffield and Clark brought his rifle back to his shoulder. Valkyrie moved over beside Doc and helped him check Sheffield. Greyeagle was already approaching the beast. It was still moving its head and reaching out with the remaining arm, even though the minigun had severed both legs and one arm.

There was a massive report as Greyeagle put a .458 SOCOM round into its head at point-blank range. Only then did it stop moving and the arm fell limply to the floor of the cave.

"Let's get that bastard in the fire," said Clark.

Kodiak began throwing all available wood onto the fire to get it burning as hot as possible. The creature that they had already thrown into it had stopped shrieking and was now nothing more than charred bones on the coals. In seconds, the fire began licking into the sky.

Clark and Greyeagle tossed the severed limbs onto the fire first, then worked together to drag the corpse of the monster out to the fire. It was so large that they had to use a tomahawk to hack it in two pieces before they threw it into the fire. It didn't shriek but it did move in jerky twitching spasms as the fire consumed it.

"Sheffield's alive," said Doc. "But he's hurt."

100

"How bad?" asked Clark.

"I won't know for sure until we get him back to Valhalla," said Doc. "He's going to need an x-ray and more help than I can give him here. I think most of his injuries are internal."

In the distance from the direction of Valhalla, they could hear the shrieking of several of the Wendigo. When they shrieked a second time, it was clear that they were getting closer.

"They're coming!" said Clark. "They must have heard the big one scream. "We've got to move!"

"Too late!" shouted Doc.

Before Clark could react, one of the Wendigo seemed to materialize right in front of him. He tried to bring up his rifle, but the beast moved impossibly fast. It backhanded him, knocking him over the fire and into the mouth of the cave. He hit hard on his back and was struggling to breathe. The blow to the chest had been meant to disembowel him, but it had only cut deeply into his ceramic trauma plate.

Doc and Valkyrie dragged Sheffield back into the mouth of the cave while Greyeagle and Kodiak took up defensive positions. As soon as they were clear, Doc released Sheffield and took up a position between Greyeagle and Kodiak.

"In for a penny," he said, glancing at Greyeagle.

Four more of the creatures materialized out of the darkness. The five of them fanned out, snarling and hissing. Kodiak kept his weapon pointed at the creatures on their left while Doc took the middle and Greyeagle covered the right. Valkyrie was checking Clark as he fought to get his breath.

Before a command to fire could be given, one of the creatures leaped over the fire and took Doc to the ground. He managed to shoot it twice in the chest, but the beast still grabbed him by the throat and began squeezing. Doc knew that this was exactly how it had torn Anderson's head off and felt his life flashing before his eyes.

As the creature's grip tightened, Doc saw his vision going red at the edges. The sheer weight of the creature was too much and he couldn't bring his rifle up to bear. Then the thought occurred to him, I still have a pistol. Reaching down, he felt the handle of the Guncrafter Industries Glock .50 GI and drew it. Putting it against the creature's ribcage, he began squeezing the trigger over and over.

As the slide locked back, the beast shrieked and released his neck. It began clawing at the massive wound in his side caused by seven .50 caliber rounds slamming into it. Doc took in lungful after glorious lungful of air and looked up as the creature fell away from him. Greyeagle glanced back at the others and had an expression of grim determination on his face.

"Cody, now!" Greyeagle roared at Kodiak.

Shrugging off the pack that held the ammo for the minigun, Kodiak roared in fury and began to shift forms. Doc had never seen the transformation and had no idea it could be done. Greyeagle roared as he threw his rifle to the side and began changing forms, too.

Kodiak turned into a massive, dark-brown bear as Greyeagle shifted into a gigantic wolf covered in dark fur. The Wendigo stopped on the other side of the fire, unsure of how to proceed. They were snarling and shrieking but made no move to attack the enraged *Hotamétaneo'o.*

Kodiak moved towards the creature and they spread out to flank him. Greyeagle dove onto the nearest creature and bore it to the ground. It suddenly occurred to Doc that unless they threw the creatures into the fire, this fight was still going to go against them.

Clark forced himself to his feet and brought his weapon up to his shoulder. He was leaning heavily on Valkyrie and his face was ashen. He was in a great deal of pain.

Doc watched all of this with calm detachment, unsure of why it seemed to be distant and far away. It was as if he was watching it on television instead of happening all around him. Then everything slowed to a stop as if time had just frozen. Out of the darkness, a Native American woman clad all in white deerskins approached him.

Kneeling beside him, he recognized her. It was Sarah *Makawee.* He remembered her from when he hunted the Dogmen with the *Hotamétaneo'o.* It suddenly occurred to him that she was dead. She died at the hands of a werewolf named Alex, months ago. She had been Greyeagle's wife. Will had reluctantly told him the story about a month after it had happened. He'd been hunting the person responsible, at the time.

"How are you here?" he asked her.

She didn't speak, just placed her hand gently on his cheek. He heard one word flash into his mind, although her lips never moved.

"Remember," was all it said, but it was her voice.

There was a flash of memory and he felt himself back in the *Inipi* with the others. He'd joined them in the sacred sweat. He'd been with them and had a vision. He was one of them. He was a *Hotamétaneo'o*.

In an instant, he was gone and he felt something rumble from deep within him. It was a roar of primal fury and it came exploding from his throat with power that he never felt before. He was changing.

Clark watched in shock as Doc got to his feet and began shifting form. While he wasn't as large as either Kodiak or Greyeagle, he was still well over nine feet tall and covered with a coat of silver-grey. His roar took Wendigo and *Hotamétaneo'o* alike by surprise. The appearance of another wolf might not be enough to stop all of the Wendigo, but it certainly changed the odds in this fight.

Leaping over the fire, Doc took the nearest one to the ground. Before it could react, he gripped its right shoulder with his right hand and its right bicep with his left. With a savage twist, he tore the arm from the socket and tossed it over his shoulder, landing in the fire.

As the creature tried to slash into his side with its remaining hand, Doc rolled over and flipped the creature into the fire. It landed on the coals and began shrieking in pain and rage.

Looking to his left, he saw Kodiak fighting two of the creatures. One on one, they couldn't hope to outmatch the massive bear but they were too fast for him to fight together.

With a snarl, Doc drove his shoulder into the lower back of the nearest creature, knocking it away from Kodiak. As he bore it to the ground, Kodiak wrapped his massive hands around the head of the other creature. With a reverberating snarl, he crushed the creature's head like an egg. Then, he casually tossed the beast into the fire.

Doc ripped into the creature's back as it fought to roll over and attack him. Drawing back, Doc drove punch after devastating punch into the spine of the beast and felt the bones breaking with each blow. As the creature shrieked, Kodiak stomped its head and crushed it beneath his massive foot.

Nodding in appreciation, Doc stood and tossed the beast onto the fire. All of the creatures were being greedily devoured by the steadily growing fire. They hissed and popped and began charring black as the fire consumed them.

Turning, they saw Greyeagle lifting the Wendigo by the neck. There was blood flowing down his chest where the creature had slashed him deeply, but Greyeagle didn't seem to feel it. Instead, he forced the creature over backward until they could hear the spine began cracking like deadwood. Once it was bent double, he held its head in the fire until it caught.

As it shrieked, he drove a fist into its chest and pulled out its heart. It was blue and covered in ice. Greyeagle stared at it for a long moment before tossing it into the fire. As the fire destroyed the heart, the creature stopped shrieking. Then it too went into the fire.

In the distance, they could hear others coming in their direction. It sounded as if there had to be several more. Glancing around to make sure there were no more in the immediate area, Greyeagle turned back to the others.

"We have to leave this place," said Greyeagle, his voice a deep rumbling growl. "It'll be faster if we carry you."

"How did you change?" asked Kodiak, looking at Doc.

"I can't explain it," answered Doc.

"We'll talk more when we're safely inside Valhalla," said Greyeagle. "We need to go, now! It'll be faster if we carry you."

Doc scooped up Sheffield and nodded at the others. Greyeagle knelt on one knee and picked up their discarded equipment. Kodiak grabbed his pack and minigun. Valkyrie climbed onto Greyeagle's back and Clark climbed onto Kodiak.

"Let's go," said Greyeagle. "Follow me!"

Streaking off into the night, he kept his pace so that both Doc and Kodiak could keep up. Even though he was not with the other *Hotamétaneo'o*, Greyeagle was still an Alpha. He was still far faster than most other creatures. Only the Wendigo was faster.

He listened to the approaching creatures and knew that they would not reach the cave in time to prevent them from reaching Valhalla. The question was, would they follow them there?

As they raced back down the creek, they paused long enough to plant a thermite charge in the chest of the body they'd left behind. Placing the head on top of the chest so it would be immolated with the rest of the body, they pulled the pin and raced off into the night.

In the distance, the Wendigo shrieked. They were getting closer with each passing second.

Chapter Eight
Touch of the Healer

"Live for something rather than die for nothing."
General George S. Patton

0045 Hours CST
14 February

Clark had to radio ahead to warn Valhalla that they were coming in. Not everyone on the team knew about Greyeagle and Kodiak's abilities. Doc was a complete surprise to all of them, even himself. Once they were safely inside, they took Sheffield straight to the infirmary. They insisted that Clark get checked out, as well.

Clark was informed that he had several bruised ribs and a mild concussion. Sheffield had a broken right arm, broken left leg, and a severe concussion. He was going to be in the hospital for a while, once they evacuated him from here. The Native American woman that they had found was still unconscious but in stable condition. Margolin was still sitting beside her bed.

"Are you okay?" Clark asked Margolin, pausing beside him.

"Yes, sir," said Margolin. "I just feel like I need to be here for her. I can't explain it."

"You don't have to," said Clark. "I understand. Let me know if there's any change or if you need anything."

"Will do, sir," said Margolin.

Clark headed down the hallway to the small common area where they gathered for meetings. He found Valkyrie, Doc, and Greyeagle waiting there for him.

"What's the verdict?" asked Valkyrie, gesturing at him.

"A few bruised ribs and a mild concussion," said Clark. "I'm fine."

"You're not fine," said Valkyrie, "but you're stubborn as hell and won't let it stop you."

Clark just smiled and shrugged.

"Sounds about right," said Doc. "I think I know another guy like that."

He glanced over at Greyeagle.

"I have no idea what you're talking about," said Greyeagle, chuckling.

"Does anyone want to explain to me how Doc turned into a gigantic wolf?" asked Clark.

"Yeah," said Doc. "Anyone want to explain how that happened?"

"Tell me what happened just before you turned," said Greyeagle.

Doc sighed and looked at his friend. He knew what he was about to say would hurt him, bringing up his wife.

"After I fell, it seemed like the world just sort of stopped," said Doc, a confused look on his face. "Then I saw her."

"Saw who?" asked Valkyrie.

"Sarah *Makawee*," said Doc. "She appeared out of the darkness, wearing all white buckskins. She put her hand on my face and I heard her voice say 'remember'. I never actually saw her mouth move. Then, I remembered the *Inipi* at your grandfather's place."

"The what?" asked Valkyrie.

"*Inipi*," said Greyeagle. "It's a sacred sweat in a sweat lodge. In Lakota, *Inipi* means to live again. It symbolizes rebirth."

"I had a vision," said Doc.

"I remember," said Greyeagle. "You never told me about it."

"Because it would only come in fragments of memory," explained Doc. "It was only after Sarah touched me that I remembered everything. I saw myself as one of the *Hotamétaneo'o* many times through different lives. I was one of the Dog Soldiers."

"That's why you could change forms," said Greyeagle. "She let you remember how."

"Will it happen again?" asked Doc.

"That I cannot tell you," answered Greyeagle. "It might happen easily or it may never happen again. I suppose that will be up to you, more than anything else. It is your path to choose. But that is a discussion for another time."

"I need to go brief All-father," said Clark. "I'm glad we got to talk first. Are you all okay?"

"I was wounded but it healed," said Greyeagle. "My wolf-form heals very rapidly."

"That must come in handy," said Clark, rubbing his ribs.

"At times," said Greyeagle.

"How's Kodiak?" asked Clark.

"He is fine," said Greyeagle. "He's resting, now. I forget sometimes that he is not as fast as I am when we change forms. The bear cannot keep up with the wolf. He was exhausted by the time we made it back here."

"Good," said Clark. "You should all go get some rest. I'll brief All-father and then hit the rack, myself."

"Sure you will," said Valkyrie as she headed for the barracks area. "I'm taking a shower and going to bed. You should do the same, sir."

Clark nodded at the others, leaving Doc and Greyeagle to talk. He could tell that Greyeagle had questions and since it was likely concerning the vision of his wife, Clark thought they would prefer privacy.

As he ducked into the Command Module, he saw Hernandez, Saunders, CSM Hammond, Gideon, Elliott, and Murdock all waiting there for him. Wilder wasn't in the room and neither were either of the Combat Controllers or the Weather officers.

"Dan, how do you feel?" asked Saunders.

"I'm alright, sir," said Clark. "Banged up a bit, but I'll live."

Henderson came over and shook Clark's hand.

"Glad to see you made it, brother," said Henderson.

"It was a close one," said Clark, patting him on the shoulder. "How's your team."

"Two injuries," said Henderson. "Neither life-threatening."

"About that," said Clark. "Wounds from a Wendigo can turn you into one, under the right circumstances."

"Runestone has been complaining of a cold feeling in his chest," said Saunders. "We've got him in quarantine until a specialist gets here in the morning."

"Who's coming in?" asked Clark.

"Gideon knew who we needed to call," said Saunders. "It's First Sergeant Greyeagle's grandfather. He'll be here around first light. There's a chopper bringing him in and will evac Sheffield at the same time."

"He's an old friend of mine," said Gideon, "and a powerful Lakota Shaman. If anyone will know what to do, it'll be Jay *Matoskah*."

"Jay *Matoskah*?" asked Clark. "As in the guy from the original Wild Hunt team back in the 1970s?"

"The same," said Gideon. "I served with him, back then. He's a good man."

"Then we should have him check the wounded from Team Four, as well," said Clark.

"Good call," said Henderson. "I don't want any of my guys turning into one of those goddamned things."

"Do we have anyone out patrolling the perimeter?" asked Clark.

"No," said Saunders. "We pulled everyone inside after you made it back. We put claymores and motion sensors out by the wire."

"They're going to want to hit us back after we hit their lair," said Clark.

"I would expect so," said Gideon, "but I doubt they come tonight. We've already bloodied their nose here. They'll regroup before they hit us, again. At least, that's what I would expect them to do."

"Makes sense," said Clark. "They've got to be off their game. I doubt that anyone has ever challenged them like that before."

"We hit them hard," said Hernandez. "We took two down. After the others ran off, we dragged the ones we dropped out of the trees and placed thermite charges on their chests. They burned up completely."

"Good," said Clark. "I wonder how many more there are?"

"After our fight," said Hernandez, "the eye in the sky was able to track six heading back your way. I think the ones you killed at the cave weren't part of that because we were still tracking them when you showed up at the perimeter."

"With any luck," said Clark, "that's all that's left."

Clark spent the next half an hour briefing them on everything that had happened, leaving out no details. They were all surprised when he told them that Doc had turned into a wolf and fought alongside Greyeagle and Kodiak.

"I didn't know Mr. Davis was one of the Dog Soldiers," said Saunders.

"He is as of last night," said Clark. "He was as shocked as anyone when he changed. We'll need to add it to his file."

"Already on it," said Saunders, making a note on his tablet.

"If there isn't anything else," said CSM Hammond, "I think these men deserve to get some rest. They've certainly earned it."

"Team Three will remain on ready alert until 0300 hours," said Elliott.

"And Team Four will take over then," said Henderson. "Team Two can take a break. We've got it tonight."

"Thanks," said Clark. "I think I'll take you up on that."

"Alright everyone," said Saunders. "Get some rest. Elliott, I'll leave you in charge of the Command Module. You should have Tech Sergeant Simpson in to take over Combat Control and Tech Sergeant Elkins on the weather station in a few minutes."

Tech Sergeant Vanessa Simpson (Code Name: Saga) and Tech Sergeant Michael Elkins (Code Name: Frostbite) had come to the team from the US Air Force ParaRescue and Special Reconnaissance. Adding Combat Controllers and Combat Weathermen to the team had already proven to be the right call.

"Copy that, sir," said Elliott. "I'll yell if anything happens."

Clark headed down the hallway towards the barracks assigned to Team Two. Gideon was right behind him. As they passed the infirmary, they were stopped by one of the nurses.

"Captain Clark," said the nurse. "The Native American woman is awake."

Clark ducked into the infirmary and found Margolin sitting beside the woman. She was sitting up on the bunk and looking around. Clark noticed she was holding Margolin's hand.

"Hi," said Clark. "I'm Captain Clark. How are you feeling?"

"Confused mostly," she said, glancing around. "Where exactly am I?"

"You're in a military facility," said Clark. "I can't go into the details, I'm afraid. You're safe. We found you tonight and you were badly hurt."

"Thank you for that," said the woman. "My name is Winter *Damashkawizii*. Do you know what happened to the others who were with me?"

"We only found two others," said Clark. "I'm afraid they were both dead."

"I fear I am the only one left," she said. "We came to try and stop the Wendigo. We did not expect there to be so many."

"We can try to get you home in the morning," said Clark.

"No," she replied firmly. "I came here to fight the Wendigo. I am looking for one in particular. He killed my mother."

"Can you describe him?" asked Clark.

"When he was alive," she answered, "he had a tattoo of a raven's wing over his left eye."

"We saw him," said Clark. "We took him down."

"Did you burn the body?" she asked, growing concerned.

"Yes," said Clark. "We've burned several of the creatures since we got here."

"Good," she said, seeming to relax somewhat.

"Who was he?" asked Clark. "If you don't mind me asking."

"He was my father," said Winter. "He killed and ate my mother after he was turned by the Wendigo. I swore to bring him down. Thank you for finishing him for me. You have saved many lives in doing so."

"We think that there are only about six of them left," said Clark. "We're going to try and finish them off as quickly as possible."

"You will need my help," said Winter.

"You're hurt, ma'am," said Clark, gently. "No offense, but let us take care of the fighting."

"I am a Medicine Woman of my people," she said. "I can help your people. Have any of them been hurt by the creatures?"

"Actually, yes," said Clark. "We have a few people who were hurt by them."

"I can protect them from the curse," she explained, "if it has not been too long since they were wounded."

"How long is too long?" asked Clark.

"It depends on the severity of the wound," said Winter. "A non-fatal wound can take days for it to turn them. Fatal wounds are much more rapid."

"We need to get her to Runestone," said Clark. "He's been hurt the longest."

"Yes, sir," said Margolin.

"Is there anyone we can contact for you?" asked Clark. "Anyone wondering what happened to you?"

"No," she said, shaking her head. "My brother was with me hunting our father. If he is dead, then I have no one and no reason to return home."

"Let's get her to Runestone," said Clark, "if you're up to it, ma'am."

"I can manage," said Winter. "I need to get to your friend as quickly as possible. The longer it has had to take hold, the more difficult it will be to remove."

"I'll take her, sir," said Margolin.

Clark glanced at Margolin, surprised that he was being so helpful.

"You feeling alright, Margolin?" asked Clark.

"I'm good, sir," said Margolin. "I'm just kinda invested in making sure she's okay."

"I am told he carried me for miles," said Winter. "I owe him my life."

"I'm glad to have done it," said Margolin.

"I have the strangest feeling that he was meant to find me," said Winter. "Two days ago, I saw him in a dream. When he was there when I woke up, I thought I was still dreaming."

"Alright," said Clark. "Take her to see Runestone. When she's done with him, if she's still up to it, there are a couple of guys from Team Four who were injured, as well."

"Yes, sir," said Margolin. "We'll take care of it."

Clark watched them head for the quarantine unit before turning towards Gideon.

"I'll hang around here for a bit," said Gideon. "Just in case they need me. You should go get some rest. No offense, sir, but you look like shit."

"Thanks, Sar-Major," said Clark, grinning. "To be honest, I feel like shit, but I'll survive."

Heading down the hallway to the armory, Clark stopped and handed off his weapons to SSG Hall.

"I'll go over everything before I get them back to you," said Hall. "Do you want me to leave the shotgun mounted or are you going back to the grenade launcher?"

"I think I'll stick with the shotgun," said Clark. "I still have the feeling that those Dragon's Breath rounds are going to come in handy. How long do you need to keep them?"

"Give me half an hour," said Hall. "I'll check over everything and make sure nothing was damaged on your last mission."

"Thank you," said Clark. "I'm going to go take a hot shower. I'll swing by when I'm done. That should take about half an hour."

"I'll have them ready for you, then, sir," said Hall.

Heading into the barracks area, Clark found part of his team had gone to bed, but the majority of them were still awake and moving around. Pausing at his bunk, he grabbed a clean set of clothes and headed into the big communal bathroom.

The only thing separating the men's area from the women's was the direction they went when they entered. He could hear a shower running on the women's side, but he was alone on the men's. Dropping his towel and clothes on a bench, he sat down and started taking off his gear. He hadn't realized just how badly his ribs hurt until he removed the tightly velcroed body armor. Wincing in pain as he dropped the armor to the floor, he stretched and grimaced as he gingerly touched the bruises on his ribs.

"Shit," he groaned.

"You alright over there, sir?" asked Valkyrie.

Clark realized it must have been her showering on the women's side. She must have recognized his voice.

"I'm good," he said. "Nothing a hot shower won't fix."

Even though there was a solid wall between the male and female sides, there were mesh grates at the top of the wall and you could hear the other side.

"Alright, sir," she said, sounding concerned. "I'll be at my bunk if you need me."

"Thanks," said Clark, turning on the hot water.

As he slipped off his clothing and stepped into the hot shower, all he could think was that he wished his wife were here to rub his back. The hot water was refreshing and he let it run down his face and chest. After a few minutes, he began lathering up with soap to wash away the grime that coated his body.

Once he finished, he wrapped a towel around his waist and headed for the mirror. Shaving wasn't going to be as much fun without his wife here, either. He missed their ritual of her sitting on his lap and shaving his face. Now that he was back in the military, he was seriously considering shaving his head.

Lathering up his face and neck, Clark took out his razor and rinsed it in the hot water. As he shaved, he noticed the dark circles beneath his eyes. He felt weary, but he wasn't going to be able to rest until he knew they were finished with the mission. Still, he was going to have to try and grab a few hours of sleep. Any more than that and he felt guilty.

Slipping into a fresh pair of underwear and a clean pair of uniform pants, he picked up the rest of his clothes and headed back to his bunk. He realized that he hadn't put a t-shirt on when he felt everyone staring at him. He could hear a few of them whispering to each other.

They were undoubtedly discussing his scars. He had a hell of a collection. Some were recent and some were old, but there were quite a few of them. Each one a constant reminder of the battles that he carried with him. Each with its specific memories and pains, some representing times he'd lost teammates and friends.

Tossing his dirty uniforms into the laundry bin, he pulled on his t-shirt and slipped into his boots. Ducking out of the barracks, he headed back to the armory. Staff Sergeant Hall was waiting for him when he arrived.

"All done, sir," said Hall. "I replaced your optic and bench sighted it. Yours had a crack in the casing, so I swapped it. I went ahead and cleaned it for you while I had it apart."

Setting an olive-drab shoulder bag on the counter, Hall nodded.

"I gave you some additional mags for the .458 SOCOM and the shotgun," said Hall. "The ones with the blue tape are the Dragon's

Breath. The red tape is flechette rounds. Those pack a hell of a punch. If it won't kill one of those things, I bet it gets its attention."

"Thanks, Sergeant," said Clark. "Much appreciated."

"When we get back to base," said Hall, "I'm going to look into specialty rounds for the shotguns. With and without the special coatings you guys use on the monsters."

"That's a great idea," said Clark. "I bet silver buckshot would ruin something's day."

"Or silver flechettes," added Hall. "Hell, they even make micro-grenades for shotguns. I could experiment and see what kinds of stuff I can come up with."

"Let me know when you have it put together," said Clark. "I've been thinking about designating a few team members to use the AA-12s."

"They're versatile weapons, sir," said Hall. "Plus, they have almost zero recoil and you can't jam one if you tried."

"I'll pitch the idea to the Major," said Clark, "but I'm already sold on it. I want to add shotguns to the rotation."

"Personally or for the team?" asked Hall.

"I might want one, myself," said Clark.

"I'll customize one just for you, sir," said Hall. "I'll set it up with a good optic and a breacher muzzle brake."

"The only thing I might miss is the range from the SOCOM," said Clark.

"With the right rifled slugs you won't," said Hall. "Those SOCOMs are only really effective at ranges less than two-hundred meters. The rounds are just so damned heavy they don't get the distance of a 5.56mm. They're better at a hundred or less. With the right twelve-gauge rifled slug, you can hit two-hundred-meter targets all day long. I'll set it up for you and I bet you won't even miss the SOCOM."

"You set it up and I'll take it out and play with it," said Clark. "If I like it, I'll probably switch over."

"Deal," said Hall. "I'll have it ready for you before we get back to base."

Clark turned to head for the barracks and found Margolin approaching with Winter.

"Sir," said Margolin. "We were looking for you."

"What's up?" asked Clark.

"We were able to help all of your men who had been wounded," said Winter. "The man you called Runestone was very close to being beyond help. He would have succumbed to the Wendigo curse before morning. The man you rescued, Sheffield, was also treated with only a few hours to spare. Had you not rescued him, he would be one of the Wendigo, now."

"Thank you," said Clark. "I think it's lucky that we found you, for all of us."

"I think that there was more than luck at work," said Winter. "I think I was meant to meet you and your team. I've felt that way since I woke up."

"How so?" asked Clark.

"My family has been hunting creatures like the Wendigo since before your people came to this continent," said Winter. "Now, I am the last one. My father was taken by the curse and my brother was killed when we came after him."

"I'm sorry," said Clark. "I know how difficult that must be."

"Thank you," said Winter, "but that was not why I mentioned it. I feel like I was brought to your team to help you with your mission. I can offer my services as a medicine woman of the *Ojibwe*. I would like to help you."

Clark instantly thought of how valuable to the team it could be, having a real medicine woman with them on missions. Not only could she help with the weapons, but her knowledge would be incredibly useful.

"I'll have to talk it over with Major Saunders," said Clark, "but I think that might not be a bad idea. I can certainly see the advantages. In the end, it will be up to General Dalton. We can present the idea to him, though."

"Thank you," said Winter.

"Don't thank me just yet," said Clark. "They haven't said yes."

"I am confident that they will," said Winter. "I think they will see the benefits that working together can bring us both."

"Margolin," said Clark. "Why don't you take Winter to one of the bunks so she can get some rest. We're going to have a busy day tomorrow."

"May I?" asked Winter, holding her hand near Clark's chest.

"What are you doing?" he asked.

"I can ease the pain you are feeling," she said.

"Okay," said Clark, curious as to what she was going to do.

Placing her hand on his ribs, she began singing softly in her language. Clark could feel her hand growing warm against his side. At first, there was mild discomfort from her touch but soon it was replaced with a warm feeling and he suddenly felt very relaxed and tired. The pain was gone.

"That's amazing," he said, yawning.

"It is only a relief of pain," said Winter. "Although, if you rest now, it will heal faster. It should be mostly gone by the time you awaken."

"Thank you," said Clark.

"You are most welcome," said Winter. "Now, much like yourself, I need to get some rest. I feel that I might have pushed too hard after my injury."

"Are you okay?" asked Margolin.

"Yes," she assured him. "I just need to get some sleep."

"I'll show you to a bunk," said Margolin, guiding her away.

"Wow," said Clark. "I think she's the real deal. Medicine woman might be an understatement. She's a bonafide healer. That could come in handy."

Heading into the barracks, Clark placed his weapons in the rack that was attached to the end of his bed. Kicking off his boots, he lay down on the bed and took out his cellphone. Checking, he discovered that he didn't have any signal.

"Figures," he thought. "I think I need to get a SAT phone."

Putting the phone away, he leaned back against his pillow and closed his eyes. His thoughts were of his wife as he drifted off into a deep and dreamless sleep. Tonight, there were no nightmares, for the first time in a very long time.

Chapter Nine
Shock and Awe

*"We sleep peaceably in our beds at night only because rough men
stand ready to do violence on our behalf."*
George Orwell

0700 Hours CST
14 February

Clark awoke and felt completely rested. Glancing at his watch, he discovered it was 0700 hours. That meant he had been asleep for almost five hours. It was the longest unbroken sleep he'd had in years. He couldn't remember the last time he had slept all night without being woke up by nightmares.

Murdock was sitting on a bunk across from him, brushing his teeth. He lifted his eyebrows at Clark as he sat up, but didn't stop brushing. Clark swung his legs off the bed and glanced around the room. There was a line at the door to the bathroom. Murdock spat into a plastic cup, then rinsed his mouth with a bottle of water.

"Why do you think I'm brushing my teeth at my bed?" asked Murdock, taking another pull from the water bottle.

"Good thing I showered and shaved last night," said Clark. "I might have to go outside to piss, though."

"It would probably be faster," said Murdock. "That's one thing they could improve about the Mimics. Bigger bathrooms. But, hey, I'm not complaining. At least we're not using port-a-potties and living on MREs[18]."

"Meals Ready to Excrete," said Clark. "No thanks."

"Same," said Murdock. "I think they've got eggs and sausage in the chow hall. I'm gonna go give it a shot."

"Grab me a couple breakfast burritos," said Clark.

"Sure thing, boss," said Murdock, ducking out the door.

---

[18] MREs – Military pre-packaged meals called Meals Ready To Eat.

Clark started getting dressed and timidly touched his ribs where they were bruised. They felt fine to the touch. There was no pain there, at all.

"Holy shit," he thought. "She's the real deal."

Once he had his armor back in place, he checked the loads on his weapons and put them back on. By the time he had all of his gear in place, Murdock came back in with a plate full of eggs, bacon, sausage, and bread. Tossing two large breakfast burritos on Clark's bunk, he nodded and sat on his bunk to start eating. Clark noticed that the burritos were bigger than anything he'd ever gotten at a restaurant.

"Thanks," said Clark. "Look at the size of those bastards."

"I gotta say," said Murdock, "the food here is better than it was with the Rangers."

"That's because the cooks are all stolen from the Air Force," said Clark. "They've been upgrading the menus for the last month. Before then, it was the usual Army crap you get everywhere."

"Well I, for one, am damned happy about that," said Murdock. "What's the plan today?"

"I'm gonna eat," said Clark, "then go brief the Major about Winter. I think we should recruit her for the team."

"Does she have a military background?" asked Murdock.

"No," said Clark. "She's a Medicine Woman of her people and she's a healer. An honest-to-god, no-bullshit healer. She healed the bruised ribs I had."

"No shit?" asked Murdock. "I mean, seriously, sir?"

"Yeah," said Clark. "I wouldn't have believed it if I hadn't seen it for myself."

Unwrapping one of the burritos, Clark took a bite and realized that there was no way he was going to eat both of them. Picking up the other one, he tossed it to Valkyrie as she headed back to her bunk from the bathroom.

"Thanks, sir," she said, catching it with her right hand. "You sure you don't want it?"

"I can't eat two of these big bastards," said Clark, still chewing.

Valkyrie shrugged and sat on her bunk, unwrapping the burrito as she leaned back against the wall.

"Hey sir," said Valkyrie. "Can I ask you something?"

"Go ahead," said Clark, taking another bite.

"Where did you get all those scars?" she asked. "If you don't mind me asking."

Shrugging, Clark finished chewing before answering.

"Some were in Afghanistan," said Clark. "A few from Iraq. Some are from when I was a cop. Some are from when I was in Kosovo. I've got at least one from everywhere I've deployed."

"How many places have you seen combat?" she asked, wide-eyed.

"Officially or unofficially?" he asked.

"Both," she replied.

"Well, the fact that you're part of this team means you've got a high enough clearance to know about some of them," said Clark, frowning. "Four continents and eight different locations."

"Is that counting fighting monsters here?" she asked.

"Yeah," said Clark. "I think that definitely counts."

"I'd like to hear about them sometime," said Valkyrie.

"Maybe," said Clark. "One of these days. I usually don't like to talk about it."

"I've had two deployments," said Valkyrie, "not counting this team. Both times to Bagram. We only left the base a couple of times to bring back downed pilots."

"I've been to Bagram," said Clark. "A couple of times."

The intercom sounded and interrupted their conversation.

"Captain Clark," said the voice of Wilder, "please report to the Command Module. Captain Clark to the Command Module."

"Duty calls," said Clark, getting up and stuffing another bite of the burrito into his mouth.

"Want me to come along, sir?" asked Murdock.

"Might not be a bad idea," Clark said through the burrito.

Murdock followed him, shoveling food into his mouth as fast as he could while he walked. By the time they reached the Command Module, Clark was shoving the last piece of his burrito into his mouth. Wilder handed him a steaming thermal mug of coffee. Instead of talking with his mouth stuffed full, Clark raised the cup to her and nodded.

CSM Hammond was sitting at a console while Saunders was in the radio room. Rainmaker was back at her post on the weather station and Overwatch was at the Combat Controller station. Chewing furiously, Clark swallowed the mouth full of food and washed it down with a drink of coffee.

"Morning, sunshine," said CSM Hammond. "Nice of you to join us."

Clark grinned at him.

"Morning, Command Sergeant-Major," said Clark.

"Levi's on the horn with base," said CSM Hammond. "We've got a VIP coming in on a chopper. They're going to evac Sheffield and get him to a hospital."

"Jay *Matoskah*?" asked Clark.

"That's him," said CSM Hammond. "He's coming in to check on the men wounded by the Wendigo."

"The woman we rescued," said Clark, "is a Medicine Woman of the *Ojibwe* people. She's also a healer. She took care of the men who'd been wounded. She also healed my bruised ribs."

"Seriously?" asked CSM Hammon. "No bullshit. Actual healing?"

"All I know is," said Clark, "yesterday I had four bruised ribs. Before I went to bed, she touched my ribs and I felt her hand get warm. Then, I slept like a baby and woke up with no pain in my ribs. Also, the best night's sleep I've had in years."

"That could come in handy," said CSM Hammond.

"She's asked to join the team and help us hunt these creatures," said Clark.

"Does she have a military background?" asked CSM Hammond.

"Not that I'm aware of," said Clark. "But she's the real deal on Native Magic. We could use her skills."

"Do you think she can be trusted?" asked CSM Hammond.

"That's what we'll have to determine," said Clark. "If she's someone we can trust, I say we bring her onboard. She could be a hell of an asset. Her family has been hunting monsters for centuries. Hell, having her around just for the knowledge they must have accumulated would be fantastic. Toss in her abilities and we'd be stupid not to bring her on-board."

"I'll pitch it to Levi," said CSM Hammond. "We're going to need Team Two outside to cover the chopper when it gets here."

"No problem," said Clark. "What's the ETA?"

"It's supposed to be here around 0830 hours," said CSM Hammond. "Doc Olivetti already has Sheffield ready for transport."

"I'll get the team prepped and ready," said Murdock, "unless you need me to stick around."

"No, son," said CSM Hammond. "You can go ahead. All I needed to tell you boys was that you've got chopper duty."

Murdock nodded and headed out of the Command Module to prep the team. Clark turned back to CSM Hammond and waited for him to speak.

"What?" asked CSM Hammond.

"What else are you waiting to say?" asked Clark, grinning.

"I just wanted to know how Murdock is doing?" asked CSM Hammond. "I know he was a bit of a hard-head when we agreed to take him on. How's he progressing?"

"He's listening well," said Clark. "He takes initiative and the team seems to respect him. So far, he's doing well. He's improved significantly since the tryouts."

"Good," said CSM Hammond. "We need him up to speed. With the way things go around here, he could be leading his own team next week."

"I'll do my best to make sure he's ready," said Clark. "Has there been any movement from the Wendigo today?"

"Nothing that we've picked up on motion sensors," said Overwatch. "We've got an eye in the sky up right now and it hasn't picked up anything."

"That could be good or bad," said Clark. "It makes me wonder what they're up to."

"I sincerely doubt that it's anything good," said CSM Hammond. "How many of those goddamned things do you think are left? I know we tracked six, but there could be more."

"The only ones we're certain of are the six," said Clark. "I hope that's all there are. We should probably not assume there's only the six."

"Yeah," said CSM Hammond, "because six of those bastards aren't enough on their own."

"Alright," said Clark. "I'll go gear up. I want to get outside and take a look around before that chopper gets here."

"Choppers," said CSM Hammond. "Plural. A new protocol for the team. All birds have to have escorts. That just came down the wire from Asgard, himself."

"It's not a bad idea," said Clark. "We've seen things throw trees at choppers before. I seriously doubt a Wendigo would fare too well against a gunship."

Heading down the hallway, Clark ducked into the barracks and found Murdock already addressing the team. He held back and let him finish.

"Alright, boys and girls," he said, chuckling. "We've got a VIP inbound on a chopper. All-father wants us on standby for the arrival. I

125

want shooters on the roof covering the closest approach vectors. Valkyrie, you take the southern corridor and Viking gets north. Hooah?"

"Hooah," said Valkyrie and Viking almost in unison.

"Outstanding," he said. "Both dog teams are on roving patrol. No closer than fifty meters to the tree line. I don't want anyone grabbed and dragged into the woods. Hooah?"

"Hooah," repeated Kestrel and Eagle.

"Everyone else," said Murdock, "see First Sergeant Greyeagle. He's got the rest of the assignments. Gear up and let's roll."

"Hooah!" shouted the team.

"Hooah!" replied Murdock.

With that, everyone began grabbing their gear and buckling on their armor. Clark gave Murdock an approving nod before heading for his bunk to grab his gear. Murdock grabbed his rucksack and started adjusting his armor.

"Nicely done," said Clark, without looking up.

"Thanks," said Murdock. "Did I miss anything?"

"Not really," said Clark. "The team is responding well to you. That's good. I felt like it took them a little bit to warm up to me. Keep doing what you're doing."

Clark grabbed the last of his gear and headed for the Command Module. As he was walking out, he spotted Margolin downing a Rip It Energy drink in a single pull. Shaking his head, Clark walked out. Murdock glanced over and saw Margolin crack open a second one.

"Those things will kill you," said Murdock. "There's nothing in them that's good for you."

"True," said Margolin. "But in this job, I think an energy drink is the least of my worries."

"Where's your friend?" asked Murdock.

"Winter?" asked Margolin. "Sleeping. She's in one of the private quarters reserved for senior officers."

"How's she doing?" asked Margolin.

"Better," said Margolin. "I hope they let her stay. Not only because it would be good for the team, but I think she kinda likes me. Also, I have this weird feeling like I already know her. Fuckin' weird, right sir?"

"Well, she's already aware of the existence of monsters," said Margolin, "not to mention she knows about the team. Unless there's something major bad in her background, I can't see why they'd say no. It would be good to have someone with her skills around. I'd certainly give her my approval, for what it's worth."

"Thanks, L.T.," said Margolin.

"No problem," said Murdock.

Nodding at Margolin, Murdock shouldered his pack and headed out the door. He caught up with Clark in the Command Module. Clark was filling his coffee mug and staring at the weather report.

"How's it look?" asked Murdock.

"Not bad," said Clark. "We could be looking at snow by nightfall, though."

"How much?" asked Margolin.

"Six to eight inches," said Rainmaker. "They get a lot of snow up here in Minnesota."

"What's the ETA on the chopper?" asked Murdock.

"About half an hour," said Clark. "We need to get the team in place. I want to be ready if anything happens."

"I'll get them stacked up by the door," said Murdock.

"I'll join you in a few minutes," said Clark. "Let me finish my coffee."

By the time he downed the rest of the coffee and made it to the primary exit, Team Two was stacked and ready to go.

"Everyone know their assignments?" asked Clark.

"Yes, sir!" snapped Team Two.

"Alright," said Clark. "Let's roll. Hooah!"

"Hooah!" answered the team.

"Lock and load!" bellowed Gideon. "Team Two is weapons hot!"

The sound of charging handles pulling and rounds locking into firing chambers filled the room.

"Thunder-god to Valhalla Control," said Clark. "Team Two exiting. Over."

"Copy Thunder-god," said Overwatch. "Happy hunting. Valhalla Control out."

Cycling the door lock, Clark was the first one out the door. The sun was bright in the morning sky and the air was crisply cold. They were the first team to exit the facility today, so Clark was on edge. Even though the cameras had shown the area to be clear, he was uncertain if the cameras could even detect the Wendigo when they were cloaked.

"Stay alert!" shouted Clark.

"Stay alive!" echoed the team.

Clark turned right as soon as he cleared the door. Behind him, the others staggered their exit, covering every angle as they emerged. Moving quickly, they fanned out and formed a perimeter around Valhalla. The dog teams moved into their positions to begin active patrols. Clark could see the dogs were eager to go, which would indicate the Wendigo wasn't in the area.

Clark scanned the trees and saw no movement in his sector. Seconds later, all of the team had taken their positions and were covering all angles of approach.

"Valkyrie in position," said Valkyrie.

"Viking in position," said Viking.

"Copy, "said Clark.

Bringing his weapon up into low-ready, Clark began pacing along the back of the positions they had taken up. Glancing at the dog teams, he saw their demeanor had not changed. Despite the training, you could see a complete change in the dogs whenever they were close to the large predators. It was especially noticeable in the case of the Wendigo. Training could only do so much, but instinct was still instinct.

"Valhalla Control to Thunder-god," said Overwatch, "Angel 1-1 now fifteen minutes out. Over."

"Copy Vahalla Control," said Clark. "We're ready. Over."

"Solid copy, Thunder-god," said Overwatch. "Valhalla Control out."

Clark rounded the corner of the Mimic Units and found Murdock coming his way. Murdock had a dark look on his face and was walking briskly.

"Got a second, boss?" asked Murdock.

"What's up?" asked Clark.

"That's just the thing, sir," said Murdock, glancing around. "Nothing is going on. Doesn't this seem too easy? Where are they?"

"You're not wrong," said Clark. "I think I've got the same bad feeling you do. Something isn't right."

"Has the eye in the sky seen anything?" asked Murdock.

"Nothing that I've been made aware of," replied Clark. "They're supposed to update us if they see anything."

"Maybe we should check-in," said Murdock, glancing around nervously.

"It's worth a shot," said Clark.

Activating his comm, Clark began looking around the area.

"Thunder-god to Valhalla," said Clark. "Any update from the eye in the sky? Over."

"Negative, Thunder-god," replied Overwatch. "Nothing on motion sensors or visual. Over."

"Have you tried thermal?" asked Clark. "Over."

"Negative," said Overwatch. "No heat patterns on visual. Over."

"Does he know those things show up colder than normal?" asked Murdock.

"I don't know," replied Clark. "But I'm going to find out."

In the distance, they heard a strange "whoop" sound coming from the south side of the clearing. It was nothing like any sound they'd previously heard the Wendigo make. It was followed by three loud knocks that sounded like wood striking against wood. Whatever it was, it wasn't close.

"That's not typical Wendigo behavior," said Murdock. "What the hell is that?"

"Thunder-god to Valhalla," said Clark. "Are you aware the Wendigo show up colder than their surroundings? Over."

There was a long pause which spoke volumes. Either Overwatch hadn't been informed of that or he had somehow forgotten it.

"Adjusting for thermal gradients," said Overwatch. "Contact! Thunder-god, we have contact. Four subjects approaching slowly on your northeast sector and seven more on the northwest. Do you copy? Over."

"Fuck, I hate being right all the time," snapped Murdock. "I'll take the northeast, you grab northwest."

Clark was transmitting as Murdock sprinted off towards the northeast corner of the perimeter. Clark started running as he spoke into the radio.

"Valhalla Control," said Clark. "Copy eleven subjects inbound. Advise Angel 1-1 of hostiles in the area. Do not approach until we are clear. Over."

"Copy Thunder-god," said Overwatch. "Valhalla Control out."

Clark turned and ran for the northwest corner. It was more than a hundred yards away. All along the line, Team Two was bringing their weapons up and searching for movement. With the Wendigo moving slowly and remaining cloaked, they were going to be very difficult to spot until it was too late.

"Valkyrie, transition to northwest quadrant," Clark said into his mic. "Viking, transition to northeast. Over."

"Copy, Thunder-god," said Valkyrie. "Valkyrie is mobile."

"Viking going mobile," said Viking.

"Understood," replied Clark. "Advise when in position. Out."

"INCOMING!" shouted a voice along the defensive line.

Clark turned his head that direction and saw a tree trunk about the size of a telephone pole come sailing through the air. It appeared that it had been aimed at Valhalla and not at the team on the ground.

"Contact!" yelled another voice.

Changing directions, Clark headed for the sound of the voice. Emerging from the trees were two of the Wendigo. They leaped into the air and easily cleared the concertina wire without touching it. For all the good it had done, they shouldn't have wasted their time placing it.

"Valkyrie is in position," said Valkyrie. "Acquiring targets. Out."

Clark was rapidly coming up behind SSG Margolin (Huntsman 2-6) and PO1[19] Bedford (Huntsman 2-5). Both were actively engaging the nearest creature, but the second creature was approaching unchallenged and it was bearing down on Margolin.

"Hey!" screamed Clark.

The creature's attention shifted from Margolin to Clark in an instant. He felt the gaze of the beast as the glowing red eyes fixed on his. Clark kept running directly at the monster as it jumped high into the air. The arc of the leap was going to bring it down on top of Clark.

Shifting at the last second, Clark spun to his left and brought his rifle to bear. He'd switched his grip from the SOCOM to the under-barrel mounted shotgun. Unable to change trajectory while still in the air, the beast could not dodge his attack.

Ka-BOOM!

The Dragon's Breath round spat incandescent death at the Wendigo, completely immolating the monster in burning magnesium before it even hit the ground. When the beast crashed to the ground, shrieking in pain, it tried rolling into the snow to extinguish the fire. Before it could make any progress, Clark hit it with another round, further engulfing the

---

[19] PO1 – Petty Officer First Class

131

monster in pyrotechnic fury. This round punched deep into the beast's chest cavity because the range was less than six feet. The multitoned screech faded out like a dying siren as the flames destroyed it's heart and other internal organs.

"Viking in position," said Viking. "Beginning target acquisition."

Another log flew into the air, this one aimed at the team on the ground.

"INCOMING!" Clark roared.

Behind him, over the roar of the fight, Clark heard a strange sound that seemed completely incongruous with the symphony of battle raging around him. Someone was singing in a language he did not understand. It was a melodic, beautiful woman's voice that filled the air. Stealing a glance back, Clark saw Winter standing on top of the Mimic Units, chanting and holding her hands in the air.

To his left, the log was bearing down on PO3[20] Reardon (Huntsman 2-3), who hadn't seen the danger. Clark sprinted the last few feet and tackled Reardon. Momentum carried them out of the way, just as the log struck the ground.

The log was approximately the diameter of a bowling ball and over ten feet long. It bounced and struck Clark in the side. Grunting in pain, he rolled with the impact as the log bounced over him. The armor had absorbed the worst of the impact, but he knew he was going to be bruised.

"Thank you, sir," said Reardon, getting to his feet.

Clark just nodded as he got slowly to his feet.

"You alright, sir?" asked Reardon, turning back to face the perimeter.

"I'm fine," said Clark.

Above him, he heard the unmistakable sound of rotors as helicopters were approaching. Before he could reach for his radio to warn them off, he heard the miniguns on the two escorts open fire.

---

[20] PO3 – Petty Officer Third Class

Glancing up, he saw two Blackhawks circling at an altitude of around a hundred feet. They were spraying tracers and directing fire into the trees along the perimeter. While they were firing, the third Blackhawk came in above the top of the Mimic Units. Before it had fully touched down, Clark saw a white-haired Native American man drop from the chopper and head towards Winter. Immediately, four people began quickly loading the litter carrying Sheffield into the chopper.

As the chopper began lifting, the older man began chanting with Winter. While the chopper climbed higher into the sky, the chanting grew louder. Clark could tell that although they were singing in different languages, whatever they were doing was in unison.

As the chopper carrying Sheffield banked and headed back to the south, the two escorts took one more pass, spraying automatic weapons fire into the trees before banking away to escort the retreating medivac chopper.

Clark couldn't take his eyes off the two shamans, chanting and holding their hands in the air. Above them, the clouds darkened and thunder rolled across the clearing. Then there was a bright flash and lightning crashed down from a clear sky, burning into the trees. It was instantly followed by a tearing metal shriek that ended abruptly.

"Valhalla to Thunder-god," said Overwatch. "Eye in the sky indicates eight targets moving away at high speed. They're clearing the area. Over."

"Copy that," said Clark. "All units, Cease Fire!"

Along the perimeter, weapons stopped chattering and silence filled the clearing. Only the sound of the thunder rolling off into the distance remaining, accompanying the chanting of the shamans.

"Son-of-a-bitch," whispered Clark. "What the hell was that?"

Behind him, Kodiak and Gideon were dragging two creatures out of the trees. Placing thermite charges on their chests, they began the process of cremating the monsters so they wouldn't come back.

Chapter Ten
White Bear

"In war, you win or lose, live or die
– and the difference is just an eyelash."
Douglas MacArthur

0900 Hours CST
14 February

Teams Three and Four took over the perimeter while Team Two went inside Valhalla. Several members of the team had to have wounds treated from being struck with large rocks or tree branches. They were fortunate that there were no broken bones but several of them would be sore for a while, Clark included.

Clark, Murdock, Gideon, and Greyeagle all entered the Command Module to find their VIP, Jay *Matoskah*, already waiting. Winter was sitting beside him while he was brewing coffee.

"Gentlemen," said Saunders, "May I present Master Gunnery Sergeant (Retired) Jay *Matoskah*. Former Marine Force Recon, Scout Sniper, and member of the original Wild Hunt team."

"Nice to meet you, sir," said Clark.

"Sir," said Murdock, nodding.

"Grandfather," said Greyeagle, smiling.

"Hi, Jay," said Gideon. "Good to see you, again."

Jay sat the coffee to brew, then turned to greet the newcomers.

"Captain Clark," said Jay, "I have heard good things about you. My grandson speaks highly of you."

He paused to shake Clark's hand. Clark was impressed with the strength in his grip. Moving to Murdock, he clasped his hand and looked him in the eyes.

"Did Gideon tell you that we both knew your grandfather?" asked Jay. "Charlie was a good friend and a hell of an officer. I can see him in you. You look very much like him, as he looked when I first met him."

"No, sir," said Murdock, glancing at Gideon.

"I did a double-take the first time I saw him," said Gideon. "I thought Charlie was back."

"The resemblance is uncanny," said Jay, nodding at Gideon.

"Thank you, sir," said Murdock.

"You have his drive to excel," said Jay. "It was one of the things I admired about your grandfather. He never wanted to be anything but the best, never content to be second at anything. I think he would be pleased to find you with this team. After all, he helped in the creation of it."

"I never knew that," said Murdock.

"Not many do," said Jay. "The formation of this team is still held as closely guarded a secret as its very existence. A word of advice, if you don't mind?"

"Go ahead, sir," said Murdock.

"Do not feel that you are competing with the legend of your grandfather," said Jay. "Whether you realize it or not, you are already building one of your own. He would be very proud of you, of that, I am absolutely certain."

Murdock nodded but said nothing. Clark could tell by the look on his face that Jay had given him a lot to think about. Gideon clasped Jay's hand and they smiled at each other.

"How many years have we been playing this game?" asked Jay.

"Far more than I care to admit," said Gideon.

"It is good to see you, old friend," said Jay.

"You, too," said Gideon, smiling.

"Grandfather," said Greyeagle, smiling.

Instead of an answer, he drew him into an embrace and hugged him. After a moment, he released Greyeagle and patted him on the cheek, touching the scars.

"Are you alright?" asked Jay.

"I will be," said Greyeagle, softly.

"I think you are where you need to be," said Jay, "for now. One day, your path will take you back to the *Hotamétaneo'o*. That is where your destiny lies."

Greyeagle nodded but said nothing.

"When last I heard," said Jay, "you had men who had been wounded by the Wendigo."

"I already took care of their wounds," said Winter.

"I see," said Jay. "It is fortunate that you were here."

"I think fate might have had a hand in it, as well," said Winter. "I think I was meant to meet this team."

"I sense the will of *Wakan Tanka* in this," said Jay.

"I am hoping to join them in their hunting," said Winter. "After all, it is what my family has done for generations."

"I think it would be a good fit," said Jay. "This team could benefit from having a shaman with them full-time. You are strong. I rarely sense this much power in one so young."

"I saw you channel lightning into one of the Wendigo," said Clark. "That was beyond amazing. I never would have believed it, if I hadn't seen it with my own eyes."

"It requires a great deal of strength to accomplish," said Jay. "Not many can summon the lightning."

"Did it take both of you to do it?" asked Clark.

"No," said Jay, smiling enigmatically. "She could have done it on her own. However, both of us together produced a much stronger effect. It was enough to kill the target. Either of us alone might not have been able to accomplish that. The magic of the Wendigo is very powerful."

"We sent a request to General Dalton," said Saunders. "It will be up to him to decide if she can join the team."

"You may give General Dalton my highest recommendation," said Jay. "I can think of no one better suited to this task. Her family knows more about these creatures than most scholars ever will. She is *Ojibwe*

Bear Clan. Her people have been healers and protectors since the *Wakan Tanka* placed our peoples on this world."

"Well," said Saunders, "I don't think we can get a better recommendation than that."

"I'm sold," said CSM Hammond.

Doc walked into the Command Module and nodded at Jay.

"Good to see you again, sir," said Doc.

"You, as well," said Jay smiling. "I see you have embraced the spirit of the *Hotamétaneo'o*."

"Uh," said Doc, confused. "You can see that by just glancing at me?"

"He can," said Greyeagle, nodding.

"Well, I bet that comes in handy," said Doc with a grin.

"Thank you for coming," said Saunders.

"Well, I might not be in the military anymore," said Doc, "but when the C.O.[21] calls, I know you don't say no."

"Well," said Saunders, "you're not under my command. You are under no obligation to follow my orders or help us in any way. I can't and won't attempt to order you to do anything."

"Call it a healthy dose of respect for the Chain of Command," said Doc. "How can I help?"

"Under normal circumstances," said Saunders, "I wouldn't send a civilian out on patrol with my team. Even a civilian with your experience."

"Like circumstances for us are ever *normal*," said CSM Hammond. "Hell, there isn't anything about us that's anything close to normal."

"Good point, Dave," said Saunders. "We certainly operate outside the definition of normal."

"How can I help?" asked Doc.

---

[21] C.O. – Commanding Officer

"Now that we have Sheffield safely airlifted," said Saunders, "we can look at ending this situation, once and for all. I'm tired of playing defense. It's time to take the fight to the Wendigo."

"I'm down like four flat tires," said Doc, smiling. "How can I help?"

"Well, your skills as a medic are worth admission, just on their own," said Clark.

"But?" said Doc.

"Your ability to shift forms might prove to be more valuable," said Saunders.

"Honestly," said Doc, "I have no idea how I did it and can't guarantee I can do it again."

"We're confident that you could, under the right circumstances," said Saunders.

"Maybe," said Doc. "Hell, probably. I don't know."

"We're going after the Wendigo," said Clark. "Whether or not you can change, you're welcome to join us."

"Alright," said Doc. "I still owe those bastards for my friends. I'm in."

"Sensors picked up eight of them leaving the area," said Clark. "The problem is, we have no idea if that's all of them. Every time we think we know how many there are, a few more show up."

"That might be partially my fault," said Winter. "I fear they turned most of the warriors who came with me to hunt them."

"How many came with you?" asked Clark.

"Seven others," said Winter.

"That would be about right," said Clark. "It would explain how they suddenly swelled their ranks."

"Well, here's hoping they don't raid a camp or town nearby," said Gideon.

"Unlikely," said Saunders. "According to the map, there's nothing for twenty miles in any direction you want to pick."

"Sir," said Overwatch. "We have something on thermal."

"Wendigo?" asked Clark.

"No, sir," said Overwatch. "This is showing body heat."

They all turned to look at the computer monitor. On the south side of the perimeter, they could see three heat signatures. They were keeping their distance, staying far enough away to not be seen.

"Who are they?" asked Saunders.

"I don't think *who* is the right term, sir," said Overwatch. "If the readings are correct, they're much larger than a normal human."

"How much larger?" asked Greyeagle, frowning.

"Hard to say, First Sergeant," said Overwatch. "Thermal isn't that precise. Let's suffice it to say they're big."

"*Chiye Tanka*," said Jay.

"What's that?" asked Saunders, turning to face Jay.

"Your people call it Bigfoot," said Winter.

"Great," said Doc. "I knew those things had to be real, too. I'm never going camping again."

"Why are they here?" asked Gideon.

"They are enemies of the Wendigo," said Winter. "The Wendigo will eat them, as well."

"They are probably an early warning system," said Jay. "There to alert their clan if the Wendigo gets too close."

"I think I saw pieces of those things in the Wendigo cave," said Clark. "Body parts were hanging inside that looked human but were too big."

"They likely suffered losses to the Wendigo, as well," said Jay, "and are looking to fight them."

"Are they a threat to us?" asked Saunders.

"Possibly," said Winter. "Some clans are peaceful and others are very violent. It is hard to say without getting closer, but then it would be too late."

"This just keeps getting better and better," said Doc. "First it's Dogman, then Wendigo, now the damned Bigfoot. What's next? The Loch Ness Monster? For the love of God, tell me those aren't real."

No one answered him.

"Beautiful," whispered Doc.

"So, how does this affect us going after the Wendigo?" asked Clark.

Saunders watched the screen for a few moments before speaking.

"It doesn't," he said, not looking back. "We continue with the planned mission. They haven't done anything or attacked anyone. Unless they bother us, we won't bother them."

"Let's hope they feel the same way," said Murdock.

"So, what's the plan?" asked Doc.

"We're going to take Team Two and go back to the cave," said Clark. "If it's empty, we'll place charges and bring it down. If it's not, we clear it out completely. We can put an end to them today."

"Eye in the sky hasn't detected any movement at the cave," said Overwatch. "Neither in nor out."

"So, we don't know if they're in there," said CSM Hammond.

"We don't know they're not," said Doc. "Unless we can send a drone inside the cave, the only way we're going to know for sure is to go there and check."

"Your call, Major," said Clark. "I think it's our best shot at nailing these things. We're going to have to put boots on the ground."

"We can get the drone closer," said Overwatch, "but not into the cave, itself. For one, the drone's too big. It would fit, but there's no room to maneuver. If they're in the cave, the drone will likely be destroyed."

"How close can you get the drone?" asked Saunders.

"Honestly, sir," said Overwatch, "with the height of the trees in the area, if we get low enough to look into the cave we're already in danger of losing the drone. We've got fifteen feet between the trees and the mouth of the cave. The best angle we can get without hovering just outside the cave is a high oblique, and we can't see more than a few feet inside."

"If they see the drone, they'll attack it," said Clark. "I think that's safe to assume."

Saunders stared at the monitors for a few moments before speaking.

"Prep your team, Dan," said Saunders. "I want you mobile in thirty minutes."

"Got it," said Clark, heading out the door.

"One more thing," said Saunders.

Clark paused at the door and turned.

"Yes, sir?" he said.

"Take Winter with you," he said. "If anyone gets wounded, she can keep them from turning. I don't want to have to put down any of our team members."

"Yes, sir," said Clark. "Winter, if you'll come with me, I'll get you some equipment."

Winter followed Clark out the door. Gideon nodded at Saunders and CSM Hammond before following. Murdock drained the last of his coffee and smiled.

"Hooah, sir," said Murdock, heading out of the room.

"Are you coming with us, grandfather?" asked Greyeagle.

"I think I will stay here," said Jay. "It might not be a good idea to have both Winter and I committed to the same mission. Should anything go wrong here, one of us should be available."

"Good idea," said Greyeagle. "I'll see you when we get back."

With that, Greyeagle headed out the door and towards the armory. Murdock, Gideon, and Winter were already there. Clark had gone to brief the team.

"Let's get you some gear," said Gideon to Winter. "Sergeant Hall, what do you have for this young lady?"

While they discussed her weapon preferences and skills, Clark began speaking to Team Two.

"Alright folks," said Clark. "Listen up!"

Everyone stopped talking and turned to face him.

"We've got a mission," said Clark. "Team Two is going to return to the cave and see if we can finish off the Wendigo, once and for all. This time, we're all going."

That brought a few cheers.

"Winter will be accompanying us on this, just in case anyone gets hurt. She'll be on-hand to keep them from becoming infected by the Wendigo curse. Margolin, since you and Winter have a good rapport, I want you to stick with her like glue and keep her safe."

"Got it, sir," said Margolin. "I'll stay close to her."

"I bet you will," said McGregor, elbowing him in the ribs.

That drew a few chuckles from the group.

"Margolin, keep her in the middle of the group," said Clark. "You can pair up with McGregor. He can be your chaperone."

That caused more chuckles from the group.

"Dog teams," said Clark. "Coventry, you stick with Sargeant-Major Gideon. Gaines, you're with Lieutenant Murdock. Hooah?"

"Hooah!" said Coventry and Gaines.

SSG Amanda Coventry (Code Name: Raven) came to the team from the US Marines 4th Law Enforcement Brigade. She had a female German Shephard named Sage. SSG Malcolm Gaines (Code Name: Eagle) came to the team from the US Army Rangers and had a Bullmastiff named Bjorn.

"We're breaking into three-man teams," said Clark. "No one goes anywhere unless you've got your team with you. I don't care if you're taking a shit, one can wipe and the other can watch."

Several people laughed out loud.

"We're taking no chances on this one," said Clark. "We find and eliminate this threat before they kill anyone else. I'll have the three-man assignments for you before we clear the gate. Everyone swing by the Armory and top off your ammo and do a weapons check. Be ready to leave in fifteen. Hooah?"

"Hooah!" roared the team.

"Dismissed!" said Clark.

Team Two quickly gathered their gear and headed for the Armory. Clark waited a moment to let them all clear out before grabbing his gear and following behind them.

Standing at the back, he watched the team topping off ammo and grabbing additional supplies. Gideon was at the front with a clipboard making notes and checking off team members as they finished. When Clark made it to the front of the line, SSG Hall smiled and motioned him over.

"I've got your AA-12 ready for you, sir," said Hall. "I think you're going to be pleased. I was really happy with the way it turned out."

"Let's have a look," said Clark, unclipping his .458 SOCOM from his single point strap.

Hall sat the modified AA-12 on the counter. Clark took a moment to look at it before he picked it up. It had a custom arctic camouflage pattern painted on it, a high-intensity Surefire M600U Scout Light, and a breecher muzzle brake on the end of the barrel. The brake had teeth around the edge to grip the wood of a door to hold it in place while a round was punched through either a hinge or a deadbolt. A thermal optic had been mounted to the top and Picatinny rails had been placed on top, bottom, and sides of the weapon for further additions.

"Nicely done, Hall," said Clark, grinning. "Any specialty rounds?"

"A few," said Hall. "I loaded Dragon's Breath rounds in the eight-round box magazines. You've got specialized tungsten tipped flechette rounds in the drums. Those things will punch through body armor like tissue paper. They should do a hell of a job to your Wendigo. They're blessed and chased with silver. I hand loaded them, myself. Those are in

143

the drum mags with the blue tape. The red taped mags have rifled slugs with silver cores."

"You've been busy," said Clark. "Thanks, Sergeant."

"No worries, sir," said Hall, grinning. "I'll be able to make a lot more custom rounds for that thing once we're back at base and I've got access to my shop."

"I can't wait," said Clark. "I'll take this with me now and give it a field test."

"Let me know what you think," said Hall. "If you like it, I can outfit as many as you like. Not many teams use those and I know a guy that can get us a truckload if we want them."

"I'll let you know how it does," said Clark, locking in a drum magazine a red taped magazine. "Thanks."

"Happy hunting, sir," said Hall.

Clark and Gideon headed down the hallway and into the Command Module.

"The team is stacking by the main door," said Gideon.

"Thanks, Sar-Major," said Clark, grinning.

"That's still going to take some getting used to," said Gideon.

"Would you prefer Centurion?" asked Clark, quietly.

Gideon just gave him an odd look but said nothing.

"Team Two's ready to deploy, sir," said Clark, turning towards Saunders.

"Outstanding," said Saunders. "Come in for a final intel check?"

"Yes, sir," said Clark.

"No additional movement from the cave," said Overwatch. "Nothing on thermal in the area."

"What about our guests to the south?" asked Gideon.

"They're still right where they were," said Overwatch. "No movement. They're just watching us."

"Once we depart," said Clark, "if they move to follow or intercept, let us know."

"Will do, sir," said Overwatch.

"What's the weather look like?" asked Clark.

"Still looks like snow by nightfall," said Rainmaker. "Probably won't start until around 1900 hours. Steady snowfall but not a full-blown storm. Temperatures should be around minus five."

"A walk in the park," said Clark, grinning.

"You should be back before nightfall, anyway," said CSM Hammond.

"That's the rumor," said Clark. "We'll see what Mr. Murphy has to say about that once we're out there."

"Good point," said CSM Hammond.

"One thing before we go," said Clark.

"What's that, son?" asked CSM Hammond.

"I want Team Four on Hot Standby," said Clark. "If we end up having to fight both the Wendigo and those Bigfoot creatures, I want additional manpower."

"I'll make it happen," said CSM Hammond. "Hernandez will be thrilled to come out and play."

"I'm sure he will," said Clark. "I hope we don't need him, but I'd rather have them ready. Just in case."

"Copy that," said CSM Hammond. "They'll be ready. Good luck, son."

"Thanks," said Clark, grinning as he headed for the main entrance.

Team Two was already stacked and ready by the door. Clark walked down the line checking his team and double-checking equipment. When he reached the front of the group, he turned back and nodded.

"Alright folks," said Clark. "Teams of three from here on out. Stick together and stay alert. We don't know what we're walking into. The Wendigo could be at the cave or they could be waiting in the trees for us. We're unable to locate them on motion sensors and thermal isn't showing us anything useful."

He nodded at Gideon who began reading off the team assignments from the clipboard.

"Listen up!" roared Gideon. "Here are your assignments. Raven and Caduceus are with me. Eagle and Shieldmaiden are with Lt. Murdock. Runestone and Viking are with First Sergeant Greyeagle. Hunstman 2-6 is with Winter and Kodiak. Valkyrie and Heimdall are with Captain Clark. Huntsman 2-1, 2-2, and 2-3 are together. Huntsman 2-4, 2-5, and 2-7 are together. Huntsman 2-8, 2-9, and 2-10 are together. Any questions?"

"Yeah," said Doc. "Where am I at?"

"Shit," said Clark. "Sorry, Doc. You stick with me and my group."

"Gotcha," said Doc.

"Murdock and Gideon's teams will be on rearguard," said Clark. "Greyagle and Kodiak's teams in the center. I'll be on point with my team. Huntsman 2-1 and his team will back me up. Hooah?"

"Hooah!" shouted the team.

"Lock and Load!" roared Gideon.

Charging handles were pulled and rounds went into firing chambers all down the line.

"God, I love that sound," said Margolin, grinning.

McGregor just smiled and nodded agreement.

"Let's roll," said Clark, activating the door controls.

They headed out the door at a quick pace, moving towards the southern end of the compound. They would follow the creek back to the cave. Team Three was already on the roof providing cover, so they proceeded without delay.

The wind was blowing softly from the south and the dogs kept looking nervously in that direction. Clark knew they had to be catching the scent of their observers in the trees. That was fine, so long as that's all they did.

Clark found himself wondering briefly, how his wife was doing. She would be taking over as the newly-elected Sheriff of Sloan County, effective this week. He found himself hoping they finished this mission so he could call her.

"You okay, boss?" asked Valkyrie.

"Uh, yeah," said Clark, "Sorry, I was a thousand miles away for a second."

"Worried about your wife?" she asked.

"Yeah," said Clark. "She's a cop."

"Is that how you met?" asked Valkyrie.

"Yeah," said Clark. "She was actually my supervisor."

"She sounds tough," said Valkyrie.

"She is," said Clark. "She saved my life a couple of times. Hell, she's a better cop than I ever was. I'm a soldier. It's all I've ever really been good at."

Valkyrie didn't say anything.

"We're almost to the wire," said Clark. "Time to get our game faces on."

"Yes, sir," she said, grinning.

Clark unlinked the wire, just as they'd done the last time they exited this direction. Gideon would seal it once the team was completely through. Once the second strand had been separated, Clark brought his AA-12 up into his shoulder and scanned the trees in front of him, cautiously, searching for any sign of movement.

"Thunder-god to Valhalla," said Clark. "We're exiting the wire. Over."

"Copy, Thunder-god," said Overwatch. "We've got you on camera. No movement in your area and nothing on thermal. You're clear to begin assigned patrol. Over."

"Copy," said Clark. "Thunder-god out."

Scanning left, right, and up, Clark moved towards the trees. Moving in a crouch, he kept continually scanning and watching the trail ahead. Although he doubted that the Wendigo would set traps, he wasn't going to rule it out.

The ground began to slope gently towards the creek and he knew that once they reached it, it would be very difficult for the Wendigo to remain above them. Moving carefully, he tried to step in the same tracks they'd made the last time they came this way.

Just ahead, there was a branch that hung low over the trail. Clark tried to recall if it had been there before but didn't remember it. Motioning for everyone to freeze by holding up his closed fist. Instantly, the team complied and stopped in their tracks.

Turning his head towards Valkyrie, Clark said softly, "Cover me."

Valkyrie brought her HK-UMP50 tight against her shoulder and began sweeping the area. Heimdall repeated the movement, scanning the opposite direction. Slowly lowering his weapon, Clark freed his hands and moved cautiously towards the branch.

Now that he was studying the foliage, he saw where it appeared several bushes and tree branches had been disturbed. Nothing was obviously out of place and who or whatever had done this had gone to great lengths to conceal it.

Moving along the branch and closely examining every inch, Clark spotted sinew wrapped around the branch behind a thick pine branch. It was completely invisible until you got close. Following the sinew, he found where it went behind the tree and led into the darker pine trees beside the trail.

Following the sinew, Clark found where a large pine tree had been pinned down with a tripwire attached to it. There were several large, sharpened sticks attacked to the bough of the tree and a crudely braided rope that was attached to a large round rock. If the tripwire were released, at least one person would have been skewered by the sharpened spikes and then pummeled by the stone.

Pointing at the trap, Clark saw Valkyrie look at him with wide eyes. Heimdall shrugged and nodded. From the looks on their faces, neither of them had seen the danger.

Clark moved carefully to the tree to see if he could release the trap safely. The bough was too thick for him to be able to handle. He could tell that whoever had set the trap had been tremendously strong. Ducking back out onto the trail, he hit the mic on his radio.

"Thunder-god to Team Two," he said. "We have a tripwire trap on the trail. I cannot disarm. I'm going to find a path around it. Watch your steps and step where my tracks are. Out."

Moving back to the branch over the trail, he examined it. He couldn't go to the right because that was where the tripwire was at. He'd have to find a way to the left. As he began checking to the left, the same instinct that had warned him about the tripwire was warning him again.

As he began searching, he spotted the deadfall trap. There was a large tree balanced against another tree, set to fall on whoever tried to go around the tripwire.

"Clever bastards," muttered Clark.

By D.A. Roberts

CHAPTER ELEVEN
THE DEVIL YOU KNOW

"I've always believed that no officer's life, regardless of rank,
is of such great value to his country that he should seek safety in the rear ...
Officers should be forward with their men at the point of impact."
Chesty Puller

1300 Hours CST
14 February

It was early afternoon before they made it to the cave. There were several traps discovered along the way, most of them deadfall or tripwire. They even found a couple of step traps with large rocks positioned to break the leg of whoever stepped into it. They'd been lucky and avoided all of them.

The fire had burned completely out in the firepit in front of the cave. They could see the charred remains of bones from the creatures that they'd burned in it. In the ashes was a charred flint arrowhead. Clark picked it up and held it in his hand. It was still warm.

The cave was dark and foreboding, but they saw no movement inside. The smell hadn't improved since their last visit, either. Clark, Valkyrie, and Heimdall moved through the trees and around to the right edge of the cave entrance. Greyeagle, Runestone, and Viking took the left edge. Everyone else stayed concealed inside the trees, waiting for the command to attack.

Reaching into a pouch on his vest, Clark took out a flash-bang grenade and nodded at Greyeagle. He pulled the pin on the grenade and held it in his hand without releasing the spoon. Glancing up at the team, he held up three fingers and nodded.

Then he silently mouthed, "Three. Two. One."

Stepping quickly around the corner, Clark threw the grenade as deep into the cave as he could. It had no sooner left his hand than he stepped back around the mouth and placed his fingers in his ears, closing his eyes tightly. The rest of the team followed his lead and prepared for the blast.

KA-BOOM!!

The flash-bang grenade detonated with a thunderous explosion, belching smoke, and small pieces of debris from the mouth of the cave. As soon as it cleared, Clark spun around the edge and into the cave. His tactical light illuminated the smokey interior of the cave. Greyeagle rolled in from the left at almost the same time, his light adding to the illumination.

Through the swirling smoke, they expected to see a Wendigo rush at them at any second, but nothing moved. Although the flash-bang had scattered some of the bones around, the interior seemed to be nearly identical to their last visit. Rounding the corner into the second chamber, they found that all of the hanging meat had been cleared out. Everything, including the body of the Native American warrior, was gone.

"Clear!" shouted Clark.

"Clear!" echoed Greyeagle.

"Clear!" called Valkyrie.

"Where the hell did they go?" asked Clark.

"I'll check the area and see if I can locate tracks to follow," said Greyeagle, turning to head back out of the cave.

Clark continued to search the chamber, hoping to find any indication of where they might have gone. After a few minutes, he returned to the front of the cave and pulled the team together. Greyeagle was still searching the area for tracks.

"They're not here," said Clark. "Plant charges all through the cave. I want to bring that entire thing down. They're not coming back here."

"On it, sir," said Huntsman 2-1.

"Copy that, sir," said Hunstman 2-4.

The teams that consisted of Huntsman 2-1, 2-2, and 2-3, plus Huntsman 2-4, 2-5, and 2-7 all headed into the cave to plant explosives. Three of them were Navy SEALs and certified explosives experts. Clark had every confidence that the cave was about to come down.

Greyeagle emerged from the trees and approached Clark. He had a disturbed look on his face and was moving at a brisk pace. Whatever was on his mind, Clark had little doubt of it being good news.

"Captain," said Greyeagle, "we have a problem."

"What kind of problem?" asked Clark, glancing back into the trees.

"The kind that will likely turn into a firefight if we're not careful," said Greyeagle. "Call the team in close and tell them to hold their fire unless ordered to."

"Alright everyone," shouted Clark. "Gather up!"

The team moved over to Clark and took up defensive positions.

"Hold your fire unless I give the order," instructed Clark.

Gideon looked quizzically at Clark but said nothing.

"Here they come," whispered Clark.

First one, then five more Bigfoot appeared from the trees. They were fanned out in a semi-circle, blocking every direction the team could have gone except back into the cave. They were wearing crude camouflage using grass, sticks, and leaves braided into their long dark hair to add to their natural ability to hide. They were also carrying an assortment of crude weapons, including spears, stone axes, and two had massive bows with arrows that were nearly four feet long.

"There's only six of them, sir," whispered Margolin. "We can take 'em."

"There are more in the trees," said Greyeagle.

"Shit," hissed Margolin. "How many?"

"I do not know," replied Greyeagle. "More than enough to give us a tremendous fight."

Winter stood up and began walking towards the largest of the creatures. He was a massive beast that was covered in thick black hair and stood close to nine feet tall. From the deference the others showed him, Clark figured he was the leader.

"What are you doing?" asked Margolin.

He reached out and grabbed her by the arm. She turned her head and smiled at him.

"Everything is alright, Frank," she said, smiling serenely. "If he had been here to fight, we would have known it already. I can communicate with him if you will allow."

The last statement was directed at Clark.

"Go ahead," said Clark. "But if he makes a move on you, he won't make it."

"Just as you have your weapons trained on them," said Winter, "there are many arrows that you cannot see that are trained on you. As I said, if they were here to fight, blood would already have been spilled."

Clark nodded at Margolin and he reluctantly let go of her arm. Giving him a reassuring smile, she turned back and moved slowly towards the big creature. As she approached, the beast seemed to loom over her tiny frame. Standing in front of the massive beast, her slender five feet two-inch frame seemed almost childlike.

Stopping a few feet away, she looked up at the massive beast and spoke in her native tongue. The creature replied with a series of intricate gestures and grunts. After several minutes, the beast reached out his enormous fist and slowly opened it. Inside its hand was a shiny piece of metal that resembled a badge. She accepted the gift and returned it by giving him several large pieces of beef jerky from the pouch on her belt.

Sniffing the jerky, the beast put one in its mouth and began chewing contentedly. With a snort, the beast turned and vanished back into the trees. The others remained still for a few seconds, then slowly stepped back into the trees and vanished from sight. Within the span of a few heartbeats, they could no longer hear any sound from the creatures, but Clark could tell that they were gone.

"Holy crap," whispered Margolin. "That goddamned commercial is right. He does love jerky."

Valkyrie gave Margolin a withering look and silently mouthed, "Dumbass."

Turning around slowly, Winter walked carefully back to the group. Going straight to Clark, she held out her hand. Clark took the badge which was scuffed but still shiny, with blood on the front of it. It was a gold badge with blue enamel and an insignia in the middle. The lettering read, "RCMP GRM."

"This is a badge from the Royal Canadian Mounted Police," said Clark.

"Yes," said Winter. "The Wendigo are heading north."

"How much of a headstart do they have?" asked Clark.

"Not long," said Winter. "They left just before our arrival here."

"What are the Bigfoot doing here?" asked Clark.

"They are hunting us," said Winter. "Or, more precisely, they were."

"What do you mean *were*?" asked Clark.

"When they realized that we were hunting the Wendigo," said Winter, "they decided to leave us alone. They have had clashes with the Wendigo as well and wish to see them gone."

"I saw pieces in the cave last night that I knew wasn't human," said Clark.

"They said that if we destroy the Wendigo, they will let us leave in peace," said Winter.

"Let us?" said Margolin. "We've beaten those things before. We can do it again."

"Why would you fight if you did not need to?" asked Winter.

"Uh, I, uh, I guess we wouldn't," said Margolin.

"Exactly," said Winter. "They are not your enemy. They only thought we were coming after them because of your buildings. The structure you call Valhalla."

"We won't go after them," said Clark, "but if they start taking down people, we'll be back."

"I think I made them understand that," said Winter. "They do not hunt men. They prefer to avoid them unless they feel threatened. With the Wendigo gone, they will help to heal and sanctify these woods.

154

Although the stain of the Wendigo will darken this place for years to come."

"Did they set those traps we found?" asked Clark.

"Yes," said Winter, "but we will not find anymore. They have not set any others since they learned we were hunting the Wendigo."

"That's good," said Clark.

Glancing down at the badge, Clark saw it was scratched but not badly tarnished. It was brass, so that meant it hadn't been away from its owner for long.

"So, I gather by this badge that the Windigo are heading for Canada," said Clark. "Or have been there recently."

"Yes," said Winter. "They said that the Wendigo were moving north beyond *Gichi-gami*."

"Beyond what?" asked Margolin.

"That is the *Ojibwe* word for Lake Superior," said Greyeagle.

"The Wendigo are heading for Canada," said Clark. "The border is only a few miles away. We need to get moving if we're going to catch them before they cross it."

"Why not just call the Canadians and let them handle it, boss?" asked Margolin.

"Because they might just kill more people before the Canadians can get a team to the area," replied Clark. "If we can end this before they leave American soil, then we're going to do it."

"You heard the man," snapped Gideon, "let's get ready to move!"

"Are the Bigfoot going to help us catch the Wendigo?" asked Clark.

"No," replied Winter. "They are returning to their homes. They will be watching us, though."

"Great," said Clark. "So, how did they slip around our thermal eye in the sky?"

"The Wendigo are not the only creatures who possess magic," said Winter. "There is ancient magic that runs deep in this place. It helps the

155

creatures you call Bigfoot to hide, no matter how hard you look for them."

The teams emerged from the cave and handed Clark a detonator.

"She's ready to blow on your word, sir," said Huntsman 2-3. "I thought you might like to do the honors."

"Thank you, Reardon," said Clark.

"Everyone, clear the area," said Gideon. "Move away from the cave."

Moving away from the entrance, Clark did a quick headcount and made certain everyone was clear.

"Fire in the hole!" he shouted, hitting the detonator.

They felt as much as they heard the detonation of the plastic explosives. The ground shook and the cave seemed to implode, pulling a good chunk of the hillside with it. It was several seconds before the ground stopped shaking and the hillside settled into place. The cave was completely collapsed.

"That was awesome!" shouted Margolin. "Can we blow something else up?"

Everyone chuckled.

"Alright folks," said Clark. "Let me check in with Valhalla and we're going after the Wendigo."

Gideon and Greyeagle began checking on the team, making certain everyone was ready to travel.

"Thunder-god to Valhalla," said Clark.

"This is Valhalla Actual," said Saunders. "Go ahead."

"Valhalla Actual," said Clark. "We arrived at our target destination and found it empty. Demolition charges were planted and the target was destroyed. Over."

"Copy Thunder-god," said Saunders. "Are you RTB, at this time? Over."

"Negative," replied Clark. "We were unable to engage tangos. We are attempting to overtake tangos before they reach the northern border. Over."

"Copy, Thunder-god," said Saunders. "Do not cross northern border unless cleared. How copy?"

"Solid Copy, Valhalla Actual," said Clark. "Will advise when we reach the border. Can you attempt to obtain permission to pursue? Over."

"I'll send it up the chain," said Saunders. "Say again, DO NOT cross northern border until approval is obtained. Over."

"Thunder-god copies," said Clark. "Out."

Clark looked around at the team.

"We aren't allowed to cross into Canada," said Clark. "Valhalla is attempting to get us permission to pursue, but we can't cross without it. So, let's catch these goddamned things before they reach Canada. Hooah?!"

"HOOAH!" shouted the team in unison.

"Let's move," said Clark. "Greyeagle, take point."

"Yes, sir," said Greyeagle.

Clark's team stayed right behind him as they headed off deeper into the forest. It wasn't long before Greyeagle had a trail and began following it. Once he had the trail, he picked up the pace.

"We're less than three miles from the border," said Clark quietly to Valkyrie.

"Are we stopping at the border?" she asked.

"Let's just catch these goddamned things before we have to find out," said Clark. "If they get across the border, then we're responsible for whoever they kill before the Canadian team can get there."

Valkyrie didn't answer. There wasn't anything she could say. He was right and they all would feel like they failed if the Wendigo killed more people.

Greyeagle quickened the pace, pushing hard to overtake the Wendigo. The trees in this area were mostly Jack Pines and pushing through was much easier than pushing through the vines and underbrush that seemed to grow in other areas of the forest.

They emerged from a thick stand of pines and saw the cabin up ahead, maybe seventy yards. Even from that distance, they could see that it had been attacked and torn apart. The walls were still standing, but the front door had been torn off and several of the windows were busted open.

"Son-of-a-bitch," said Doc. "They tore that place apart."

"Yeah," said Margolin. "Makes you wonder why they didn't do that when you were locked inside."

"That's a frightening thought," said Doc.

While they were watching, a large table came sailing through the open window.

"Fuck," said Margolin. "They're still inside."

"At least one of them is," said Doc.

As they continued towards the cabin, two of the creatures emerged from inside. They hadn't noticed the team approaching and seemed to be fighting over something. They were tall and gaunt, with their skin an ash-grey color. One of them still had straggles of black hair still stuck to its skull-like head.

"I think that's the guy that was hanging in the cave," said Clark. "I think he turned."

"What are they fighting over?" asked Margolin.

"Looks like a bag of beef jerky," said Valkyrie.

"They better watch it," said Margolin. "Bigfoot gets pissed when you mess with his beef jerky."

Margolin chuckled at his joke and Valkyrie rolled her eyes.

"Take them out," said Clark.

Numerous rifles rang out as the team engaged the two Wendigo. Both creatures shrieked from pain and surprise as they were hit multiple

158

times with both silver-tipped and incendiary rounds. Clark quickly switched magazines on his AA-12, loading in a fresh mag of Dragon's Breath rounds.

The creatures shook under the impacts but didn't drop. Instead, they turned towards their attackers and roared their challenge. Then, in a flash, they shot towards the team with incredible speed, dodging as they came. They were too fast to track and it was nearly impossible to hit them.

Clark waited for them to move within thirty yards of the team. When they veered towards each other, he fired ahead of them with a Dragon's Breath round. The cone of burning magnesium engulfed both creatures, stopping them in their tracks. They both dropped to the ground and tried to use the snow to extinguish the fire that was now rapidly covering their entire bodies.

Running towards them, Clark put the rest of the magazine of Dragon's Breath rounds into the creatures, immolating them in the process. As they shrieked and sizzled, the rest of the team moved up. Valkyrie used her HK-UMP50 to stitch a burst into each of their chests. When the powerful incendiary rounds pierced their hearts, the shrieking abruptly ceased.

"Two more down," said Murdock.

"God knows how many more to go," said Clark.

"At least six," said Greyeagle.

"Then we've still got work to do," said Clark. "Have you got a trail?"

"Yes, sir," said Greyeagle. "They're heading north."

"Have we gained any ground?" asked Clark.

"I think so," said Greyeagle. "They stopped here long enough to rip this cabin apart. These two were stragglers."

"Must have stayed for the jerky," said Margolin, laughing.

"Asshole," said Valkyrie, shaking her head in mock disgust.

"Let's get on their trail," said Clark. "We're nearly two miles to the border and they're still ahead of us."

Both dogs were eager for the chase. There had been a complete change in their demeanor since they now understood the monsters could be killed. They no longer felt like they were prey. Instead, they wanted to hunt them down, eager for the kill.

"Let's go!" shouted Clark, heading after Greyeagle.

They were gaining ground but running out of time.

CHAPTER TWELVE
RACE FOR THE BORDER

"What counts is not necessarily the size of the dog in the fight
—it's the size of the fight in the dog."
President Dwight D. Eisenhower

1500 Hours CST
14 February

Clark found himself almost running to keep up with Greyeagle. There was no need to track anymore. They could hear the creatures ahead of them, almost taunting them. Now that the Wendigo were aware of their pursuit, they were tormenting them by staying just ahead. Clark could only wonder if the Wendigo retained enough human knowledge to know they were close to the Canadian border or if they were just mocking them with their speed. Either way, it pissed him off.

"Valkyrie, Viking," shouted Clark. "Get ready! When we reach the shore of Caribou Lake, they're going to be out in the open. I want you both engaging them before they reach the opposite shore. Drop as many as you can!"

Valkyrie let the HK-UMP50 drop on its sling and brought her custom sniper's rifle around from her back while she ran. Viking tossed his over his shoulder as he pulled his own sniper's rifle back to the front.

"Kodiak!" roared Clark. "Swing to the left when we hit the lake and engage with your minigun."

"Yes, sir," said Kodiak.

"If we don't stop them at Caribou Lake," shouted Clark, "we've only got one more shot before the border. Clearwater Lake is about a mile on the other side of Caribou. We've got to bring them down before they reach the border!"

"What about launching grenades?" asked Margolin.

"Negative," said Clark. "Only as a last resort. If we crack the ice, we'll have to go around and they'll be too far ahead to catch."

"Copy that!" shouted Margolin.

161

"When the sniper's drop," yelled Clark, "everyone get the fuck out of their way!"

They could see through the trees that they were nearly at the lake.

"Get ready!" roared Clark.

As they burst through the bushes at the edge of the lake, they could see seven of the Wendigo running across the ice and heading for the opposite shore.

"NOW!" roared Clark.

The snipers both dropped to the ground and started acquiring targets. The team split to keep their line of fire open. Kodiak took a position to the left of the snipers and the electric motor began spooling up the rotary barrels, bringing them to firing speed.

Just before the minigun engaged, there was a sharp snapping sound. Bjorn had broken his leash and streaked out ahead of them, racing after the Wendigo.

"Bjorn!" roared Eagle. "Fuß[22]!"

Any other commands were drowned out in the roar of the minigun spitting three-thousand rounds per minute at the fleeing Wendigo. Over the roar of the minigun came a louder boom. Valkyrie had fired her first round. It was closely followed by Viking's first round.

The high-velocity lead covered the distance and tore into the unprepared Wendigo. The long burst from the minigun chewed up the last three Wendigo in the line, sheering off legs and destroying most of their lower torsos.

Valkyrie's round burst the head of the creature in the lead. It stumbled and fell to the ground. Viking's round struck another creature in the middle of the back and exploded out the creature's chest. Shrieking, it toppled forward and slid to a stop on the snow-covered ice.

The remaining two vanished into the trees on the far side of the lake. Clark ran out onto the ice, eager to finish off the creatures that had fallen before they could recover and escape. They were wounded, but he knew that would not keep them down for long.

---

[22] Fuß – German language dog command – pronounced FOOSE. Command to Heel.

"Let's move!" roared Clark.

The team followed behind him as they covered the distance rapidly. The three who had lost their legs were desperately trying to crawl away before they could finish the job. The other two were not moving. Their wounds had been incapacitating, but not fatal.

One of the creatures that were crawling towards the opposite shore was suddenly pinned to the ice by nearly a hundred and fifty pounds of an angry bullmastiff. Bjorn grabbed the monster by the back of the neck and pinned it to the ice. It tried to reach the dog that was violently shaking it, but the massive canine stood on the creature's back and avoided all attempts to grab it.

Clark ran up and put a flechette round through the other two crawlers' heads. They immediately stopped moving.

"Bjorn, Fuβ!" shouted Eagle.

Obediently, Bjorn released his grip and leaped away from the beast, returning to Eagle.

"Good boy," said Eagle, his tone both high-pitched and affectionate. "Who's a good boy?"

While Bjorn was being praised and petted, Clark and Margolin put rounds through the heads and hearts of every creature laying on the ice.

"Quickly," said Clark. "Let's drag these things off the ice and plant thermite. We've got to get back on the trail before the last two hit the border."

Seconds later, they were running while dragging the creatures to the shore. No sooner had they reached the edge of the lake, they started gathering loose pieces of wood and anything that they thought might be combustible. Once it was piled up, they shoved thermite into the chest cavities of the creatures and yanked out the pins. They were already running into the trees when the thermite began to glow bright incandescent red.

"Let's move!" shouted Clark. "We've got just over a mile left to the border."

Ahead, they could hear the remaining Wendigo racing off through the trees. They were far enough ahead now that they would have only seconds of visibility on the lake before they reached the other side.

"Keep moving!" shouted Clark.

Clark pushed as hard as he could go, knowing full-well that they were less than half a mile from the border. Their chances of catching the creatures before they reached Canadian soil were diminishing by the second. The next time they reached a clearing would be the Mountain Lake, which sits right on the line.

"Valkyrie!" shouted Clark without turning around. "You've got to tag them before they get past the center of the lake!"

"On it!" she shouted.

Bursting through the trees, Clark didn't move to the side. He trusted Valkyrie with his life. Running flat out, he was determined to catch the beasts before they reached the center of the lake. They were less than twenty yards from leaving American soil. On the far side of the lake, directly across from them, two men in dark-colored uniforms emerged from the trees. They were in the line of fire.

"I don't have a shot!" yelled Valkyrie.

"Goddamn it!" shouted Clark, not slowing down.

Clark knew with those two on the other side of the creatures, he couldn't risk a shot either.

"Valhalla Actual to Thunder-god," said Saunders via the radio. "GPS indicates you are dangerously close to entering Canada. Stop now before we cause an international incident."

"Fuck!" snarled Clark, sliding to a stop in the middle of the lake.

The two Wendigo sped directly at the two men on the far side of the lake. Before they could draw their weapons, the creatures were upon them. Clark watched helplessly as they ripped the two men apart.

"Shit!" he roared, angrily. "We could have stopped that!"

Rapidly changing magazines, Clark loaded a drum of rifled slugs. Bringing the AA-12 to his shoulder, he put four rounds into one of the creatures. It staggered back and fell into the trees. The second one

164

grabbed one of the fallen men and dragged him into the darkness of the Jack Pines. Somewhere in that darkness, the one that had been wounded screeched that telltale multi-tonal cry.

Clark stood indecisive in the center of the lake. Glancing at the team, he considered his options. Glancing back at the far shore, he could still hear the screeches of the Wendigo as they tore into the dead man.

"Don't do it, sir!" called Valkyrie. "They'll court-martial you!"

"Thunder-god to Valhalla Actual," said Clark. "They just killed two foreign nationals. Requesting permission to pursue. Over."

"Negative, Thunder-god," said Saunders. "We do not have permission to cross the border, at this time. Do not, say again, DO NOT cross the border. How copy?"

Looking back once more at his team, Valkyrie saw the decision in his eyes. Clark took off his radio which had his GPS built into it, dropping it on the ice. He looked at Valkyrie for a long moment before turning and running towards the Canadian shore.

"Aw, shit," said Murdock, taking off his radio and tossing it into the snow.

"What are you doing, sir?" asked Valkyrie.

Murdock drew in a deep breath and let it out slowly.

"I'm not letting him go alone," he replied. "Sar-Major Gideon, you're in charge. I won't let any of you risk your careers over this."

Turning away, he raced out onto the ice, following after Clark. Greyeagle tossed his radio beside Murdocks.

"I was already retired," he said. "What are they going to do, make me go back to it?"

Greyeagle headed out onto the ice. Kodiak tossed his radio down and started after him.

"Where he goes, I go," said Kodiak with a shrug.

Winter followed right behind him.

"I'm not in the military," she said, smiling.

"Me either," said Doc. "I guess I'm going with them."

"Well, shit," said Margolin, tossing his radio down. "My last orders were to protect her. Guess I'm in, too. Come visit me at Leavenworth[23]."

Valkyrie shrugged and tossed down her radio, then headed across the ice without another word.

"Goddamn it," said Gideon. "Somebody pick up those goddamned radios. We're going to need them."

"On the way back to Valhalla?" asked Raven.

"No," said Gideon. "I'm going after them. If any of you want to go back to Valhalla, there won't be any bad feelings. I can't and won't order you to go."

"What are we waiting for?" asked Shieldmaiden. "They're just getting farther ahead of us."

Gideon shook his head.

"If they ask at the court-martial," he said, "tell them I ordered you to go."

"Fuck that, Sar-Major," said Runestone. "We're all going to Leavenworth together."

Shaking his head, Gideon headed across the ice.

"I suggest you all turn off your radios for a while," said Gideon. "You can't be ignoring orders if you can't hear them."

All down the line, everyone switched off their radios as they ran across the lake. Above them, the drone was capturing footage of the entire thing, in crystal clear hi-definition video. Back at Valhalla, Saunders was rapidly approaching a nervous breakdown.

"Sir, eye in the sky indicates the entirety of Team Two is crossing the border," said Overwatch.

"Why am I not surprised," said Jay, chuckling softly.

"Son-of-a-bitch!" roared Saunders. "They're going anyway! Shit!"

Saunders kicked over a desk chair.

---

[23] Leavenworth – referring to the military prison at Fort Leavenworth, Kansas

"Calm down, Levi," said CSM Hammond. "Clark will bring them all home."

"Yeah, so we can all stand a General Courts-Martial together when Asgard finds out," replied Saunders shaking his head. "So much for retiring a Colonel."

CSM Hammond chuckled as he took out a cigar.

"Command Sargent-Major," said Wilder. "There's no smoking in the Command Module."

"Fuck it," said CSM Hammond. "We're so far down the rabbit hole, smoking is the least of our problems, now. Might as well enjoy myself."

Wilder just smiled and turned on the ventilation fans and calmly went back to her console.

"Sir," said Overwatch, turning to Major Saunders.

"Go ahead," said Saunders.

"We have a priority video message coming in, coded your eyes only," said Overwatch. "Asgard wants to speak to you on a secure line."

"Well, fuck," said Saunders, heading for the communications room. "That didn't take long. Been nice working with you, Dave."

CSM Hammond blew a smoke ring into the air and leaned back in his chair.

"Hell of a way to end a career," said CSM Hammond with a chuckle.

"I've got a good bottle of bourbon in my bag," said Jay *Matoskah*.

"Don't mind if I do," said CSM Hammond.

By D.A. Roberts

Chapter Thirteen
The Invasion Of Canada

*"Soldiers can sometimes make decisions that are
smarter than the orders they have been given."*
Orson Scott Card, Enders Game

1800 Hours CST
14 February

Clark burst through the trees and had his AA-12 ready to engage the Wendigo. He found a large bloody spot on the ground, but no sign of the creatures. There were no tracks, no bloody spots, and no indication that they'd even been here other than the blood.

"Where the fuck did they go?" whispered Clark, scanning the area.

He spun around when he heard the sound of something approaching rapidly and pulled up short when Murdock broke through the trees.

"Shit, I almost shot you, Nate," said Clark. "What are you doing here, anyway?"

"Watching your back," said Murdock. "Some asshole once told me to forget that lone ranger bullshit and start showing some teamwork. We have to rely on each other to make the mission a success."

"Sounds like a real dumbass," said Clark, chuckling as he turned around, scanning for signs of the creatures.

"You could say that," said Murdock. "It was the advice you gave me when we met at the team tryouts."

"I thought that particular brand of bullshit smelled familiar," said Clark. "Seriously though, Nate. Get the hell back across the border before All-Father figures out you're here. You're going to get yourself court-martialed."

"And you're not?" asked Murdock.

Greyeagle and Kodiak emerged through the trees.

"Looks like someone else will be going with us," said Murdock.

"I'm pretty sure the entire team is right behind me," said Kodiak.

Clark shook his head in mock disbelief.

"I guess I shouldn't be shocked," said Clark.

Valkyrie ducked beneath the branches and stepped up beside Kodiak.

"Trying to leave without us, boss?" she asked.

"Wouldn't dream of it," said Clark. "I don't suppose I could order you all back across the border?"

"Probably not, sir," said Valkyrie. "I think you're stuck with us."

"Fine," said Clark. "Greyeagle, can you find a trail? I can't find where they went."

"They're up in the trees," said Greyeagle. "It's going to be difficult to track them."

"Wonderful," said Clark. "It's almost dark. Finding them is not going to be easy. Especially since we don't have the eye in the sky, now. We're on our own."

Clark looked around at the growing darkness in the woods. There was no sound of animals or movement. The silence was oppressive and unnatural.

"Get a few people on the thermals," said Clark. "Scan the area. Watch for those cold spots."

Several of the team began sweeping while Clark took out his map. Kneeling, he unfolded it and brought out his lensatic compass. Gideon and Murdock knelt beside him and looked at the map.

"We're here," said Clark, gesturing at a point on the map. "Depending on which way these things go, they could reach a couple of places with people."

"What are we looking at?" asked Murdock.

"If this map is right, we've got a couple of Provincial Parks," said Clark, "a campground, and a Nature Preserve. I have no idea if any of those places are occupied."

"Probably only Park staff, rangers and maybe a few die-hard winter campers," said Gideon.

"That's a food source," said Murdock. "Or new recruits. I'm not sure which is worse, them eating the locals or turning them into more Wendigo."

"How long does it take to transform into one?" asked Clark.

"Hell if I know," said Murdock.

"Winter," said Clark, motioning for her to join them.

"Yes?" she said as she approached.

"How long does it take for someone to turn into a Wendigo?" asked Clark.

"It varies," she said, thinking. "If the person was killed by the Wendigo, it is significantly faster than it would be from a wound. There are also tales of Wendigo possession."

"What's that?" asked Murdock.

"Some of the old stories say that the spirit of the Wendigo could corrupt otherwise healthy people," she said, frowning. "They would become Wendigo without ever encountering one."

"Well, we've got something else to worry about, now," said Clark.

"These tales were usually of people stuck in snowstorms," said Winter, "or running out of food in a remote cabin during the deep winter. I have never heard of one where it happened to a person who was not starving."

"Well, that's something at least," said Gideon. "So we're still faced with the decision of what to do here. Do we keep pursuing the Wendigo or get back across the border and leave it to the Canadians?"

"If I was sure they were here," said Clark, "that might be an option. Unless they can deploy a hell of a lot faster than we can, it's going to take them a while to get here."

"They work faster than we do," said Gideon, "but even if they mobilized as soon as they were contacted, they're still hours out."

"How do they move so fast?" asked Clark.

"Their military doesn't have the same restrictions about operating on their own soil as we do," explained Gideon. "Canadian Special

Forces are top-notch units. I've worked with a few of them in the past. Joint Task Force Two is on par with Delta. Plus their law enforcement is set up differently. They play seamlessly with the military. It's a good system. America could learn a lot from how they do it."

"So, what would you say their ETA will be?" asked Clark.

"Twelve hours from contact," said Gideon. "But that's just a guess. If they had a team closer, then it could be any moment. Without comms, we don't have any way to find out."

"Twelve hours is still pretty fast," said Clark. "But we're only a few miles from the closest possibly inhabited area. If we don't catch those things, then those people won't know what hit them."

"Assuming Greyeagle can find their path," said Gideon.

"He'll find it," said Clark.

"But if he doesn't?" asked Gideon.

"If that happens," said Clark, pausing, "then we'll head back across the border. If we don't have a trail to follow, then we've got no reason to be here."

"Some might argue that we don't anyway," said Murdock.

Clark took in a deep breath and let it out slowly.

"You might be right," said Clark, after a moment. "The longer we stay here, the more trouble we're going to be in. Unless we can locate a trail to follow or show direct cause, we're going to have to go back and face Valhalla. I'll take full responsibility for this."

"Of course you will," said Gideon, "right along with the rest of us."

Clark just shook his head.

"Here comes Greyeagle," said Murdock.

They both glanced up as he came walking back from the woods with a dark look on his face. They had the feeling that he wasn't bringing good news.

"I don't like that look," said Clark as Greyeagle crouched beside them.

"Nor should you," said Greyeagle. 'You're not going to like it."

"What happened?" asked Gideon.

"They went up the trees," said Greyeagle, "just like I suspected. That's where things get tricky. I could shift into wolf form and try to follow them, but they left no trail to follow. This isn't like the *Oolonga-Doglalla*. The Dogmen I've tracked leave something at least. The Wendigo leave nothing. Not so much as a scratch on the bark."

"That's not good," said Clark. "Could you point us in a direction?"

"Not reliably," said Greyeagle. "I'm not even certain that they stuck together. They know they're being chased. It's reasonable to believe that they split up."

"Alright," said Clark. "Get everyone together. We're heading back to Valhalla to face the music. I guess it's the Canadians' problem now."

"I'll get everyone ready to move," said Murdock.

"I want to move out as soon as they're ready," said Clark.

"On the plus side," said Gideon, "we haven't been here long enough to cause a problem. We might just get chewed out for this."

"Maybe," said Clark, "but unlikely. Especially if Asgard knows about it."

"We know for a fact that he listens to our radios," said Gideon.

"True," said Clark. "I suppose we'll know if the other teams meet us with handcuffs."

Gideon cocked his head to the side and pointed up.

"Do you hear that?" asked Gideon.

Clark slowed his breathing and strained to hear the sound, expecting to hear the Wendigo approaching. Instead, he heard the deep thump-thump of approaching rotors.

"Choppers," said Clark. "Where are they going?"

"Sounds like they're getting closer," said Greyeagle.

"I think they're coming in low," said Gideon. "Sounds like they're landing on the lake."

"Let's move," said Clark, motioning for the team to follow.

He headed back through the trees and emerged on the edge of the lake that sat on the border. Two Blackhawk helicopters were approaching, preparing to land side by side on the ice.

"They're Canadian," said Clark, gesturing at the markings on the sides.

"Somehow I don't think we're going back to Valhalla, just yet," said Gideon. "Looks like we're about to be in the middle of an international incident."

No sooner had the choppers touched down, the sides opened and men began pouring out. Twelve armed personnel in each chopper emerged, all armed with armament very similar to what the Wild Hunt carried. It was obvious to everyone present that they came expecting trouble.

The two groups of troops fanned out and brought their weapons up into high-ready and began advancing towards them. One man stepped out in front of the others as he scanned the group. Adjusting his direction, he headed directly for Clark.

"I think it's safe to say they know who we are," said Gideon.

Clark just nodded as the man approached. He had the bearing of a soldier to him, walking confidently and with purpose. He also looked cautiously up and down the line of Team Two.

Clark could see he wore the rank of Major and he wore military insignia instead of police. He was carrying full equipment and Clark recognized the type of rifle he was carrying. It was the same as the Hunt carried. A custom-built Wilson Combat .458 SOCOM.

"Captain Clark, I presume," said the man in a slight French accent. "I'm Major Renee Tremblay, Joint Task Force Two. Cryptid Containment and Elimination Detachment."

Clark saluted and held it until Tremblay returned it.

"Major," said Clark. "I think we have quite a bit to talk about."

"Absolutely," said Tremblay, "but that can wait for later. I want to thank your team for coming to help."

Clark and Gideon exchanged a confused look.

"Your General Dalton contacted my superiors and explained the situation," said Tremblay. "How long have the creatures been on Canadian soil?"

"Not long," said Clark. "They took out two officers as soon as they hit the border. I think they were Mounties."

Clark pointed at where the body of the officer had been covered with a poncho.

"The Wendigo carried off the other one," said Clark. "I wasn't able to stop them."

"Thank you," said Tremblay.

Nodding at two of his people, they headed over to the fallen officer and began placing him in a body bag. Gently, they placed the fallen officer in the bag and zipped it up.

"On behalf of the Canadian Government," said Tremblay, "I formally welcome you to Canada and thank you for your help. I was also asked to pass on a message."

"What's that?" asked Clark.

"To check your radios," said Tremblay. "Your Valhalla has been unable to contact you."

Clark chuckled and glanced at Gideon.

"Sounds like some type of interference," said Gideon with a grin.

"I'll check our comms and check-in," said Clark, smiling.

"Have you been able to track the Wendigo?" asked Tremblay.

"Unfortunately, we lost them in the trees," said Clark.

"If we could get our drone in position," said Tremblay, "we would be able to track them."

"With us able to contact Valhalla," said Clark. "We have a drone in the area already."

"With the snow coming in," said Tremblay, "it will likely be grounded."

"Damn it," said Clark. "I forgot about the weather coming in. It should start snowing soon."

"So, without a direction of travel," said Tremblay, "we can only guess where they're going."

"What are the closest places with people?" asked Clark.

"There are only two within easy distance," said Tremblay. "Both are on Arrow Lake. One is a small village on the south shore and the other is the park offices. There's a small staff there year-round."

"We should split the teams," said Clark. "Part of the team pursues along the path we expect them to take. Then we send people to both locations to wait for Wendigo to arrive. We can get ahead of them with your choppers."

"How do you want to do the split?" asked Tremblay.

"Well, sir," said Clark, "this is your show. Not only are we in your country, but you're also the ranking officer."

Tremblay looked at Clark with an odd look on his face.

"Honestly," said Tremblay, "I assumed you'd want to be in charge."

"Because I'm American?" asked Clark.

"Partially," said Tremblay. "Mostly because our team doesn't have the experience fighting these things that yours does."

"It's your show, Major," said Clark. "You make the calls. I'll offer my advice if you want it. But you're the senior officer."

Tremblay nodded, frowning.

"Alright, then," said Tremblay, "I like your suggestion. We'll split the teams. I think we should keep them mixed. As long as some of my men are with yours, their authority will not be questioned should you run into anyone locally."

"I agree," said Clark. "I think we'll be able to work together without any issues. How do you want to make the split?"

"I will take five of my men with me," said Tremblay, "and you choose five of your own. Our group will go to the little village. My exec and yours will each take five of their men and go to the park offices. Both teams will go by helicopter. The rest will pursue overland."

"Sounds like a plan, sir," said Clark, smiling.

Turning to address the team while Tremblay did the same, Clark started pointing at people as he spoke.

"I'll take Doc, Valkyrie, Heimdall, Raven, and Runestone," he said. "Murdock, you take Gideon, Viking, Eagle, Shieldmaiden, and Kodiak. Greyeagle, you've got command of the ground team. Radios active. If anyone encounters the creatures, all units will converge on the area. Hooah?"

"Hooah," said the team.

"Form up in your groups and let's get moving," said Clark. "Now, if you'll excuse me, I have a radio call to make."

Clark took a few steps away from the group and turned on his radio. Once it completed the power-up sequence, he waited to see if the channel was clear.

"Thunder-god to Valhalla," said Clark, hesitantly.

"Thunder-god, this is Valhalla Actual," said Saunders. "Status report."

Clark noted that he didn't sound happy.

"We've made contact with the Canadian team," said Clark. "We're organizing continued pursuit. We crossed the border when two Canadian law enforcement officers were killed by the creatures. Over."

"Copy that," said Saunders. "Keep us posted and we'll discuss further when you return for debriefing. Out."

"Well, that could have gone worse," said Clark as he turned to head back to the group.

As he approached, he could see that Tremblay was already directing the teams to the helicopters.

"Captain Clark," said Tremblay. "We need to get moving. The choppers won't be able to fly much longer with the snow getting worse."

Clark stopped long enough to check with Greyeagle.

"You ready for this?" asked Clark.

"I've worked with other teams before," said Greyeagle.

"That's not what I meant," said Clark. "If you have to turn, they might not react well."

"Then let us hope it does not come to that," said Greyeagle, nodding grimly.

"Good hunting," said Clark.

"You too, sir," said Greyeagle.

Clark crouched and headed for the chopper his team was in. Climbing in, Clark took a seat beside Valkyrie. Taking out his can of chewing tobacco, Clark put in a dip and offered it to her. She just chuckled and shook her head no. Clark tossed the can to Heimdall who took a pinch and passed it to Raven and Runestone. They both took a pinch and then tossed it back to Clark.

"Anyone else?" asked Clark, offering the can to the Canadian team.

"Chewing tobacco?" asked Tremblay.

"Yeah," said Clark. "Bad habit, I know. But I've been doing it for years."

Tremblay wrinkled his nose but held out his hand. Taking the can, he offered it to the rest of his team. Two of them took him up on the offer. Clark tucked the can back in his pack once they were finished.

The pitch of the rotors changed and the Blackhawk began climbing into the sky. Clark looked down and saw the rest of the team moving off into the trees. The other chopper was lifting just below them.

Once they were clear of the trees, their chopper banked around and circled wide, heading due east. The plan was to fly far enough away to not alert the Wendigo of their destination. After a few miles, they headed northeast towards Arrow Lake. The other chopper was on a similar course, although their destinations were a few miles apart.

Below them, the team had nearly five miles to cover to the nearest of the two destinations. They were to drive the Wendigo towards the teams on the choppers. Clark just hoped that the Wendigo hadn't beaten them to the village.

177

CHAPTER FOURTEEN
BLACKHAWK DOWN

"Discipline is the soul of an army. It makes small numbers formidable; procures success to the weak, and esteem to all."
George Washington

2030 Hours CST
14 February

Circling out over the frozen lake, they surveyed the tiny village. It consisted of only half-a-dozen permanent buildings and several smaller shacks that were likely used for smokehouses or outhouses. The village was dark and there was no movement. This wasn't that unusual since no roads or powerlines led to the village. The only access was by boat or snowmobile.

"Is it always this dark?" asked Clark, leaning towards Tremblay.

"They live primitively up here," said Tremblay. "First Nations people. *Ojibwe* and *Chippewa,* mostly. They don't have power or phones. Maybe a generator, if they want lights and refrigeration. Special consideration for their status from the government. They live off the land, for the most part. What they refer to as subsistence living."

Clark nodded and leaned back.

"Maybe twenty or twenty-five people live there," said Tremblay.

The pilot began dropping altitude and slowing his approach. They were going to land on the frozen lake about fifty yards from the village. The snow was now coming down in heavy flakes and the temperature was steadily dropping.

As the chopper settled to the ground, Clark began to get apprehensive. There was no reaction coming from the village. There was no way they couldn't hear the chopper landing beside them.

"Where are they?" asked Clark, rhetorically. "I'd be finding out what was going on if a helicopter landed in my front yard."

"I agree," said Tremblay. "This is most unusual."

179

They all exited the chopper rapidly, fanning out and kneeling in a semi-circle, facing the village. Everyone had their weapons in the high-ready position and they were watching every angle of approach. The village remained eerily silent with no signs of movement.

As soon as they all were clear, the chopper began to lift back into the sky. Turning to the east, the pilot began to gain altitude as it prepared to return to base. The weather was getting worse and there was already a no-fly order for aircraft.

Dipping the nose, the pilot began to pick up speed while he climbed. Just as he was passing the edge of the village, a tree trunk about the diameter of a softball and close to fifteen feet long came streaking out of the trees like an arrow. The pilot attempted to dodge, but instead of the tree striking the rotors it drove through the cockpit canopy like a spear. Clark wasn't on their radio frequency, but he could imagine the alarms and mayday calls coming from the wounded aircraft.

To his credit, the pilot fought valiantly to save the aircraft. It was spinning wildly and moving out over the ice. Before he could level out and make an emergency landing, two more trees flew out of the dark woods and struck the dying aircraft like ground-to-air missiles.

The first smashed into the main rotor and came apart, disintegrating part of the rotors in the process. The second punched through the side of the chopper and into the engine compartment. Smoke poured out of the doomed chopper as it plummeted towards the ice.

"Valkyrie!" shouted Clark. "Find and eliminate those targets!"

"On it," she said, dropping to the snow and preparing her rifle.

Heimdall hit the ground beside her and brought up his spotter's scope. They were already panning the trees for targets.

The chopper spun around once more and slammed into the ice, going in nose-first. There was a sickening crunch of aluminum and breaking ice as what remained of the rotors dug into the lake's frozen surface. Smoke was billowing from the debris but it didn't catch fire. There was the groaning of metal as it settled onto its side and the rotor hub continued to spin slowly with a few shards of the rotors still attached.

Tremblay was already on the radio when Clark, Doc, Raven, and Runestone began sprinting towards the wreckage. Over the dying sound of the engines, they could hear the thick ice beginning to break. Clark was the first to reach the aircraft, leaping up onto the side of the aircraft. Runestone went around to the front, hoping to find the pilot or co-pilot. Clark yanked the side door open and dropped down inside.

"The ice won't hold much longer!" screamed Doc. "I can hear it breaking beneath us."

Clark dragged himself up over the side, pulling the badly wounded crew chief with him.

"Doc!" yelled Clark. "Take him. I'm going back in."

Doc took hold of the crew chief and eased him down to the ice. Dragging him away from the cracking ice, Doc began assessing his wounds and rendering first aid.

"I think the pilot's dead!" shouted Runestone.

"Get to the front!" roared Clark. "I'm getting the crew out!"

Runestone started breaking out the rest of the canopy to make it easier to hand out the wounded. Inside, he could see Clark pulling the other crewman from the back towards the front. The pilot had been struck on the first impact. Part of his face had been torn away, stripping away his lower jaw and nose. The co-pilot hung limply in his harness, blood dripping from his face.

"Take him!" said Clark, handing the crewman to Runestone.

Runestone took him without hesitation and began carrying him away.

"The ice is separating!" shouted Raven. "You've got to get out of there."

Clark noticed that the aircraft was already starting to roll more towards its top. Water was starting to seep into the back of the aircraft. They only had moments left before it disappeared beneath the surface of the lake.

"Hang on!" shouted Clark, pulling out his knife.

181

Cutting the straps on the co-pilot's harness, he caught him as he started to fall.

"Here!" shouted Clark, handing the co-pilot through the canopy. Raven took the man and hooked her arms under his, then began dragging him away from the sinking aircraft. Clark glanced at the pilot and decided he had to be dead. The head trauma was severe. He wasn't sure he would have time to get the body out before the chopper sank. Divers would have to recover the body later.

"I'm sorry, man," said Clark, turning towards the opening in the canopy.

Movement caught his eye just as he was starting to turn. The pilot's hand had twitched. Turning back, he saw the pilot slowly reaching out for him. His eyes were wide open and pleading, but only a gurgling sound escaped his ruined face.

"The pilot's alive!" shouted Clark, cutting the straps on the harness.

Water was now coming over the toes of his boots as he cut the final strap away. Grabbing the pilot, Clark cradled him as best he could.

"I'm getting you out of here, brother," he said, trying to sound reassuring. "I've got you."

Stepping out onto the shifting ice, Clark saw that an area around the chopper had broken apart and was slowly pulling it into the icy water. The larger pieces of ice were beginning to tilt sharply, opening up a place for the chopper to fall through into the frozen depths below.

Clark felt the ice beneath him shifting, making it almost impossible to walk. Glancing to his left, he saw an opening but it would take him farther away from the team. He knew that if he kept trying to climb the ice, both he and the pilot were going down with the chopper.

Turning to his left, he leaped onto another chunk of ice that wasn't tilted as far. Using the momentum, he jumped to another ice shelf and slid the last few feet to the solid ice beyond it. Lowering the pilot to the ice, Clark began to assess his wounds. Behind him, the chopper continued to sink into the water.

As the chopper took on more water, the nose dipped into the lake and the tail climbed back into the air. Slowly, the water continued to pull in the fuselage down into the dark depths of Arrow Lake. He could hear the others calling his name, not knowing he'd already made it to safety.

"Thunder-god is clear," he said into his mic. "We need a medic over here. The pilot is severely injured, but alive. Over."

"Copy, Thunder-god," said Valkyrie. "Medics are on the way. Over."

"Copy," said Clark. "Thanks. Out."

"Valhalla Actual to Thunder-god," said Saunders. "Can we get a SitRep? Over."

"Standby, Valhalla," said Clark. "I'll advise shortly. Out."

Clark continued to administer what first aid that he could until the Candian medic arrived and took over.

"I've got it from here, sir," said the medic.

Clark stepped back and let the medic take over care. Scooping up some snow, he used it to clean the blood from his hands.

"That was a hell of a thing to do," said Tremblay as he approached.

"Not really," said Clark. "There was no way I was going to sit there and watch those men go into the water. Not if I could help."

"Still," said Tremblay, "I wasn't even off the radio before you were diving inside that chopper. You Americans certainly aren't afraid of anything."

"Never saw the point," said Clark. "Did we get any of the creatures?"

"No," said Tremblay. "They were too far back in the trees for the sniper to get a shot."

"We've got to get these men inside and out of the cold," said Clark. "We're not going to be getting a medivac until this weather breaks."

"We might have bigger problems than that," said Tremblay.

"How so?" asked Clark.

"Since we landed," said Tremblay, "I've seen more than a dozen sets of glowing red eyes in the woods around us."

"Shit," said Clark. "We've got to get to a defensible position. It's going to be hours before our backup gets here."

"And it's unlikely that this weather will break before morning," said Tremblay.

"Let's get the wounded inside and set up a defensive perimeter," said Clark. "We'll figure out our next move once the wounded are stabilized."

Tremblay nodded and moved over to check on the pilot.

"Alright folks," said Clark. "Sound off. Can the wounded be safely moved?"

"We need to get this man on a stretcher," said Doc, "preferably with a backboard. I think he's got spinal damage."

"Well, we don't have either of those," said Clark.

"I've got a folding stretcher in my pack," said Runestone.

"Good," said Clark, "get that over to Doc."

"On it, boss," said Runestone, turning and running towards Doc.

Raven glanced over at Clark from where she was working on the co-pilot.

"He's got head trauma," said Raven. "I can't say moving him is a good idea, but staying here will kill him. We've got to get him warm."

"We can move the pilot," said the Canadian medic. "He's got severe facial trauma, but I think with a C-collar in place, he'll be alright to move. Besides, it's not like we've got any choice."

"The crewman's got a broken arm," said Runestone. "Maybe a collarbone fracture, too. He can walk."

"I'll walk, sir," said the crewman. "Can I help?"

Clark walked over to the crewman. He was a kid of about nineteen or twenty. His arm was in a sling and the pain was etched on his face, but he was determined. Clark took out his Guncrafter Industries Glock .50 GI and handed it to the kid.

184

"It's hot," said Clark. "Round in the chamber. You get seven shots and she's empty. Make them count."

"Yes, sir," said the young man.

"What's your name, kid?" asked Clark.

"Cloutier," he said. "I just made sergeant."

"Alright, Sergeant Cloutier," said Clark. "We're going to get the others to safety and we're surrounded by some nasty creatures. Conserve your ammo and stay close to us. Don't get separated."

"Yes, sir," said Cloutier.

"Good man," said Clark. "Now, let's get the others inside a building and get them stabilized."

Clark started organizing the move.

"I want two people on each of the wounded," said Clark. "Everyone else, form up around them and keep your weapons up."

Runestone and Doc put the stretcher together and locked it into place. Gently, they moved the wounded man onto it. He never even woke up enough to groan. That might have been the kindest thing that they could hope for, under the circumstances. Once he was on the board, Doc secured him in place with rolls of gauze.

"It's not ideal," said Doc, "but it'll do for now. We're ready."

"Let's move!" said Clark.

Runestone and Doc lifted the crew chief while four of the Canadians lifted the pilot and co-pilot. The rest of the team fanned out to form a protective perimeter around the wounded. Clark motioned for Cloutier to stay beside him.

"Stick close, Sergeant," said Clark. "I'll cover you and you keep your eyes open for movement."

"Yes, sir," said Cloutier.

"Let's move!" said Clark.

Glancing behind him, he noticed that Tremblay seemed more than content to let Clark make the calls. Tremblay looked nervous and unsure of himself. Clark made a mental note to talk with him once they were safely inside a building. As they moved across the ice, Clark was taking a good long look at the buildings. Valkyrie moved up beside him and glanced at him.

"Looking for the most defensible building?" she asked.

"Yeah," he said, not looking her way. "Something that might keep them out while we treat the wounded."

"I think that big cabin in the middle looks the best," she said. "I got a good look at the buildings while I was looking for the creatures. It's the sturdiest looking of the group. Thick log construction."

"That works for me," said Clark. "We just have to make sure it's secure once we're inside. Plus clear the building before we go in."

As they continued across the ice, Clark could feel the creatures watching them. He felt their cold hunger reaching out for them. Deep in the darkness of the forest, he could see the faint glow of many sets of eyes. As some would fade out, others would appear. It was impossible to tell exactly how many there were.

Approaching the big cabin, Clark could hear the sound of movement in the darkness. They weren't getting closer, but they weren't making any attempt to hide the fact that they were there.

"Thunder-god to Mjolnir," said Clark into his mic.

"Go ahead," said Gideon.

"Be advised," said Clark, "we're encountering numerous creatures near the village. Are you encountering any at the park? Over."

"Negative," said Gideon. "This place is as empty as the proverbial tomb. No signs of life, so far. We're still searching buildings. Over."

"Copy that," said Clark. "Stay alert. We are encountering heavy presence here and we have wounded from the chopper crash. We're going to find shelter and button-down, for now. Over."

"Clear," said Gideon. "We'll head your way as soon as we finish clearing the park. Over."

"Copy that," said Clark. "Advise when you're close. Over."

"Fenrir to Thunder-god," said Greyeagle. "We're heading in your direction. We'll be there ASAP. Over."

"Copy, Fenrir," said Clark. "We'll hold. Be careful on your approach. Numerous hostiles in the trees. Over."

"Solid copy, Thunder-god," said Greyeagle. "We'll be ready. Out."

As they grew closer to the cabin, the sounds in the woods became louder. The creatures were moving closer but it was still impossible to see them. Bringing their weapons up and aiming at the trees, the team kept sweeping back and forth when sounds were close.

"They're getting brave," whispered Valkyrie.

"We've got to get inside before we get swarmed," said Clark. "Once we're inside, we can set up choke points and maybe thin the herd down."

As they approached the front of the cabin, they could see that the front door was standing open. Clark lit up his tactical light on the AA-12 and shined it inside the building. Valkyrie switched to her HK-UMP50 and activated her tactical light.

"Alright," said Clark. "Cover both sides and the roof while Valkyrie and I clear the building."

"Make it quick," said Doc. "Those things are getting brave. It won't be long before they rush us."

The other members on the team began covering the roof and edges of the building. Clark nodded at Valkyrie and brought his AA-12 up to his shoulder. She stepped behind him and brought her weapon up.

"Ready?" asked Clark.

"As I ever will be," she replied.

"I'm going left," he said.

"I'll take right," she replied.

"Let's go," said Clark. "On three. Three. Two. One."

Clark moved rapidly through the door and swept to the left, trusting Valkyrie to cover her zone. The deep darkness inside the cabin was instantly flooded with the bright tactical lights. There was simple furniture inside with a large stone fireplace that had gone cold.

The small kitchen area was clean and featured a wood-fired cooking stove. Sweeping quickly, Clark saw no movement. The main room was empty, but there were three side rooms.

"Main room clear!" said Clark.

"Clear right," said Valkyrie.

"Three rooms on the left," said Clark.

"I'm right behind you," replied Valkyrie.

Clark waited until he felt her hand on his shoulder before turning into the first room. It was a large pantry, stocked with canned goods and food that had been canned in mason jars. Other than that, it was empty.

"Clear," said Clark.

They reversed position and Clark put his hand on her shoulder. Valkyrie led out of the pantry and into the next room. This was a bedroom and it was also clear. The small closet was open with clothes still hanging and the bed unmade.

"Clear," she said.

Reversing again, she put her hand on Clark's shoulder and they quickly exited and turned the corner into the final room. It was another bedroom but was in more disarray. It looked as if there had been a struggle in the room. Clark could see where someone had been dragged from the bed and out of the room. Whoever had been sleeping in this bed had been surprised in their sleep and dragged away.

"Clear!" said Clark.

"Clear," echoed Valkyrie.

Moving back through the living room, Clark stepped out the door.

"Building's clear," he said. "Let's get everyone inside."

"You heard the man," said Tremblay. "Let's get these men inside and get a fire going."

Clark kept his weapon up as they all filed inside. He was the last one through the door, backing up through with his weapon at the ready and Valkyrie's hand on his shoulder. Shutting the door behind him, Clark saw where the locking mechanism had been tampered with.

Somehow, the Wendigo had destroyed the lock without alerting the sleeping man inside.

Shutting the door, Clark looked around for a means to secure it. There was a crossbar bracket where a beam could be placed across the door to prevent it from being opened. Clark noted that the door was of thick wood, partially to help keep out the cold but to also prevent it from being forced open by bears. Glancing around, he found the crossbar and dropped it into place.

"That should hold for now," said Clark. "Heimdall, Raven, go check windows and the back door. Make sure they're secure."

They both moved off quickly. Two of the Canadian team were breaking up kindling and starting a fire in the fireplace. In minutes, they had it burning and crackling. By the time it was going, Heimdall and Raven returned.

"We're clear, sir," said Raven. "The windows are covered with wood and nailed shut from the inside. Looks like they were already defending from something."

"Back door is solid," said Heimdall. "Not only is it locked, its got a heavy wooden crossbar. It should hold."

"I want someone watching the doors and windows at all times," said Clark.

"Yes, sir," said Heimdall.

"On it, sir," said Raven.

Clark looked at Raven's dog, Sage. The German Shepard was cowering in the corner, staying away from the doors. Shaking his head, Clark knew that meant the creatures were all around them.

"I hear movement," said Valkyrie.

"They've surrounded us," said Clark.

People began to move and for the second time, Clark noticed that Tremblay was hanging back and not making any move to give orders or instructions. While everyone was busy, either covering points of entry or treating the wounded, Clark pulled Tremblay to the side.

"Are you alright, sir?" asked Clark, keeping his voice low to avoid being overheard.

"I'm fine," said Tremblay. "Why?"

"This is your mission," said Clark. "I don't have a problem with running things, I'm just not sure why you do."

"To be honest," said Tremblay, "this is my first deployment with my team. I was just posted to the Cryptid unit. I've never faced a real paranormal threat before."

"They're just like any other enemy," said Clark. "Tougher to kill, maybe, but still an enemy. These things seem to be vulnerable to fire. Every creature we've encountered has a weakness and that's what we have to use against it. Have you served in combat before?"

"Yes," said Tremblay, "twice in Afghanistan. I was the assistant team leader for Joint Task Force Two."

"Then this is no different," said Clark. "Your men will take their cues from you. To be an effective leader, you have to lead. Show them you're in charge and not just waiting for things to happen. No matter what happens, I have your back. My team might have more experience, but this is my second deployment as the team leader. Before that I was Delta."

"I've worked with Delta before," said Tremblay. "Good people."

"Honestly, I don't know much about Joint Task Force Two," said Clark, "but my Sergeant-Major has good things to say. I trust his judgment."

There was a thumping sound from the roof and they all glanced up. It was the unmistakable sound of the hooves that the Wendigo had.

"They're on the roof," whispered Valkyrie.

"So long as they don't get inside," replied Runestone.

"Everyone stay sharp," said Clark. "They're looking for a way in."

Clark could hear the sound of gloves tightening on pistol grips all around the room. Glancing over at Tremblay, Clark made eye-contact and nodded at him. Tremblay paused for a moment and took a deep breath.

190

"Alright everyone," said Tremblay. "Stay calm. We're safe for the moment. If they force their way through anywhere, we treat it as a choke-point and start taking them out."

There were a few glances from the Canadians at him. Their confidence in their commanding officer was shaken. Clark knew it was going to take more to restore that trust. He just hoped that he hadn't done enough to completely lose their trust. Then it was going to be almost impossible to regain it.

"What if they cover the chimney?" asked Runestone.

Clark stopped himself from answering, letting Tremblay take the question.

"We can't let them do that," said Tremblay. "If it starts backing up, we'll put a few rounds up there to discourage them."

"I've got Dragon's Breath rounds for the AA-12," said Clark.

"Perfect," said Tremblay. "That'll clear it."

Clark moved over beside Valkyrie and leaned over to peer through a crack in the boards, straining to get a glimpse of the creatures outside. Even with the heavy snow, it was still too dark to see anything.

"See anything?" whispered Valkyrie.

"No," replied Clark. "It's too dark."

"We can't last in here for very long," said Valkyrie.

"We've got plenty of supplies to last until the rest of the team gets here," said Clark. "Even if they break through a window or a door, we can start stacking bodies. We're not low on ammo."

"I'm glad you're so optimistic, sir," said Valkyrie.

Clark grinned at her and headed over to the couch where Doc was still taking care of some of the injured. He was working on the pilot and had his head wrapped in bandages.

"How's he doing?" asked Clark.

"Not good," said Doc. "He's lost a lot of blood. His injuries are extensive. He'll be lucky to make it until morning. I had to do an emergency tracheotomy. His airway is in really bad shape. Severe damage to the mouth, throat, and nasal cavities."

"What else can we do for him?" asked Clark.

"I've used up all my kit treating everyone," said Doc. "Between me and Anderson, the Canadian medic, we've used most of our trauma supplies stabilizing him."

"Can you give him some blood?" asked Clark. "Would that help?"

"Yeah, if we could find any of his type," said Doc.

"Well, I'm O Negative," said Clark. "I can give blood to about anyone."

"It's worth a shot," said Doc. "You sure you want to do this?"

"We've got the doors and windows covered," said Clark. "I should be good, for a while."

"Well, this isn't like giving blood at the hospital," explained Doc. "This is a transfusion. I'll hook the two of you up and let your blood flow into him. It's a battlefield transfusion, not nearly as pretty as you'd see it in the hospital."

"I figured," said Clark. "Let's do it."

"Alright," said Doc. "Take off your jacket and roll up your sleeve."

Clark sat his gear down and took off his winter coat. Rolling up his sleeve, he sat in a chair beside the couch and waited for Doc to get ready. He caught a glimpse of Valkyrie watching him as Doc cleaned a section of the skin on his arm with an alcohol swab.

"This might hurt a bit," said Doc.

Clark didn't watch and kept his attention focused on the far side of the room. There was only a slight bit of discomfort as Doc put in the IV needle and set up the transfusion. Moments later, blood was flowing into the wounded pilot from Clark.

"What's his name?" asked Clark, nodding at the pilot.

"Mike Clarke," said Tremblay.

"Now, that's ironic," said Clark.

"Yeah, but his is spelled with an E on the end," said Tremblay.

"Still," said Clark. "What are the odds?"

Sergeant Cloutier came over and sat beside Clark.

"That's a great thing you're doing there, sir," said Cloutier.

"Not a big deal, "said Clark. "I've got some to spare and right now he needs it more than I do."

"Captain Clarke is a great guy," said Cloutier. "Thank you for saving him."

"He's not out of the woods yet," said Clark, "both figuratively and literally."

"Still, sir," said Cloutier. "He wouldn't even have made it out of the chopper if it hadn't been for you. None of us would have."

Clark just smiled and shrugged.

"You let me know if you start feeling light-headed," said Doc.

"Will do," said Clark. "I just hope I can give enough to give him a fighting chance."

"If not, we'll see if anyone else can donate," said Doc. "But right now, anything is better than nothing."

"Mjolnir to Thunder-god," said Gideon via the radio.

"Go ahead," said Clark.

"We've located a group of survivors sealed in a building," said Gideon. "We've also encountered several of the Wendigo. With worsening visibility, we can't track them with thermal. We've got too much background interference from the snow. Over."

"Copy," said Clark. "Button-down with the survivors, for now. Protect them until the weather breaks and we can get an evac chopper to extract them. Over."

"Copy that," said Gideon. "What's your status? Over."

"We're stable at this time," said Clark. "We're holding. Over."

"Understood," said Gideon. "Mjolnir out."

"I guess that just leaves Greyeagle and the rest of the team," said Valkyrie softly.

"We'll be fine," said Clark. "We're holding. We just have to keep those things from getting inside."

"We'll hold," she said. "Or we'll make it damned expensive to get in."

Valkyrie gave Clark a reassuring smile and headed back to her position near one of the windows. The snow was coming down in thick flakes bringing with it a steady wind that reduced visibility to less than twenty feet. If it continued, it could reach total white-out conditions before morning. Clark was starting to grow concerned for the rest of the team that was approaching overland.

CHAPTER FIFTEEN
VILLAGE OF THE DAMNED

"If you find yourself in a fair fight,
you didn't plan your mission properly."
David Hackworth

2145 Hours CST
14 February

Half an hour passed in silence, as everyone was listening for any sounds of the Wendigo trying to force their way inside. It was eerily quiet as the only sounds in the room were their own breathing and the occasional soft groan from one of the wounded. Doc moved over beside Clark and checked his heart rate and blood pressure.

"I think you've given all you safely can," whispered Doc. "Any more and you'll be putting yourself at risk."

Clark nodded as Doc began removing the IV.

"How's he doing?" asked Clark, nodding at the pilot.

"He's resting," said Doc. "I've given him something to help him sleep and hopefully not in pain. He needs a major trauma center. He's lucky to be alive."

"He's in for a long recovery and a lot of reconstructive surgery," whispered Clark.

"True," said Doc, "but his wife won't be handed a folded flag. Thanks to you."

Clark just shrugged noncommittally.

"I was just the first one to get there," said Clark. "We all went to help save the crew. You deserve just as much credit as I do."

Clark slipped his gear back into place and rolled his sleeves down. Glancing around the room, he did a quick check on their people. They were all on high-alert and Clark knew that they wouldn't be able to maintain that without the entire team being exhausted soon. Clark nodded at Tremblay and motioned at the room. Tremblay glanced around and nodded.

"Why don't we start taking shifts," said Tremblay. "We've got enough people to watch doors and windows and still let some of you take a break. My people will take the first shift. Captain, you and your team try to get some rest. It could be hours before the rest of the team can get here."

"You heard the man," said Clark. "Grab some floor and try and catch a nap, if you can."

As they started to move away from their posts, there was a massive impact against the front door. It shook the wall and dust came down from the ceiling. The door held but they all knew it couldn't keep taking hits like that. All around the room, everyone brought their weapons up and covered the door. They were fully expecting the creature to come through on the next strike.

"Reinforce that door!" shouted Clark. "Get something against it!"

BOOM!

The door was struck again and shook the doorframe. Clark rapidly changed magazines in the AA-12. He couldn't risk using Dragon's Breath inside a wooden building. He'd have to use the custom slugs. Chambering a round, he glanced around the room. Two of the Canadians were moving a heavy wooden cupboard over against the door.

Valkryie was covering the door with her HK-UMP50 while Heimdall was moving obstacles out of the path of the cupboard. Raven had her weapon ready but Sage was only whimpering in the corner. Clark suddenly had the thought that some of the dogs might need more training and exposure with cryptids before they returned to the field.

BOOM!

This time, they heard the cracking of wood. Clark couldn't tell if it was the door, the frame, or the crossbar that was cracking.

"They're breaking through!" yelled Tremblay.

The sound of splintering wood filled the room, instantly followed by screaming. Only the sound had come from behind them. Clark spun around to see one of the Canadians being dragged through the smashed window. He was already halfway through and his legs were kicking wildly.

Clark rushed over, releasing his grip on his weapon and grabbed the man's legs at the knees. Hooking his arms under the knees and holding the feet beneath his armpits, Clark began pulling back with everything he had. Valkyrie ran over and leaned out the window. She stuck the muzzle of her weapon as far out as she could and started putting rounds into the creature that had hold of the man.

Shrieking in rage and pain, the beast released its hold with a wet tearing sound. Clark felt the resistance go slack and hauled the man back inside. Clark knew that something was dreadfully wrong when the man stopped struggling and went slack in his arms.

"Oh my God!" gasped Valkyrie as Clark pulled him back inside.

Clark pulled completely back through the window and found that his head and arms were torn from the body. The body just sort of ended at the top of the ribcage. Blood had already stopped pumping out and was now merely seeping from the ragged wounds.

"Get something over that window!" roared Clark.

Valkyrie looked over at Clark with her eyes wide in shock. She was covered in blood. She'd been leaning out the window when it happened. She looked like she was about to faint. Blood was flowing down her face and covered the front of her uniform.

Runestone and Heimdall rushed forward and scooped up a thick wooden table. Slamming it into place over the window, they held it while Doc rummaged around in the kitchen area looking for tools. Yanking open a drawer, he found a hammer and large nails. Rushing over to the window, he began nailing it into place.

"Nail it good," said Runestone. "We don't want them getting in again."

Clark glanced over and saw that the front door was heavily barricaded with the cupboard and a chair. Turning back to Valkyrie, he went to her and took her by the arm.

"Sit down," he said softly, guiding her to a wooden chair.

Grabbing a towel from the counter, he dipped it in a basin of water in the kitchen. Then he gently began cleaning the blood from her face.

"It's alright," he said softly. "It's different through a scope, isn't it?"

197

She just nodded and stared straight ahead.

"You're okay," he assured her.

"It was horrible," she said, her voice quivering quietly. "I've never been that close before."

"I know," said Clark. "It never gets easier. You just sort of keep going. You can't let it stop you or you're the next victim. You're strong. You can get through this."

She just nodded and sat there while he finished wiping the blood from her face.

"Take a few minutes," he said, gently. "We've got this, for now. You're alright. I'm here and I'll get you home safe."

Valkyrie nodded and leaned back in the chair, breathing deeply. Clark glanced around and Tremblay wasn't doing anything. He was just staring around the room like he had no idea what to do next. Clark wanted to say something but bit his lip and shook his head.

"Alright," he thought, "if we keep waiting for this moron to take charge, we're going to get ripped apart."

Glancing around the room, he saw that the Canadian soldiers looked like their morale had just died. They were unsure of what to do and weren't getting any leadership from Tremblay.

"Alright folks, listen up," said Clark, loudly. "Someone cover him up. We need to make sure his remains go home to his family. Everyone else, get back from those windows. That attack on the door was just a distraction. These things are smart. No one gets closer than three feet from any entrance. Hooah?"

"Hooah!" said his team.

"Hooah," said Valkyrie, weakly.

"I want to reinforce those windows so this doesn't happen again," said Clark. "Look around for anything we can use. Boards, tables, break the furniture if you have to. Move!"

Even the Canadians snapped into motion, happy to have a task to focus on. Clark went over and tossed a few more pieces of wood into the fire. They began hammering planks and pieces of wood across the windows, reinforcing the already covered windows.

"Thunder-god to Fenrir," said Clark into his radio. "What's your ETA? Over."

"Thunder-god," said Greyeagle, "we're encountering resistance. We've engaged multiple targets, but they strike and run. Zero casualties but we haven't taken out any of them, either. They've slowed us to a crawl. Over."

"Copy that," said Clark. "We're holding, for now. We're unable to move until our wounded have been medevacked out. Over."

"Copy," said Greyeagle. "We'll be there, it just might take us a while. Over."

"Copy, Fenrir," said Clark. "Good luck. Out."

"Well that's not good," said Doc. "Those things know that if we can get everyone here, then we'll start taking the fight to them."

"If they can keep us all separated," said Clark, "we're easier to fight. As a group, we've been effective at eliminating them."

There was a crackle of static over the radio, then the signal cleared up.

"Broadsword to Thunder-god," said Hernandez.

"Go ahead," said Clark.

"Team Four is mobile," said Hernandez. "We're en route to your position. Not sure of our ETA, but we're on our way. Over."

"Copy, Broadsword," said Clark. "We'll try to save a few for you. Over."

"Solid copy, Thunder-god," said Hernandez. "See you soon. Out."

"Well, that's good news," said Doc. "Now, all we need is for this weather to break so we can get a chopper in here for the wounded."

"Do your best for them, Doc," said Clark.

199

Doc nodded as Clark went back to double-checking the defenses. Once he was sure that the doors and windows were solid, he went back to check on Valkyrie.

"How are you?" he asked, smiling softly.

"I'm alright," she said quietly. "But I think I'll be seeing that in my dreams for a while."

"I'd worry about you if you didn't," said Clark. "Make sure you schedule some time with one of the team therapists when we get back."

"I will," she assured him.

"If you need to talk about it before then or even after," said Clark, "just let me know. I'm happy to listen."

"Thank you, sir," she said, nodding.

Clark nodded and headed for the front door of the small cabin. Stopping at the door, he listened for any sound of movement or indication that the creatures were still close by. Motioning for everyone to be quiet, Clark strained to hear any sound. He could hear the wind blowing outside as it brought in more snow. He could hear the occasional drip of water as icicles were forming from the roof. He could even hear the howling of wolves in the distance, but there was no trace of the Wendigo.

Just as he was getting ready to move back, he heard it. There was a faint sound that he barely registered but it screamed out a warning in his head. Forcing himself to breathe shallowly and closing his eyes, he waited in anticipation of the sound. When it came, he was certain what he was hearing. It was the sound of something with very large lung capacity trying to breathe without making noise. It was followed up by the soft crunching of snow as the beast shifted its weight slightly.

Moving back away from the door, Clark motioned at the door then held up one finger. He was informing the team that there was one at the door. Crossing to the back door, he repeated the process. Now that he knew what to listen for, it was only a matter of a few moments before he heard it there, as well. The creatures were patiently waiting for them to either open a door or make noise close to one. It was likely they were waiting at every window, as well.

Backing away slowly, Clark motioned for everyone to get away from the windows. Shaking his head, he called for everyone to get close enough to hear him whisper.

"They're listening to us," he said softly. "I think there's one on every window. Either they're waiting for us to make a move to escape or they're going to make a coordinated attack. We need to make them move when we're ready for them."

That drew a few nods. Clark glanced at Tremblay and noticed he seemed to be even more withdrawn than before. Something was wrong with him. He wasn't acting like a leader of a Tier One Special Forces Unit. He was acting more like a newly commissioned officer, unsure of every decision. Whatever it was, Clark intended to find out as soon as this mission was over.

"Alright," whispered Clark, "this is what I want to do. All of you get ready. I think all they're waiting for is a sign that we're moving near a window. I'm going to poke the bear and see if I can draw them out. Cover me and cover every entrance. I'm willing to bet that when they hit one, they hit all of them."

They all nodded that they understood, then began covering both doors and the four windows. Clark waited until they were all in position before moving forward. He was heading for the window beside the front door. When he was close enough, he made one more glance at everyone and nodded. Stepping forward, he tapped the wood over the window twice with the end of the barrel.

Nothing happened. After a tense moment, Clark tapped it again. He intended to tap it twice, but as soon as the first tap hit the wood it was answered with the tearing-metal shriek sound. Instantly, the window exploded inward. Clark leaped back, narrowly avoiding being grabbed by the massive beast as it came through. The right arm and head emerged first.

All around him, Clark could hear the splintering of wood as windows exploded inwards at the same time. The chatter of weapons erupted as they began repelling the attack. Roars of pain and rage filled the room as the creatures were met with coordinated fire instead of unsuspecting victims.

The creature in front of Clark reached for him, but he batted its arm aside with the stock of the AA-12. Snapping the weapon back to his shoulder, Clark put a 12-gauge slug into the shoulder joint of the beast. Before it could react, he stepped close and stuck the breecher brake to the beast's head.

"Breech this, motherfucker!" said Clark, squeezing the trigger.

The Wendigo's head exploded in a shower of bone, brains, and dark blood. It fell limply and was immediately yanked backward through the window. It was instantly replaced by another creature.

Clark was expecting just that and cut loose with the automatic shotgun, putting five slugs into the creature's head, neck, and chest. A third creature tried to reach through, only to meet another burst of automatic fire. Clark stitched it from throat to navel. Stepping away from the window, Clark let the AA-12 drop to the single-point sling. He pulled out a grenade from his vest pouch and yanked the pin.

"Frag out!" he yelled and tossed the grenade through the open window.

As another creature appeared in the window, the grenade went off with a dull "CRUMP" and the creature flew through the air and didn't return.

"Changing mags!" screamed Runestone.

He was covering the window to Clark's left. Lifting the AA-12, he brought it up just as a creature was reaching through to grab him. Clark pulled the trigger and emptied the remainder of the magazine through the beast, knocking it back through the window. Runestone nodded at him.

"Thanks, boss," said Runestone.

Clark nodded and began changing his magazine. This time, he loaded the Dragon's Breath rounds. Turning back to his window, he saw another creature was trying to climb through. It snarled at him and opened its mouth wide, revealing three-inch-long canine teeth. Shrieking, the beast grabbed both sides of the window frame and began dragging itself through the window.

Stepping up rapidly, Clark shoved the end of the barrel in the beast's mouth and squeezed the trigger. The force exploded the creature's head like an over-ripe melon and the incendiary Dragon's Breath round both cauterized the wound and immolated the creature behind it. It began flailing its arms and screaming as the burning magnesium ate through its flesh and began devouring the beast from within.

Clark risked a glance around the room. They were holding their ground well, but he knew that they wouldn't be able to hold forever. They simply didn't have enough ammo for a sustained firefight. The plan was to inflict massive casualties on the creatures in as short a time as possible. Once there were numerous creatures down and the others fell back, Clark was going to take a team out to plant thermite on the fallen beasts to prevent them from coming back.

Clark caught a glimpse of Tremblay. He was hiding in a corner and wasn't even engaging the creatures like the rest of the team. Before Clark could say anything, another creature reached through the window and he had to redirect his attention. He silently promised himself that once this fight was over, there was going to be a reckoning with Tremblay. He no longer cared that they were guests in this country.

Punching out two Dragon's Breath rounds, Clark caught one creature on fire and badly burned another one as it fled shrieking away from the window. Turning to help another section that was having trouble, Clark looked just in time to see one of the creatures throw a four-foot-long, sharpened tree branch like a javelin. It flew straight as an arrow and punched through Heimdall's neck. He fell gurgling to the ground, clawing at the four-inch diameter projectile sticking out of his throat.

"Frag out!" yelled Valkyrie, tossing a grenade out the window that the attack had come from.

It fell into the darkness beyond and seconds later erupted in a "CRUMP" that shook the wall of the cabin. At least three of the creatures shrieked in pain and Clark could hear them racing away from the window. Turning back to his window, it was clear. All around the room, weapons ceased and silence once more returned.

"I think we're clear," said Clark. "At least, for the moment."

Valkyrie was kneeling beside Heimdall. His eyes were wide open and staring blankly at the ceiling. He was dead. From the sheer amount of trauma, there was nothing that any of the medics could have done. The wound had almost severed his head.

"Get him covered up," said Clark, nodding at Runestone. "Everyone else, let's get those windows covered again. Use whatever you have to."

While part of the team covered the windows, others began ripping apart furniture, pulling boards off interior walls, and yanking doors off the bedrooms.

"I'm sorry," said Clark to Valkyrie, kneeling beside her.

She glanced at him and nodded without saying anything. Clark was beginning to worry that she might not be able to return to duty after this mission. Patting her on the shoulder, he got up and went back to overseeing the repairs.

Tremblay stood up and walked over to the window Clark had been shooting through. Glancing outside, he saw the pile of bodies.

"Outstanding," said Tremblay. "Nicely done."

Clark noticed that even his teammates were looking at him with utter disdain. Clark reloaded the AA-12 with a drum magazine of slugs as he moved towards Tremblay. Then, he let it drop to hang from the strap. Grabbing Tremblay by the arm, he yanked him away from the window and dragged him towards one of the bedrooms. Once they were alone, he shoved Tremblay onto the crude bed.

"Listen to me you stupid asshole," snapped Clark. "You can't hide in the goddamned corner during the entire fight then come out once the shooting stops like you actually did something."

"But..." began Tremblay.

"Fucking save it," said Clark. "I don't know how the fuck you got command of a Tier One Unit. You're either a coward, incompetent, or both. My fucking money is on both. I swear to God, if I see you hiding in the corner next time, I'll fucking feed you to the goddamned Wendigo, myself."

"You can't talk to me like that," said Tremblay, his French accent becoming more prominent. "My father is a member of Parliament!"

"Well, that explains it," said Clark. "You're a political appointee. No one would dare fail you because of your political connections. You make me fucking sick. Those men under your command earned their positions. You undermine everything they stand for just by existing."

"I still outrank you, Captain!" he snarled. "I'll have you up on charges of insubordination."

"Oh no," said Clark, sarcastically. "I've never been brought up on charges before. I'll tell you what. Bring your fucking charges. I'll stand the courts-martial just so I can call everyone in the other room to testify how you hid in the corner like a fucking child while the fighting was going on."

That seemed to knock the wind out of Tremblay's sails. He seemed to shrink back almost into himself. Clark had the feeling that he'd never met anyone who would stand up to him before.

"Guess what, asshole," snapped Clark. "You don't scare me. I don't give a fuck if your father is the goddamned Prime Minister. I intend to make sure my report of your behavior goes all the way to the president so he can file a formal complaint with your PM. We'll see how much your father protects you from that. I'm warning you right now, if I even suspect you're staying out of the fight for the rest of this engagement, I will fucking leave your ass here. I'll take my team and leave. I'll put money on your team going with me."

Tremblay said nothing but glared death at Clark.

"You've got nothing to threaten me with," said Clark. "We both know you won't fight me. Your daddy won't hold any water with my general and I don't give a fuck what you or your daddy think. So, either get your shit together or stay the fuck out of my way."

Clark turned and walked out of the room without another word, leaving Tremblay alone in the room. Clark knew that everyone had to have heard the exchange. The cabin wasn't that big and he hadn't bothered to keep his voice down. If any of Tremblay's team disagreed with him, they didn't voice their opinions.

"Alright folks," said Clark. "I want to take a team out and plant thermite on the ones that are down. If we don't, they'll be back in the fight before too long. Give me three people."

Runestone stood immediately. Valkyrie started to but Clark shook his head.

"You take care of Heimdall," he said softly. "You've been through enough for a while."

She just nodded gratefully and sat back down. Two of the Canadians stood up and moved to follow him.

"Alright," said Clark. "We're going out the back door. You three cover me. I'll plant the thermite. As soon as we're done, we get right back inside. Everyone sticks together and you don't have to wait for a fire command. If you see a target, engage it."

Heading over to the back door, Clark nodded at Doc and Raven.

"You two stand by the door to let us in," said Clark. "We might be coming rapidly. I'll either use the radio to let you know to open it or I'll do the shave and a haircut knock."

"Gotcha," said Doc, chuckling.

"Alright, on three," said Clark.

Raven and Doc got ready while Clark mouthed "three, two, one". He already had his AA-12 at the ready and the others followed his lead. When he reached one, they pulled the crossbar and swung the door open. Clark had his rifle ready to fire but there was nothing there.

Filing out the door, they scanned left and right as they moved. While Runestone and the Canadians covered him, Clark planted thermite on eleven of the Wendigo. They could hear movement in the trees but nothing was getting close enough to take a shot. Two minutes later, they were back inside and slamming the crossbar back into place.

"Eleven down," said Clark. "God knows how many to go."

CHAPTER SIXTEEN
WITCHING HOUR

"The brave die never, though they sleep in dust:
Their courage nerves a thousand living men."
Minot J. Savage

0000 Hours CST
15 February

Clark paced the room from door to door, watching every direction as he moved. The radios were dead now. He'd tried to check in with the other teams but hadn't received anything back. Either the storm was interfering with the signal or the Wendigo were somehow responsible. Either thought wasn't exactly comforting.

Runestone had been trying for the last half an hour to find a way to boost the signal. He was carrying a larger SINCGARS[24] on his back. It had far more power and range than the handsets that the rest of them carried. Clark hoped that it could punch through the interference but didn't hold out much hope. He knew that they were still in range of Valhalla even with the smaller handsets.

Clark glanced over at Runestone and met his gaze. Runestone frowned and shook his head, indicating nothing was getting through. There was no sense asking the Canadians if they could get through. They were using identical radios, just on a different frequency.

"They've got to be getting close," said Runestone. "Both Team Four and the rest of our team. They have to be close, right?"

"I would think so," said Clark. "Even in the snow, it's only about seven miles."

"If the radios are out," said Runestone, "I bet the GPS is out, too."

Clark checked his GPS unit and confirmed it. There was no signal from the satellite. Clark just glanced at Runestone and nodded.

---

[24] SINCGARS - Single Channel Ground and Airborne Radio System

"That's what I figured," said Runestone. "They could walk right by us in the dark and not even know we were there without the GPS to tell them."

"The Wendigo are responsible," said Cloutier. "I remember hearing the stories when I was a kid. I never thought they were real, but there's no denying that now."

"What did the stories say?" asked Clark.

"They're evil magic," said Cloutier. "Supposedly they can control the weather and work evil spells on their intended victims. That's why the radio and GPS don't work."

"I've got a few flares for my grenade launcher," said Runestone. "If we could get outside, we could put a couple in the air."

"That's better than anything else I've thought of," said Clark. "Get it ready. We'll see if it's clear enough to try."

Runestone started digging out the 40mm grenades from his pack, stacking the flares to the side.

"There's another cabin about thirty yards to the east," said Clark. "If I can hit it with a couple Dragon's Breath rounds, I bet I can set it on fire. That should get everyone's attention."

"There are several bottles of lamp oil under the kitchen counter," said Valkyrie. "We can hit the next cabin with the oil before you shoot it. It'll catch fire for sure."

"Okay," said Clark, "here's the plan. We'll go out the back door. I want four people guarding the door. I'll take Runestone, Doc, and Raven. Everyone else, cover the doors and windows until we get back. We hit this fast and get back inside before they figure out what we're doing."

"I'm going, too," said Valkyrie.

"Why don't you sit this one out," said Clark. "You've done plenty already."

"I'm going, sir," said Valkyrie. "I'll help cover you while Runestone puts the flares in the air."

Clark looked at her and saw the determination in her eyes.

"Alright," said Clark. "I'll throw two of the bottles of oil then hit it with the Dragon's Breath. The rest of you cover me. Hooah?"

"Hooah," said the others in unison.

They all gathered their gear and doubled checked the load on their weapons. Clark put in a fresh magazine of Dragon's Breath and let it hang on the strap. Picking two glass bottles of lamp oil, he stuffed them into the cargo pockets on his pants, then brought his weapon up to his shoulder.

Clark, Valkyrie, Runestone, Doc, and Raven all stacked on the left side of the door. Four of the Canadian team stacked on the right side. They were going to cover the door for them. Once they were all in place, Clark nodded. Cloutier nodded and lifted the crossbar from the braces with his good arm.

Once it was clear, he stepped back. Clark mouthed "on three" at the other side of the door and began counting down. When he reached one, he yanked the door open and immediately swung around the frame with his weapon ready. There was nothing there, so he turned left and headed for the other cabin with his team right behind him.

Continually panning back and forth, he expected the Wendigo to be waiting for him. He was starting to wonder where they were when he heard one of them scream in the distance. It wasn't close, but that didn't mean others weren't lurking in the darkness around them.

Reaching the end of the cabin, he swung his weapon to the left to check the opening. The snow was still coming down in thick flakes with a moderate wind. It did seem to have picked up since he was last outside and that bothered him. It seemed as if the weather was getting worse, not better.

Moving into the opening between the two cabins, he saw no signs of movement. He did see the odd hoof-like tracks of the Wendigo in the snow, but they were rapidly filling in. At the rate of snowfall, he estimated that they were more than twenty minutes old.

He began moving towards the other cabin to make certain he could hit it with the lamp oil when something caught his attention. Turning to look out towards the lake, figures were standing out on the ice. They were just at the edge of visibility due to the storm. They weren't

209

Wendigo. They were human and they were just standing there. Clark froze in his tracks and motioned for the others to look at what he was seeing.

"Is that the rest of the team?" whispered Valkyrie. "They look like they're in uniform. I can see weapons."

"Then why aren't they moving?" asked Clark. "Why are they just standing there?"

"I have no idea," said Valkyrie.

"Runetone, get those flares in the air," said Clark. "Let's get a little light on the area."

"Copy that, boss," said Runestone.

THOOP!

The first flare launched at an angle that would take it out over the lake. It bathed the entire area in its eerie green light. Clark saw shadows move back into the trees, away from the light. The shadows on the lake seemed to shimmer and disappear.

Clark yanked the first bottle of oil from his pocket and threw it at the other cabin. It smashed against the wall beside and broken window. Clark quickly threw the second bottle and it sailed through the open window and he heard it shatter inside.

"Nice shot, sir," said Valkyrie.

Bringing the AA-12 to his shoulder, he fired twice with the Dragon's Breath rounds. He aimed directly at the window. There was a whoosh of air as the oil ignited and the cabin began burning rapidly. Through the window, he could see the flames begin spreading inside.

THOOP!

The second flare went into the air.

"Let's fall back to the cabin," said Clark.

The flickering green light of the flares gave the area an odd appearance, almost otherworldly. He could see the green light was attracting the red eyes of several Wendigo. They were appearing in the darkness of the woods, careful not to give them a clear shot.

210

"We're in the open," said Valkyrie as they reached the edge of their cabin. "Why aren't they rushing us?"

"Your guess is as good as mine," said Clark. "Keep moving."

Clark was walking backward, covering their retreat. The others were covering every direction of approach. Just as they were reaching the door, they heard a voice from the trees.

"Help me!" called the voice.

"That sounded like Margolin," said Runestone.

"Help me!" the voice repeated.

"That's him," said Runestone. "I'd know his voice anywhere."

"Shit," said Clark. "He's close."

"Hang on," said Doc. "Those things can mimic voices. They've tried to fool us before."

"Help me, Clark!" called the voice.

"That's not Margolin," said Valkyrie. "He'd never call you by name. That's a trap."

"Everyone inside," said Clark. "We can't risk getting caught out in the woods and surrounded. I hope you're right."

With that, everyone filed back inside and Clark slammed the door shut. Immediately, they dropped the crossbar into place. As soon as it was in place, something hit the door hard enough to shake it.

"Let me in," said the voice that sounded like Margolin. "It's me! I'm hurt! I need a medic."

"Fuck you!" roared Runestone. "You're not Margolin."

"It's me," insisted the voice. "Open the door."

"Embrace the suck!" shouted Valkyrie.

"What the hell is that supposed to mean?" asked the voice. "Just open the door."

"That confirms it," said Valkyrie, softly. "If that was Margolin…"

"He'd be doing pushups in the snow," finished Doc. "Nice one."

"These things are smart," said Valkyrie, "but they can't know personal information. They're just mimicking the voices they hear."

"Yeah, but those shadows on the lake were creepy as hell," said Runestone.

"The Wendigo has strong magic," said Cloutier. "The ones we've fought have all been the ones that were turned. The spirit of the Wendigo, the true Wendigo, will be much bigger."

"How much bigger?" asked Doc.

"The old First Nations stories I heard said as tall as a lodge," said Cloutier. "I would guess like at least fifteen feet."

"That's not good," said Clark. "Can we kill it the same way?"

"I don't know," said Cloutier. "The stories I heard said it was an evil nature spirit and it couldn't truly die."

"Well, we're going to find out," said Clark. "If it can't die, we're still going to hit it with everything we have."

The radio activated but the only thing they heard was static. All conversation stopped while Runestone grabbed his pack radio. He adjusted the signal and continued to try to clear up the static. Then, a partial radio transmission came in.

"...ord...go...say..."

Runestone made a few more adjustments and the signal suddenly cleared up.

"Broadsword to Thunder-god, do you copy, over," said Hernandez.

Clark grabbed the handset from Runestone and active it.

"Thunder-god copies," said Clark. "Go ahead. Over."

"Good to finally hear your voice," said Hernandez. "We've been trying to reach you for the last couple of hours. What's your status? Over."

"We're stable at this time," said Clark. "Two casualties. We're holding position, over."

"Did you launch flares?" asked Hernandez. "Over."

212

"Affirm," said Clark. "We were unable to establish contact with the radios. Over."

"We've made contact with Lieutenant Murdock and his people," said Hernandez. "We're going to head your way as soon as we finish with the creatures in our sector. Over."

"How many have you see?" asked Clark. "Over."

"We've engaged and eliminated nine," said Hernandez. "With at least six more in the area that we're aware of. Over."

"Copy," said Clark. "We're holding. Let us know when you're heading our way. Over."

"Will do," said Hernandez. "Broadsword out."

"Looks like the handsets aren't strong enough to punch through the interference," said Clark, "but the big radio has more range."

"Think it will reach Valhalla?" asked Runestone.

"I don't know," said Clark. "Let's see if we can reach Greyeagle, first."

"Good call, sir," said Runestone.

Clark activated the handset again.

"Thunder-god to Fenrir," said Clark. "Do you copy? Over."

After a moment, they heard a static-filled reply. It was garbled but they could understand it.

"Fenrir copies," said Greyeagle. "Go ahead. Over."

"What's your status?" asked Clark.

"We've engaged and eliminated nine creatures," said Greyeagle. "Our radios and GPS stopped working. Even my compass was off. The creatures led us away from your position. We have four wounded and two down. We're west of your position. We've got a bearing on your flares, now. Over."

"Copy," said Clark. "We're holding. Get here as quickly as you can. Over."

"Solid copy," said Greyeagle. "We're on our way. Out."

Clark waited for the line to clear and activated it again.

"Thunder-god to Valhalla," he said. "Do you copy? Over."

"Valhalla copies," said a voice. "Go ahead."

Clark recognized it as the other new Combat Controller, Tech Sergeant Emily Drake (Code Name: Saga). He also noticed that the signal was considerably clearer than it had been with Greyeagle. Whatever was causing the interference was now between Greyagle and their position. Its power over the others had weakened.

"Is Valhalla Actual available?" asked Clark. "Over."

"Stand-by, Thunder-god," said Saga. "Over."

After a long pause, the voice of Major Saunders came over the radio.

"Go for Valhalla Actual," said Saunders. "Over."

"Valhalla," said Clark. "We are stable but have taken two casualties. One ours and one Canadian. We're holding position but surrounded by the creatures. Can you request an aerial asset from our Canadian friends for possible Close Air Support? Over."

"We can try," said Saunders. "What did you have in mind? Over."

"We're not picky," said Clark. "We'll take anything they can send in this weather. Over."

"I'll send it up the chain," said Saunders. "I'll let you know when we have confirmation. Over."

"Copy that," said Clark. "Out."

"Do you think we can get Air Support?" asked Doc.

"Rotorcraft, no," said Clark. "Fixed-wing, maybe. Depends on what they have available and close enough to respond."

"Why don't we have Mister My-Father's-In-Parliament ask for air support?" asked Valkyrie, softly.

"Valkyrie," said Clark, with a scowl. "That's *Major* My-Father's-In-Parliament. I don't think we can count on his help for anything, to be honest. Whatever happens, it's going to be us that gets it done."

BOOM!

Something impacted with the side of the cabin. Not on a window or door, but directly against the wall. It shook the entire cabin and knocked loose dirt and pieces of the tacking from between the logs.

"What the hell was that?" yelled Doc. "They hit the damned wall!"

"They're trying to bring the cabin down on us," whined Tremblay. "They're going to bury us alive!"

Fortunately, no one paid any attention to him. All eyes were on Clark, both American and Canadian.

"We can't let them bring this place down on the wounded," said Clark. "Grab weapons and ammo from the wounded and the dead. Distribute the ammo to anyone who needs it. We have to go out there and push them back."

BOOM!

Another impact shook the cabin, sending books flying from a shelf and knocking a mirror off the wall. Doc leaned over the unconscious pilot to keep anything from falling on him.

"Doc," said Clark. "You stay in here with the wounded, Tremblay, and Raven. Give Cloutier one of the HK-UMP50s. Lock the doors as soon as we exit."

Raven nodded and headed for the back door. She stood by, waiting to move the bolt and let them out.

"Everyone else," said Clark, "lock and load! We move as a team and stick together. We've got to take the heat off the cabin. The wounded won't stand a chance if we don't. Any questions?"

"I have one," said one of the Canadians.

Clark saw that his name was Levesque.

"Shoot," said Clark.

"Are all American Officers like you?" asked Levesque. "If so, where do we sign up?"

Clark just chuckled.

"Ask me again if this actually works," said Clark.

Valkyrie handed him Heimdall's pistol to replace the one he'd given Cloutier. Clark took it and nodded, checking the load and slipping it into his holster. Then she handed him the extra magazines and he put them in the mag pouches on his vest.

"Stack up at the door," said Clark. "I've got point. We move around to the west side and engage whatever is out there. We can't let them bring this cabin down. We hold as long as we can. If you run out of ammo, grab some from anyone around you. We fight until we push them back or we fall. Anyone who wants to stay in here, speak up now."

No one said anything. Clark just nodded at them.

"Alright folks," said Clark. "Some of you don't really know me. I'll say this, just so we're clear. We come back together or not at all. I'll come back with you on your feet or over my shoulder. As Sargeant-Major Gideon would say, come back with your shield or on it. We fight and move as a team. Hooah?"

"Hooah!" roared everyone, including the Canadians.

Clark moved to the side of the door and the others stacked up behind him. Once everyone was in place, Clark noticed Tremblay get up and move towards them.

"I should be going with you," he said hesitantly.

"Yes, you should," said Clark. "The question is, are you?"

Tremblay stood there, indecision on his face. Clark could see that he wanted to stay and hide but something had awakened within him. It was starting to sink in that even his men were now following Clark without hesitation.

BOOM!

Another impact shook the cabin and more dust fell from the roof.

"Decide now!" shouted Clark. "We're going with or without you."

Tremblay walked over and stepped between Clark and the door.

"I should go first," he said, softly.

"You're the Major," said Clark. "Go ahead."

216

Tremblay nodded at Raven and she pulled the crossbar out of the door. Then she grabbed the door handle and pulled the door open as she stepped clear of the opening. Tremblay moved hesitantly around the corner and into the doorway. He was slow to bring up his weapon. Clark saw all of this happening in an instant, as time seemed to compress and slow down.

He saw the look of bewilderment on Tremblay's face as he saw something in the darkness. As he was opening his mouth to say something and raising his weapon, what looked like a blackened tree branch punched through his armor and chest, going out his back and through the backpack. For a split second, he locked eyes with Clark before he was yanked out the door.

"Move!" screamed Clark, swinging out the door with the AA-12 ready to fire.

Outside the door was something that made the other Wendigo look like children's toys. This creature was close to twenty feet tall and walked hunched over. Its limbs were skeletal and black. Tremblay was impaled on one of its hands. The rear legs were hooved with the front arm ending with hooves at one part with claw-like hands-on shorter appendages that connected at the elbow.

The head was like a rotting deer's head with huge antlers and massive sharp teeth in its mouth. This was the true Wendigo. The others had all been lesser creatures that had been turned. It was the evil nature spirit that they had been warned about. It suddenly occurred to Clark why some of the others had fashioned masks from deer and elk skulls. They were trying to look like their creator.

Clark began firing the AA-12 as soon as he saw it. Three burning Dragon's Breath rounds lit up the beast's side and it shrieked in pain. When it took off, it was incredibly fast. It raced around the side of the cabin and towards the lake.

"What the hell was that?!" roared Valkyrie as she moved in behind Clark.

"The true Wendigo," yelled Clark. "The others are just foot soldiers."

217

The team was moving rapidly towards the side of the cabin, pursuing the fleeing Wendigo.

"Can we kill it?" she asked.

"We're about to find out!" replied Clark, turning the corner of the cabin.

The entire area was lit up in an orange flickering light from the burning cabin. It produced enough light that they could see movement and shapes, but not for very far.

"Contact left!" roared Valkyrie.

Clark swung his weapon left and saw two of the lesser creatures emerging from the trees. Clark engaged at the same time as Valkyrie. Emptying the magazine, Clark put five Dragon's Breath rounds into the two creatures. They instantly began shrieking in pain but that was abruptly ended as Valkyrie put a three-round burst into each of their heads. They knew the fire from the burning magnesium would be enough to prevent them from coming back, so they kept moving.

Clark reloaded as he moved, switching to the rifled slugs. As they reached the front of the cabin, they saw that more than a dozen of the creatures were waiting for them. The True Wendigo was out on the frozen lake with the lesser minions blocking the path. Clark could see it was devouring Tremblay.

Bringing the AA-12 to his shoulder, he estimated the distance to the True Wendigo at approximately sixty yards. That was easily in the range of the rifled slugs.

"Concentrate your fire on the others!" roared Clark. "I've got the big bitch!"

Clark began firing, aiming at the creature's head. The AA-12 has very little recoil on automatic and Clark continued firing as he moved, never wavering from his target as he moved. The first two rounds impacted the beast, then it moved and avoided the next three rounds. Clark could see the silver-cored rounds did damage but seemed to anger the beast more than anything else.

"Contact on our six!" roared Levesque.

Glancing back, Clark saw eight more of the creatures emerging from the trees. There was more than a dozen in front of and at least eight coming up behind them. They were cut off with no way to get back to the cabin.

"Form up!" shouted Clark. "Backs to each other. We're going to hold!"

They quickly formed a tight circle and began engaging creatures as they approached. As the creatures moved in closer and closer, Clark knew that there was no way they were going to fight their way clear of this. All they could do now was to try and take as many of them down with them as they could.

"Concentrate your fire!" screamed Clark. "Make your shots count!"

Clark engaged two of the closest creatures with a burst of automatic fire. The first creature's chest was shredded and it fell over backward, shrieking as it dropped. The other creature took two rounds to the abdomen. It roared in anger, but it had no other effect on the beast.

Valkyrie was putting short bursts into the chests of creatures, putting two down before they had closed the distance. Runestone put three rounds into one with his .458 SOCOM, obliterating the chest and exploding the head of one creature.

"Contact on our nine o'clock!" roared Levesque.

Clark glanced that direction and saw nearly a dozen more of the creatures burst from the trees, running as fast as they could go. Clark was convinced that they were about to be overrun, but the creatures ran right past them heading for the ice, shrieking a warning as they ran.

The other Wendigo glanced back the way they had come and there was more movement in the trees. Clark held his breath, expecting more of the monstrosities to emerge. There was a long, tense moment when all they saw was the movement.

"Changing mags!" roared Runestone.

Clark felt his heart beating in his temples and he felt like the end was about to hit them. Instead, his fear became elation as First Sergeant William Greyeagle emerged from the trees leading the rest of Team Two and the Canadian team.

The creatures that had been surrounding them fled out onto the ice with the other creatures. They formed a ragged line between them and the massive Wendigo behind them. They were staging for a battle and Team Two was going to give it to them.

"Sorry we're late," said Greyeagle. "Traffic was Hell."

CHAPTER SEVENTEEN
GAUNTLET

"They're on our right, they're on our left, they're in front of us,
they're behind us; they can't get away from us this time."
Chesty Puller

0230 Hours CST
15 February

Greyeagle led the team directly over to where Clark stood.

"We're here, sir," he said, smiling.

"And your timing couldn't have been better," said Clark. "We've got well over twenty of the little ones and the big bastard is out there on the ice."

"We saw the big one earlier," said Greyeagle. "We hit it with everything we had and it shrugged it off. I don't know if we can stop it."

The creatures started making weird noises, looking to their left and back at their group.

"What the hell are they looking at?" asked Valkyrie.

From the far side of the burning cabin, they saw more people emerging from the trees. It was Team Four arriving with the people they'd pulled from the cabin in the park. Clark held up his hand and the gesture was returned by Hernandez. With the combined might of Team Two and Team Four, they might be able to take them all down.

They could see the Wendigo were nervous. They kept looking back and forth at the teams, then they would look over their shoulders at the opposite side of the lake. Clark thought they were planning to flee into the woods on the far side of the lake, but they made no move to get closer. They were nervous.

"Valkyrie," said Clark.

"Yes, boss," she said.

"Get on your scope and tell me what's on the far side of the lake," he replied.

221

"On it," she said, changing to the sniper's rifle.

After a few moments of scanning the trees on the far side, she looked up.

"That's why they're not running that way," said Valkyrie. "There are about fifty of those Bigfoot creatures we saw at the cave blocking their escape."

"Do you think they're going to help us?" asked Clark.

"Doubtful," said Winter, walking up behind him. "It's far more likely that they will only fight if the Wendigo charge them."

"Well, if all they're doing is preventing them from escaping," said Clark, "I'll take it. We're going to finish this here and now."

The creatures continued to back up until they were near the middle of the lake. They were in a ragged line running almost perfectly east to west. The True Wendigo seemed confused and unsure of what to do next. It was used to having the upper hand in fights. Clark guessed that it had been centuries since it had been directly challenged like this. Before he could think about it more, his thoughts were interrupted by the radio.

"Valhalla Actual to Thunder-god," said Saunders.

"Go for Thunder-god," said Clark.

"Your Close Air Support is inbound HOT to your position," said Saunders. "Call sign is Hitman. You get one pass and that's all we can give you. Make it count. Out."

Clark adjusted the radio to the pilot's frequency and hit transmit.

"Thunder-god to Hitman," said Clark. "Do you copy? Over."

"Hitman copies," said the pilot. "Standing by for my run. Over."

"Copy Hitman," said Clark. "Approach running east to west, targets are in a single line. Over."

"Affirmative Thunder-god," said Hitman. "Can you paint the target? Over."

"Standby," said Clark, nodding at Valkyrie.

Valkyrie opened her pack and pulled out a laser target designator, nodding at Clark.

"Paint the east end," said Clark.

"Got it," said Valkyrie, aiming the designator. "Target painted."

"Hitman, you have a go," said Clark. "Target is painted and you're clear to begin your run. Over."

"Solid copy, Thunder-god," said Hitman. "Run commencing in ten seconds. You called the thunder, here it comes. Hitman out."

"Ten seconds!" roared Clark. "Everyone down!"

The teams hit the deck and brought their weapons up in case the Wendigo were to charge them. The Wendigo were confused as to what was happening. More than twenty of the creatures were shrieking and screaming. Only the True Wendigo seemed to sense something was wrong. It was looking around at the sky.

At first, they only heard the rumble of a distant aircraft, but it was steadily getting closer. The clouds hung low, still dropping heavy snowflakes, but the rumble continued to get louder. Then a shape streaked out of the clouds, diving for the lake. At first, it was difficult to determine what it was but in seconds it became clear.

"That's an A-10 Warthog!" roared Margolin. "Holy shit!"

Hitman banked in and lined up his run. When the GAU-8/A Avenger nose gun thundered to life, spitting fire and death as it made it's run. Usually, the GAU-8/A was loaded with a mixture of armor-piercing rounds and incendiary ammunition. This one had been loaded exclusively with incendiary rounds.

Hitman came down the line of Wendigo spewing a firestorm of death and destruction. The Lesser Wendigo were immolated instantly, turning them into screaming matchsticks in an instant. The heat and the power of the 30mm rounds punched through the ice, ripping a large path down the center of the lake. The charred remains of the Lesser Wendigo fell into the frozen depths, never to be seen again.

The True Wendigo had proven to be too fast, again. It sensed the coming aircraft and leaped away in the instant before the conflagration engulfed the others. Clark could see it shrieking and jumping around in anger on the other side of the flames. In its blind rage, it was slamming its fists on the ice and staring directly at Clark. He could feel the heat on his face, but he wasn't sure if it was from the fire or the creature's rage.

When Hitman completed his run, only the True Wendigo remained. He ceased firing as he approached the far end of the lake and climbed back into the sky. Waggling his wings, Hitman vanished into the clouds and the engines were slowly fading away.

"Thunder-god to Hitman," said Clark. "Nice shooting. Thanks for the assist. Over."

"Happy to help, Thunder-god," said Hitman. "Catch you next time. Hitman out."

Clark watched as the True Wendigo paced back and forth behind the wall of fire. It was waiting for it to die down. It was going to attack as soon as it could get past the fire.

"Get ready!" roared Clark. "It's coming for us!"

There was a thunderous scream and the Wendigo flew through the air, sailing over the rapidly diminishing flames. When it landed, it skittered on the ice but kept its footing. Then it charged directly at the teams.

"Fire!" screamed Clark.

All along the line, both teams were engaging the creature, but it seemed like it was not affecting the beast. It didn't even seem to react to the impacts. It continued to charge right at them like an unrelenting juggernaut, not slowing down for anything. Clark could see the rounds striking the beast, but they passed through without causing any serious damage. The magic of this beast was truly powerful.

Above the roar of the battle, Clark could hear Winter chanting. She was trying to counter the magic of the beast. As soon as she began, Clark saw the Wendigo change is focus from him to her. It headed right at her, intending to stop her magic.

"Protect Winter!" screamed Clark.

Margolin put himself between her and the creature, firing continually at the oncoming monster. When the beast reached the firing line, it swiped it's powerful hand and sent six men flying through the air, screaming as they flew. Clark knew that some of them might never get up again.

Standing, Clark went full automatic and put his entire magazine into the beast. The creature ignored the hits and sent another group of soldiers crashing into the trees. Through the flashes of light from the weapons, Clark could see movement. Standing like a statue between the charging creature and Winter was First Sergeant William Greyeagle.

With a roar of challenge, Greyeagle began shifting into his wolf form. The Wendigo slid to a stop, unsure of what it was seeing as Greyeagle came to his full height and howled into the night. While he wasn't as big as the Wendigo, the magic of the *Hotamétaneo'o* was strong.

The Wendigo took a few steps back, considering what was now standing before it. Greyeagle pressed the attack and leaped directly at the beast. The Wendigo tried to bat him away with a swing of its arm, but Greyeagle caught the arm and used leverage to flip the creature and send it flying into the snow. Roaring in rage, the beast scrambled to its feet as Greyeagle slammed into it again. This time, it met the attack with strength on strength.

"All units!" screamed Clark into the radio. "Do NOT fire on the wolf. Say again, DO NOT fire on the wolf. He's on our side!"

Slashing and punching each other, the two titans slid out onto the ice and continued fighting. While Greyeagle fought with intensity, it was clear that the Wendigo was the stronger of the two. In seconds, the Wendigo pinned him down on the ice and brought up its hand to finish the job.

A second howl split the night as Doc shifted form and raced into the battle. Before it could deliver the killing blow, Doc slammed into the side of the beast and knocked it off Greyeagle. Tumbling together as they slid, Doc bit the beast in the left arm and held on tight.

Greyeagle got to his feet and raced back into the fight. The two of them were pushing the Wendigo farther down the lake, but even the two of them together seemed to not be causing significant damage while it was drawing blood with almost every attack that hit them.

A thunderous roar split the night and Kodiak shifted into his bear form. Racing out onto the ice, he joined the pitched battle and added his power to the fight. Slamming into the side of the Wendigo, Kodiak took it to the ground and the three of them pressed the attack, landing blow after blow on the beast. While the blows seemed to stun it, they weren't doing any significant damage.

Clark knew that with the way the battle was raging, he couldn't risk a shot without hitting one of his people. Getting to his feet, he glanced around. A figure was approaching him out of the darkness. It was Gideon and he nodded grimly at Clark.

"They're going to need help," said Gideon, drawing his Gladius.

"That's what I'm thinking, too," said Clark, drawing his sword.

"They're almost to that dock," said Gideon pointing. "If we go out on it, we should have enough height to attack it directly."

"Let's go," said Clark.

Turning, the two men raced off towards the dock with their swords held high. Valkyrie got to her feet and followed after them, along with Margolin, Murdock, and Henderson. They were ready to help take the fight to the Wendigo.

Out on the ice, the battle continued to rage. A powerful blow from the beast sent Doc sliding away towards the center of the lake. Digging his claws into the ice, he barely managed to keep himself from sliding off into the water where the ice had been blasted apart by the attack run.

The Wendigo got back to its feet and turned to face Greyeagle and Kodiak, turning its back on Doc. Getting to his feet, Doc launched himself at the creature and leaped high into the air. He landed on the beast's back and sunk claws and teeth into the beast's neck and shoulders.

Howling in pain, the Wendigo reached for Doc but couldn't reach him. He held fast and remained just out of reach. While it was distracted, Kodiak slammed into the creature's waist, driving it sideways and toward the dock. Greyeagle leaped into the air and landed on the beast's left arm, trapping it and digging in his claws.

226

Seeing what Greyeagle was doing, Doc released his grip and slid onto the right arm. Pinning it down, he sank his teeth into the creature's shoulder and dug his claws into the flesh of the upper arm. They had both arms pinned down.

The Wendigo drove its knee upward and into Kodiak's face. Breaking his grip, the beast kicked him in the chest and knocked him sliding away on the ice and beneath the dock. With its mobility restored, it leaped into the air and came down on top of Doc. The force knocked the wind out of him and Doc thought his shoulder might be separated. At the very least, it was fractured.

Once Doc's grip was knocked free, the Wendigo grabbed Greyeagle and threw him out onto the ice. Before he could regain his balance, he slid off into the frozen water and vanished beneath the ice.

Getting back on its feet, the Wendigo raised its hands in front of its chest and screamed into the night. The strange muli-toned cry reminded Clark of the Tyrannosaurus Rex in the movie Jurassic Park. The roar shook the night and Clark could hear the ice around the beast crackling.

Kodiak got back to his feet, but they could tell that he was hurt. Doc shook his head and got to his knees. He was spitting blood onto the ice and shaking his head. Neither looked like they were in any shape to continue fighting.

Stepping towards Kodiak, the Wendigo snarled and narrowed its red eyes. This time, it was intending to kill him and they all knew it. Kodiak stood to his full height and roared back at the creature, defiant to the bitter end.

Just as the Wendigo was preparing to charge him, the ice beside the creature erupted and Greyeagle burst through it, roaring and slashing into the beast's side. The creature drove its right fist into Greyeagle's face, but he grabbed the arm and locked it in an armbar.

Doc spat bloody phlegm onto the ice and charged at the beast. He was limping badly but still moving impossibly fast. As the creature continued to flail at Greyeagle, Doc grabbed it's left arm and repeated the armbar. They now held the creature immobile, but it was still kicking at them. The sharp edges of the hooves would be enough to disembowel if it scored a hit.

227

Before it could do more than cut their legs, Kodiak slammed into the beast's waist and wrapped it in a bear hug. The beast was trapped, but they all knew it was only a matter of time before they grew tired and it broke free.

Clark and Gideon reached the end of the dock and racked down the length of it. When the got to the end, they were ten feet over the ice below them. The Wendigo was fifteen feet away from the end of the dock with its back toward them.

Glancing at one another, they jumped from the end of the doc with their swords held in both hands, above their heads and aimed to stab into the Wendigo's back. Clark's blade sank to the hilt just above the creature's left shoulder blade and Gideon's just above the right. They were hanging from the hilt and pulling the blades down into the beast's chest cavity.

Screaming in pain, the beast flailed but the three *Hotamétaneo'o* held fast and refused to be knocked away. As the blades sliced deeper into the creature, they severed ribs and muscle until there was a tearing sound and both arms came off in the hands of Greyeagle and Doc. Leaving behind the head and spine sticking straight up out of the lower torso and legs.

Kicking straight back, the creature knocked both Clark and Gideon sliding away onto the ice beneath the dock. Clark felt dizzy and nauseous. His vision was spinning and he fought to get his breath. Glancing to his right, he saw Gideon. He was staring at him with his eyes wide open, staring unfocused at nothing. His neck was at an odd angle. Clark knew it was broken and the older warrior was likely dead.

Tossing aside the severed arms, Grey eagle and Doc dove back onto the creature, each grabbing a different piece. With a roar of fury, the three *Hotamétaneo'o* pulled in separate directions. Doc pulled away with the spine and head, while Greyeagle and Kodiak each took a hip with a leg attached.

Clark stared at Gideon and tried to reach out to him. He felt like his right arm was dislocated and he couldn't lift it. Turning his head the other direction to call for help, he couldn't seem to find his breath to yell. He watched the last few seconds as they tore the Wendigo apart and held up the pieces. There was a popping sound and he heard Gideon take a deep breath. Turning back, Gideon was blinking and shaking his head.

"Are you alright?" asked Gideon, his voice raspy.

"Help me up," wheezed Clark, unsure what had just happened.

Gideon helped him to his feet and they headed for where the pieces of the Wendigo now lay on the frozen lake.

"What do we do with it?" asked Doc, favoring his arm and limping.

"We can't wait too long," said Greyeagle. "It will pull itself together and heal."

"Throw it in the fire," wheezed Clark, pointing at the burning cabin.

"And we can have Winter sing a *Blessingway*," said Greyeagle. "That should banish the Wendigo spirit."

Clark nodded and the began gathering up the pieces, heading for the burning building.

"What now?" asked Gideon.

"Take me over to the team," said Clark. "I need a medic."

Together, they began limping in that direction. Gideon was taking the bulk of Clark's weight when Valkyrie slipped beneath his other arm. Between the two of them, they helped him back to the others.

They watched as Greyeagle, Doc and Kodiak threw the pieces of the Wendigo into the flames. Winter began singing in *Ojibwe* and the pieces began to sizzle. An oily black smoke rose from the burning creature and climbed into the air.

The thick smoke turned north and floated away over the lake. It was moving against the wind.

"That's odd," said Gideon. "I've never seen smoke move against the wind before."

"That is the *manitou* of the Wendigo," said Greyeagle. "The spirit."

"What does that mean?" rasped Clark.

"It means that we didn't kill it," said Gideon. "It'll be back."

"Yes," said Greyeagle, "but it will take it a while."

229

"Well, when it comes back," said Gideon, "we know what to look for."

"What's the status?" asked Clark, glancing around.

"We lost six to the Wendigo attack," said Hernandez as he approached. "Four of them were Canadian and two were mine. No one else from Team Two."

Clark nodded.

"He needs to have a medic look at him," said Hernandez. "Get him inside the cabin."

"Get me some clothes," said Doc, " and I'll take care of him. It's the least I can do. They just saved us out there. If they hadn't cut into that thing, I don't know how much longer we could have held it."

Clark blinked a few times and passed out.

"Get him inside," said Doc.

As they carried him away, Valkyrie looked at Gideon.

"Are you alright?" she asked.

"I'm fine," said Gideon. "A few bumps and bruises but nothing that requires a medic."

"Looks like the storm is breaking up," said Valkyrie, glancing at the sky.

"I think you're right," said Gideon. "Maybe we can get some choppers in here to lift the wounded out."

"I'll make the call," said Hernandez.

CHAPTER EIGHTEEN
DEBRIEFING

"To get the best out of your men, they must feel that you
are their real leader and must know that they can depend upon you."
Gen*eral of the Armies John J. Pershing, U.S. Army*

1400 Hours PST
16 February
Fort Leonard Wood
Missouri

Clark awoke to find he was in a hospital bed. Since military hospital rooms look alike all over the world, he had no idea where he was. He hoped that he was back at Fort Leonard Wood. The room was empty but he could see where someone had recently been sitting. A drink was on the table and a jacket was laying in the chair.

Taking a quick self-assessment, he found that his right arm was in a sling but the pain wasn't bad. His head hurt and his vision was still a bit fuzzy. There was an IV in his arm and he wasn't strapped to the bed.

"Well," he thought, "at least I'm not in irons waiting for a court-martial."

He felt stiff and sore, but otherwise in good shape. His legs both responded when he tried to move them, his left arm felt fine and he could move the fingers on his right hand.

"Well, nothing's missing," he thought.

His mouth felt dry and his lips felt cracked. He wanted a glass of water and a pinch of chew, in the worse way possible. When he heard the door click open, he glanced over and saw his wife walking in.

"Amanda," he rasped. "What are you doing here?"

"They brought me here when you got hurt," she said, smiling. "Are you okay?"

She came over and sat beside him, taking his good hand in hers.

"Headache mostly," he said. "Other than that, I'm just thirsty as hell. Can I get a drink?"

231

"I'll call the nurse," she said, hitting the call button.

"I missed you," he said. "I was out of cell range or I've been texting you but they wouldn't send."

"I know," she said, smiling at him. "I got a bunch of texts from you all at once when your phone came back into range."

He chuckled then groaned.

"Don't make me laugh," he said, softly. "It makes my head hurt."

"There are several people that want to see you," said Amanda. "Do you feel up to it?"

"I suppose," he said.

The nurse walked in and smiled.

"Can I help you?" she asked.

"Can I please get a glass of water?" asked Clark.

"Let me check your chart," she replied, lifting the clipboard and glancing at the paperwork. "Looks like you don't have any restrictions. I can get you water, soda, tea, or coffee. Whichever you prefer."

"Water is fine," said Clark. "Thank you."

"Yes, sir," she said. "I'll be right back."

"I'll go tell the people in the waiting room that you can have visitors now," said Amanda.

Both women left the room and Clark leaned back in the bed. He was expecting members of his team or possibly Major Saunders to come through the door. He was shocked when General Joshua Dalton walked in wearing his dress uniform. Major Saunders and Command Sergeant-Major Hammond came in behind him but didn't say anything.

"Captain Clark," said General Dalton. "How are you feeling?"

"All things considered, sir," said Clark, "I've felt better, but I certainly have been worse."

"I understand," said Dalton. "That was quite the hit you took. I've been reviewing After Action Reports from everyone involved. By the way, you made a Hell of an impression on the Canadians. I got glowing reports from them about you."

"I'm happy to hear that, sir," said Clark. "The Canadians were good to work with. Well, except for Major Tremblay. I'll put all of that in my AAR[25] when I write it."

"I've heard all about his behavior from the others that were there," said General Dalton. "It's been noted. But, since he died in the battle, the Canadians are burying him with full honors. He's posthumously being awarded the Cross of Valour."

Clark just shook his head.

"The man was a coward," said Clark.

"They're also awarding you the Victoria Cross for pulling that helicopter crew to safety," said Dalton.

"I'm not sure how much that means since they gave an award to a coward, sir," said Clark, shaking his head.

"Well, you've already been given the award," said Dalton. "I'm here to present it to you."

"Thank you, sir," said Clark. "How are the crew from the chopper?"

"They all survived," said Dalton. "The pilot will have to go through total reconstructive surgery, but he made it."

"I'm glad to hear that, sir," said Clark. "Now, if you don't mind me asking, am I going to be court-martialed for entering Canada without permission?"

"No," said Dalton. "I don't want you to make a habit of violating the borders of sovereign nations, but under the circumstances, you made the right call. The Canadians agreed and sent their own team to back you up. So, no formal charges. Besides, considering your service record, I don't think anyone was going to come after you too harshly."

Clark didn't say anything. Dalton handed him an award box, opening it as he presented it. Inside was a purple ribbon with a bronze straight-armed cross attached.

---

[25] AAR – After Action Report

"By the way," said Dalton, "at the request of the president, Major Saunders has been elevated to the rank of Lieutenant Colonel and you have been promoted to Major."

"I've been a Captain like three months," said Clark, shocked. "How does that happen, sir?"

"Don't consider it a promotion," said General Dalton. "Think of it more like a correction. Your little transgression into a foreign country forced us to reevaluate our teams as compared to the nations with similar teams."

"You mean that there are more teams like us than just Canada, sir?" asked Clark.

"There are more than a dozen nations that field teams like the Wild Hunt," said General Dalton. "Some, like the Canadians, are very good. Others not quite so much. We have mutual aid agreements in place with six countries who utilize similar teams and methods."

"Who are they, if I may ask, sir?" said Clark.

"Canada, you already know," said General Dalton. "In addition, there is the United Kingdom, Germany, Norway, Australia, and The Vatican."

"The Vatican?" asked Clark, incredulously.

"The Vatican is the single best source on the planet for paranormal lore," said General Dalton.

"I suppose that makes sense, sir," said Clark.

"Of all of those teams," said General Dalton, "only two have teams commanded by officers at the rank of Captain. Major seems to be the minimum for a field command. I don't want any foreign team pulling rank on my teams."

Clark merely nodded. He was still absorbing that so many places had teams like the Hunt.

"Which brings me to the next issue," said General Dalton. "You're border transgression brought a glaring problem to light. Something we need to address, and soon."

"What's that, sir?" asked Clark.

234

"What to do when a cryptid hunt jumps jurisdictions," said General Dalton. "Up until now, it hasn't been an issue."

"So, how do we resolve this issue, sir?" asked Saunders.

"Right now, the idea is still in the planning stages," said General Dalton, "but you can expect us to begin implementing it as soon as the details are worked out with the governments of the teams involved. We're looking at forming the first International Team. Members will be selected from all of the existing teams as well as the Special Forces of member nations. After all, we do have agreements with several countries that don't have the resources to field teams on their own. That would give an International Team the ability to hunt anywhere in the United States, Canada, Mexico, Europe, Australia, and large parts of Central and South America."

"Wow," said Clark. "That's a lot of ground to cover, sir."

"Of course, that team would not be the primary in every incident involving those countries," said General Dalton. "Only the ones without field teams and those who request the presence of the International Team."

"Will a new team be founded for this purpose, sir?" asked Clark.

"I'm volunteering Team Odin to be the inaugural team," said General Dalton. "Of course, more would follow. We would have to open the team to other nations, as well. That shouldn't be an issue since we've already had four members of the Canadian team request to be assigned to Team Odin. Specifically, they requested to work on Major Clark's team."

"Levesque?" asked Clark, chuckling.

"He was one of them," said General Dalton. "The others were the men that followed you when you led them to the cabin."

"I'll take them all, sir," said Clark. "They did well."

"We're still working on the details," said General Dalton. "This isn't going to happen today, but it is going to happen. The doctors tell me you'll likely be released from the hospital sometime tomorrow if there are no additional complications."

"Thank you, sir," said Clark.

"Don't thank me, just yet," said General Dalton. "You have no idea the can of worms that has just been opened for us. Gentlemen, Team Odin will be going international. That means your workload just increased dramatically."

General Dalton exchanged salutes with them and exited the room. Saunders sat there quietly until he was sure that the General was well out of hearing range.

"Holy shit," he said, exhaling loudly. "Dan, I thought both of us were done when you crossed that border. You're damned lucky that didn't blow up in our faces."

"I know, sir," said Clark. "I'm sorry."

"No need to apologize now," said Saunders. "I came away from it with a promotion and we're going to be going international. I'd say it turned out far better than I ever expected it to."

"Congratulations, Lieutenant Colonel," said Clark, grinning.

"To you, as well," said Saunders, grinning, "Major."

CSM Hammond just shook his head.

"Now what do we do?" asked Clark.

"We go back to Missouri and start preparing," said Saunders. "We've got a hell of a lot of work to do. I'm not waiting for the official word before we start preparing. Team Odin International. I like the sound of that."

"I doubt they're going to call it that, Levi," said CSM Hammond. "I doubt the name will change at all."

"Still," said Saunders. "Now I feel like James Bond. International Man of Mystery."

"You're more of an Austin Powers, Levi," said CSM Hammond.

That drew chuckles from all three of them.

"So, where do we begin?" asked Clark.

EPILOGUE

"The best way out is always through."
Robert Frost

2100 Hours CST
18 February
Steve's Pub and Grub
Missouri

Clark sat at the bar and ordered a large glass of Scotch. His arm was still in the sling and Doctor Olivetti said it should be for another week. He was ordered to take it easy until cleared to return to full duty. That was fine since he still had a mountain of paperwork to finish.

The memorial for the fallen team members had been earlier and they'd said their farewells and burned the wooden ship to send them off to the afterlife. There was a speech from General Dalton, but no mention of the International Team was made. That wouldn't come for a while. Only a handful of people knew about it and they were all told to keep it quiet until the team was formally announced.

Steve sat the glass of Dalmore in front of Clark and smiled. Sensing Clark wasn't in the mood to talk, he just nodded and moved off down the bar to fill other orders. Clark was content to just sit quietly and enjoy his drink until the others arrived.

It wasn't long before the rest of the team began filtering in. Margolin was carrying the elk skull mask that he'd taken off the lesser Wendigo that they'd killed on the first day of the deployment. He was pacing around the room, holding it up and looking for the perfect spot to hang it. Steve grabbed a hammer and nails, then went to help Margolin hang it.

Soon, everyone from the team was there, lifting glasses for absent friends and fallen teammates. They were toasting their loss, but also celebrating the team's victory. This had certainly been one for the record books. Clark had heard the story of the fight at the end of the dock and even he couldn't believe how much it had already grown. He was sure that it was going to continue to grow with each retelling.

237

They all sat, sang, talked, cried, and even hugged each other, dealing with the stress of the event. This mission had taken its toll on all of them. Clark hadn't worked up the courage to ask Gideon what had happened to him. Part of him still believed that he'd seen Gideon with a broken neck and part of him thought it had to be the concussion. He couldn't be sure so he hadn't asked. Although, he was beginning to suspect that there was far more to Sergeant-Major John Gideon than he'd previously suspected.

Moving over to the bar, Clark slid onto a barstool and ordered another whiskey. While he was waiting, a man sat down next to him and placed his cellphone deliberately on the bar between them. Clark glanced at the man. He was Hispanic and in his late forties or early fifties. He was about average height and had dark hair, beard, and mustache. He was wearing khakis with loafers and a t-shirt that read "May The Force Be With You." He took off a leather jacket and hung it on the back of the stool before sitting down. Perched on his head was a straw porkpie hat with a black and red band around it.

"*Una cerveza por favor,*" he said, nodding at Steve.

"Coming right up," said Steve. "Any preference."

"Sure, do you have Guinness?" replied the man.

That got Clark's attention. It was unusual to hear someone ask for a beer in Spanish, then request an Irish beer.

"And one for my friend here," he said, nodding at Clark.

Steve grabbed two of the large quart mugs and began pouring from the tap.

"Thanks," said Clark.

"Sure," said the man. "It's the least I can do."

"For what?" asked Clark.

"For a bonafide hero," said the man.

"Do I know you?" asked Clark, looking at the man suspiciously.

"No, we've not met," said the man. "My name is Roger Noriega with NDB Media. We're an online news podcast and blog."

"A reporter?" asked Clark.

"Investigative reporter, yes," said Roger.

"I'm sorry," said Clark. "Is there something I can do for you, Mister Noriega?"

"Please, call me Roger," he replied. "Mister Noriega was my father."

He chuckled at his own joke, but Clark never cracked a smile.

"Well, I suppose it was a bad joke," said Roger, shrugging.

"Thank you for the beer," said Clark, picking it up, "but I think I should be going."

"You're Daniel Clark," said Roger.

"How do you know my name?" asked Clark.

"Well, you're kinda famous," said Roger. "You're a highly decorated war hero. Which makes me wonder what you're doing assigned here in the ass-crack of hillbilly nirvana."

"I work in logistics," said Clark. "It's not very exciting."

"Logistics?" said Roger. "Yeah, sure. What can you tell me about a highly-trained military team that hunts cryptozoological and paranormal threats to the citizens of the United States?"

"I wouldn't know anything about that," replied Clark.

"Or a team called The Wild Hunt?" asked Roger, taking a sip from his Guinness. "Man, that's good. So much better when its from the tap instead of the bottle."

Clark sat back down.

"Never heard of it," he replied.

Now he was really curious. He wanted to find out just how much this man knew.

"How about an incident at Kimberling City last year where you and other deputies from the Sloan County Sheriff's Office battled a creature called a *Gugwe*?" asked Roger, taking another sip.

"How do you know anything about that?" asked Clark.

"Who do you think broke the story and got the sheriff recalled?" said Roger with a shrug.

"How did you even hear about things like this?" asked Clark.

"Well, it's kinda crazy," said Roger. "A year ago, I never would have believed that creatures like that even existed. Then I saw a YouTube video of two werewolves battling it out in Eureka Springs, Arkansas. I thought it was a hoax, at first. But, something told me it wasn't. When I started digging, I found out it wasn't a hoax. There were dozens of eye-witnesses, photos, videos, surveillance camera footage, and even footprints. That was enough to convince me it was real. I mean, come on, people have been believing in Bigfoot for decades on far less than that. Once I knew it was real, I started looking into other supposed sightings. Some were bullshit but others were the real deal. Then I knew I was onto something."

Clark said nothing.

"So, I did some digging and started a new show on the channel," said Roger. "I call it the Nightmare Hunter series. I investigate stories of strange and bizarre sightings, encounters, and attacks. So far, it's been a highly successful show. Especially once I put two and two together and realized that if I figured it out, the government had probably done so a long time ago. That led me down a series of rabbit holes until someone whispered a rumor they heard about a military team called The Wild Hunt. Am I getting close?"

"It sounds to me like you have a wild imagination," said Clark, shrugging.

"Congratulations on the recent marriage," said Roger. "I wish you and the new bride a long and happy life together."

"Thanks," said Clark. "But I still think your story sounds a little far fetched."

"No more so than a guy with more awards than I can count including the highest award our nation bestows," said Roger, "who's working in logistics. You were... excuse me... are a Tier One operator. Guys like you don't work in logistics. It would be like using a thoroughbred racehorse to pull a plow."

"You seem to have all the answers," said Clark. "I still say this alleged team doesn't exist."

"You don't have to admit it," said Roger. "Let's just say, I have my sources and leave it at that."

Roger placed a twenty on the bar and nodded at Steve.

"That should cover it and the tip," said Roger, getting up from the stool and slipping his jacket back on. "I'll see you again sometime, sir."

Clark watched him go, curious at just how much he knew and who his source was. Just as he reached the door, he stopped and glanced back, making eye contact with Clark. Smiling, he flicked his gaze towards where Margolin and Winter were sitting. Winking at Clark he whistled loud enough that he got everyone's attention. Once everyone was looking his way he yelled out a phrase.

"Embrace the suck!"

"Goddamn it!" yelled Margolin, dropping to the ground and starting to do pushups.

Roger disappeared out the door with a wink.

"Son-of-a-bitch," whispered Clark.

AUTHOR'S BIO: D.A. ROBERTS

D.A. Roberts is an author of primarily in the horror/dystopian and fiction genres. Born in Lebanon, Missouri, he now lives in Springfield, Missouri with his wife and sons. When writing, D.A. serves his community in Law Enforcement.

Best known for his "Ragnarok Saga," he blends the zombie genre with elements of Norse Mythology. The series has been called "a thinking man's apocalyptic world." This is a unique approach that creates a new sub-genre in Apocalyptic Fiction.

He is also known in science fiction for "The Infinite Black Series." This series is based on the hit video game from Spellbook Studio. Download and play the game for free at www.Spellbook.com.

In November of 2018, D.A. took on the challenging role of C.E.O. of J. Ellington Ashton Press.

In March of 2020, D.A. was elected as the president of the Horror Author's Guild.

Find more about his work at

www.daroberts.net

www.jellingtonashton.com

www.amazon.com/author/daroberts

https://www.facebook.com/DARobertsAuthor/

https://www.haguild.com/

DARK ANGEL
MEDICAL
VITA VEL NEX
WWW.DARKANGELMEDICAL.COM

Also by this author: JEA

CODE NAME: WILD HUNT
ODIN'S CALL

WILD HUNT

D.A. ROBERTS
THE END IS ONLY
THE BEGINNING

By D.A. ROBERTS

248

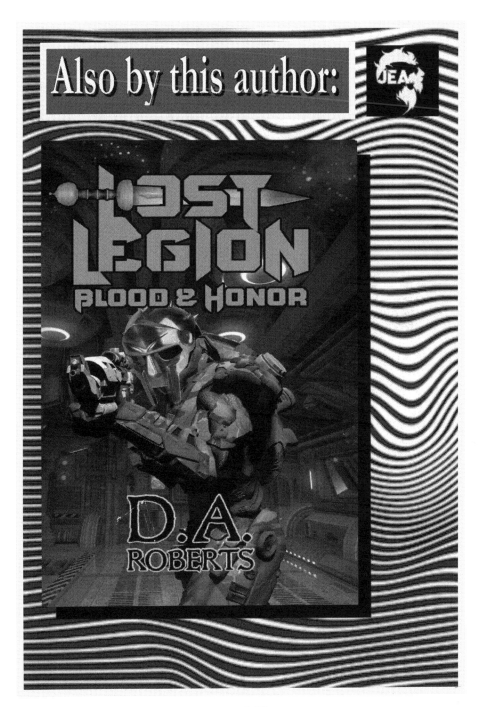

Made in the USA
Middletown, DE
13 July 2021